AGAIN *and* AGAIN

ALSO BY JONATHAN EVISON

All About Lulu

West of Here

The Revised Fundamentals of Caregiving

This Is Your Life, Harriet Chance!

Lawn Boy

Legends of the North Cascades

Small World

AGAIN *and* AGAIN

A NOVEL

Jonathan Evison

DUTTON

DUTTON

An imprint of Penguin Random House LLC
penguinrandomhouse.com

LIBRARY OF CONGRESS CATALOGING-IN-PUBLICATION DATA

Names: Evison, Jonathan, author.
Title: Again and again: a novel / Jonathan Evison.
Description: New York: Dutton, [2023]
Identifiers: LCCN 2023007427 (print) | LCCN 2023007428 (ebook) |
ISBN 9780593184158 (hardcover) | ISBN 9780593184172 (ebook)
Subjects: LCGFT: Novels.
Classification: LCC PS3605.V57 A73 2023 (print) |
LCC PS3605.V57 (ebook) | DDC 813/.6—dc23/eng/20230221
LC record available at https://lccn.loc.gov/2023007427
LC ebook record available at https://lccn.loc.gov/2023007428

Printed in the United States of America

1st Printing

Book design by Nancy Resnick

For my beloved kids:

Owen and Emma and Lulu;

may they lead many happy lives

AGAIN *and* AGAIN

I

The Most Beautiful of All Possible Worlds

Don't tell me life is short. With the benefit of my considerable experience, or should I say in spite of it, I'm still willing to buy that life is beautiful if you dress it up right, that people are basically good, or that love can save you. I still want to believe. Tell me that life is meaningful, and you've got my ear. Tell me that life is a journey, and I'll nod in agreement. But try convincing me that said journey is short, and you've lost me; that's one cliché I can't abide. If you think life is short, just wait. One of these days it might not end for you; it'll just keep going and going and you'll see that life is not a breathless sprint to the grave, gone in a heartbeat, but an odyssey that stretches on and on into eternity. Once it starts, it never ends, not even if you want it to. I should know.

I have gone by other names: Euric, Pietro, Kiri, Amura, York, and Whiskers. Currently I answer to the name of Eugene, though the attendants here at Desert Greens call me Mr. Miles. In August, I turn 106 years old. Wow, you'll say, what a full life! Impressive! What's your secret? But the fact is, I'm ready to die. There is nothing holding me here. I only hope that I am not born again, for I don't think I could endure another loveless existence.

As far as I know, I first came to live on the Iberian Peninsula in

the town of Seville, or Ishbiliyah as it was then known, during the
golden age of Abd al-Rahman III in al-Andalus. If you've read your
history, you probably know something about Spain under the Moors:
how it was a global seat of wisdom, a paradise for scholars and poets
and artists, philosophers, historians, and musicians, how Arabic was
the language of science—mathematics, astronomy, and medicine.
You've likely heard about the wondrous architecture of the mosques
with their flowing arabesques and honeycombed vaults, their domed
tops echoing the hypnotic suras of the Quran. You've probably heard
about the great walled alcazabas, and the splendor of the riads and
gardens. That is where the story of Euric and Gaya begins.

Of all my lives, this has been the longest, at turns the most re-
warding and the most fruitless, the most satisfying and the most
trying, and, accounting for the enduring awareness and attendant
weight of all my previous follies and failures, the most exhausting.
So don't tell me life is short.

But I digress.

Now I live here at Desert Greens, an eldercare facility in Lucerne Valley. I've been here for twelve years. It's a nice enough place,
I suppose, though there exist no actual "greens" on the premises,
unless you count the blighted buffalo grass on the west end of the
facility. There are a few picnic tables—four, to be exact—out there
amidst the thirsty palms, which, depending on the direction you
choose to face, confer views of the Ord, Granite, or San Bernardino
Mountains, the craggy Ords and Granites brown most of the year.
It's a stark landscape, yes, but a beautiful one; timeless, like me.

I still get around well enough. I can go to the bathroom on my
own, or walk down the corridor to the common area, or the cafeteria, or the aforementioned "greens," where a more sociable soul than
myself might find a game of dominoes, or even chess, if he were so
inclined. Were it my wish to learn to paint landscapes, or achieve

computer competency, I could do that, too, here at Desert Greens. But I don't.

Though there is no denying a slight antiseptic air here at the Greens, don't imagine it as a hospital or an institution exactly. I have my own quarters, albeit small, populated with my own things, though if eleven centuries have taught me anything it's how to travel light. Thus, I possess comparatively little next to most of the tenants: two shelves' worth of cherished books, from Virgil to Proust to O'Connor, and of course my dear Oscar; a few dozen history texts, ranging from the Greeks to the Romans to the Moors to the Americans; and an old Gideons Bible swiped decades before from the Oviatt Hotel in downtown Los Angeles (not by any means to be confused with the lavish Oviatt Building on Olive Street), along with a dozen jigsaw puzzles at any given time and a shoebox half-full of keepsakes, including my tags and medals from the war, a typed letter from one of my high school history students twenty years after I taught her, and the bone-handled jackknife my war buddy Johnny Brooks gave me. Then there's my paperweight on the dresser, a walnut-sized spherical rock I found along the Oregon coast on my honeymoon with Gladys. Oh, what a beautiful wedding it was! Oh, what a lovely time we had in Cannon Beach!

Evenly spaced atop the dresser I keep three framed photographs of my beloved Gladys (or Gaya, if you will), gone these eight years. Still not a day goes by that I do not gaze at these photographs and think of her. In the first picture, a black and white portrait, Gladys is but a young woman of nineteen or twenty, many years before I'd found my way back to her. She looks at once delicate and formidable with her dark, intelligent eyes and her generous lips. She's not smiling in the photo; rather her face is at rest for the occasion, her hands folded neatly in her lap.

In the second photograph, Gladys is in the prime of her life,

1948, flanked by her two girls, Donna and Nancy, six and eight years old respectively, the three of them clad in bathing suits and floppy sun hats, waving at the camera from Pismo Beach or some other California seaside retreat. I didn't know Gladys then, either. Our fateful reunion was still twenty years in the future. Had I known it was coming, I might have done more with my life. If you look close enough at the photo, you'll see that Gladys is still wearing the wedding ring from her first husband, Richard, who lost his life at Guadalcanal years before the photo was taken.

The final photograph depicts Gladys and me in midlife. It would have been the late-1970s, not long after we bought the house in Hesperia. There's nothing particularly memorable about this instant frozen in perpetuity, no special occasion or importance attached to it. The photo was snapped by a busboy upon my request. Gladys and I are sitting at a table at King George's Smorgasbord, wineglasses half-full, our dinner plates clean, both of us smiling, although Gladys cannot disguise a bit of a deer-in-the-headlights look, as though she wasn't expecting the photograph. God, we were happy; for the whole of our thirty-five years together it seemed we were happy every step of the way; through every peak and valley our love abided surely and steadily. And why not? Our reunion was, after all, eleven hundred years in coming. And never once did we take it for granted.

But again, I digress.

The attendants here at Desert Greens are invariably cheerful, though most of them speak to me with that cloying condescension of the sort one might employ with a toddler or a puppy. I play along with them to some degree, though despite my vintage I am still "quite sharp," an observation staff members share with me weekly. They are all very professional, which is to say attentive, even-tempered, if not consistently measured in their distance. While the others are fastidiously unyielding in their professionalism, which is fine by me, the one called Marguerite has been known to harmlessly flirt with me on occasion, a kindness I oblige as if it flatters me, though in truth nothing could arouse my ardor at this point, not with Gladys dead and gone. Aside from Marguerite's occasional playful antics, the rest of the staff here at Desert Greens maintain a polite deference and patient disposition that never quite achieves warmth.

When Gladys died, there was nothing left for me to lose. Had I believed for one minute that it would've relieved my suffering, I would have taken my own life without question. But I knew that any such merciful conclusion was beyond my reach. Chances were, I would only be reborn one step further removed from Gladys, one more lifetime distant from Gaya.

After the memorial service, my slide into decrepitude was sudden and sweeping. It seemed I aged twenty years in a matter of weeks. The dishes piled up. The phone went unanswered. I stopped eating beyond the bare minimum, stopped bathing, and I hardly got out of bed. The mail piled up and the bills went unpaid. Neighbors' casseroles were left untouched, until they eventually stopped coming around. Gladys's daughters dropped by on occasion, invariably attempting to roust me out of my isolation for a meal in town or a walk in the park, but even Donna and Nancy gave up eventually. I was unreachable. A normal person would have given up the will to live and followed Gladys to her grave, but I was a preternaturally hearty physical specimen for any age, and besides, I knew that such a notion was futile. I'd been lucky enough to find my true love twice, but surely lightning would not strike thrice.

And so, I languished, holed up in my house, resigned to my isolation. To be honest, it was only the grubby state of the house, and the constant upkeep required to render it barely habitable, that finally drove me to Desert Greens.

While it is true that in my tenure here at Desert Greens I have been far from a gadabout, and for the most part a certifiable recluse,

I am not unacquainted with my fellow denizens. Namely, there is Irma McCleary across the hall, who smells of wilting gardenias and the inside of pill bottles. I would put Irma's years somewhere between eighty-five and ninety, although decorum necessitates that I never solicit a woman's age. An interesting fact about Irma: Her hair is quite literally blue, and I don't mean grayish blue, rather somewhere between baby blue and cornflower blue. Only recently did I discover that this fact is not owing to some unfortunate mishap involving off-brand hair dye, or an unforeseen chemical reaction, but instead to personal preference. As it turns out, Irma willfully cultivates her azure hair for reasons I'm not given to understand. Unerring in her politeness, though she's been calling me Benson for nearly a decade now, Irma is quick with a compliment, as recently as last week commending my choice of moccasin-style slippers.

Two doors down from me resides Herman Billet. Herman is an unnaturally lean, bullet-headed old buzzard who is about as hale and hearty as a paper bag full of cobwebs. The next stiff breeze could be the end of Herman. While Herman might appear to be even more decrepit than yours truly, I have it on good authority that the man has not yet lived to see his ninetieth birthday. Mr. Billet is just a babe still, though you wouldn't know it to see him wandering the hallways, stooped and listless, Danish crumbs ringing his slackened jaw. My exchanges with Herman have been limited mostly to assisting him in locating the commissary or helping him find his way back to his quarters from said commissary. More than once he has mistaken me for his son, and once for a former business partner, a certain Phil Jacoby, who, I've come to learn, died an untimely death some forty-odd years ago.

In the next corridor over resides Bud Brewster, he of the ceaseless fly-fishing adventures and intolerant politics, who calls himself a patriot and claims to have fought in the 478th Infantry Division, though no such outfit ever existed. Despite my own service, I have no interest in exposing Bud Brewster as a fraud, and even less interest in talking to him.

Across the hall from Bud Brewster resides Iris Pearlman, a charming if not overly talkative woman, who has cultivated an unimaginably large family and likes nothing more than to inform people on the particulars of their existence. To wit, there is daughter Judith in Fort Worth, a retired school administrator. Judith's husband, Mac, a retired oil executive, converted to Judaism thirty-seven years ago. Great-grandson Levi was just accepted at Brown University. His mother, Barbara, a former Ms. Schenectady, is over the moon about this acceptance. Then there's Iris's son, Adam, a playwright allegedly of some renown, and his wife, Natalie, and their three sons and two daughters: Todd, Mira, David, Hannah, and Caleb, in descending order. We are only grazing the surface here, but I'm sure you get the idea. In the sum of my exchanges with Iris, which total four, I have contributed all of twelve words.

But at least Iris Pearlman is not nosy like Mrs. Messinger, who sees fit to entrust me with any and every shred of gossip she can amass, a litany of dubious particulars comprising sexual innuendo, marital complications, deaths, near deaths, projected deaths, alleged UTIs, and colorectal surgeries. As an intensely personal sort, I could never abide gossip. I find Mrs. Messinger to be, in a word, odious, and to be avoided even more emphatically than Mrs. Pearlman, who means no harm.

There are dozens of others here at Desert Greens, too many to catalog, thus I'll spare you a further inventory. Apologies if these assessments of my peers seem unkind. I harbor for these venerable souls no grudge whatsoever. Like me, many of my elderly neighbors live in relative isolation, receiving infrequent visitors. Their lives have become very small. I feel for them, I do. But not even one of them carries a light in their eyes that suggests they have ever lived before and remember it. Some of them can hardly remember their own names. I want to pity them. But the truth is I envy them, because most of them will probably win the death lottery. A few more years of habitually eating their big meal early in the day, collecting newspaper clippings for the sons and daughters who never call on them, and watching the five o'clock news, and the six o'clock news, and the seven o'clock news. Most of them will likely enjoy the opportunity to call it quits, while it seems that I am destined to go on living again and again.

I've not received a visitor in eight years. Such is my desire for isolation at this point that I have zero interest in talking to anyone beyond my perfunctory exchanges with the staff. Instead, I keep to myself, confounding my meaningless but endlessly stubborn life force. I soothe my restlessness with jigsaw puzzles depicting cats sprawled on bookshelves, lighted cityscapes, national parks, famous book covers, and locales familiar to me, most of them five to fifteen hundred pieces. It's not that I take any joy in jigsaw puzzles beyond the small satisfaction attending their completion, it is simply that they keep me occupied and focused, anchored to the one existence I hope to be my last.

Understand, I am not depressed, merely resigned to my isolation because it takes the least amount of effort. All my life I've tried to connect, and most of my life I've failed. My lone aspiration now is to ride this life out, and it seems that the less connecting I do, the less I reach out to the world, the less I'm inviting future probabilities.

Noncompliance

Just as I avoided contact at Desert Greens, so I avoided movement, reasoning similarly that the less mobility I employed, the less I would be forced to engage the world. Thus, I marked the bulk of my days at my desk puzzling, and my afternoons and evenings in bed reading. I was doing just that one evening when I pretended not to notice the young housekeeper who trundled his cart of cleaning supplies into my quarters and set directly to work putting my room in order. With his back facing me, I watched him tend to his charge, wiping down flat surfaces and straightening what little clutter there was as he moved along the back wall. It was clear that he was a conscientious enough worker, methodical and thorough in his tasks. But I'd be lying if I said that his presence in my room didn't feel like an unwelcome infringement on my solitude.

"Good evening," he said, turning to face me, rag dangling in hand.

I kept my face buried in my book, offering no rejoinder. But it was an omission, alas, that failed to dissuade the young man.

"I'm the new guy," he said. "Angel."

"Mm," I said, eyes still glued to the page, where I proceeded to read the same sentence for a third time.

Angel shrugged off my aloofness and resumed his cleaning.

I snuck another furtive glance from behind my book at Angel as he busied himself wiping down the TV remote, which he then replaced atop my bedside table. He was a young Chicano, maybe twenty-two or twenty-three, short of stature and stocky of build. He wore his hair cropped and neat on top, and shaved to a stubble on the sides. I believe the style is referred to as a *fade* in the modern parlance. Though he attempted to hide his tattooed arms, the stylized numerals 1 and 3 occasionally peeking out from beneath his left sleeve, there was no disguising the lion's head below his left ear, already beginning to fade slightly. He boasted a ring-studded septum that, coupled with his compact frame, lent him a distinctly bullish aspect.

"So, what're you reading, there?"

I deemed this query unworthy of reply.

Undaunted, Angel leaned in to get a closer look at my book.

"*Twilight of the Gods,*" he read aloud. "*War in the Western Pacific.* So, a history buff?"

"Mmph," I said.

"Not much for conversation, huh?" he said.

Bristling, I lowered my book long enough to break my silence.

"As a matter of fact, no, I'm not an avid conversationalist, thank you. So, if you wouldn't mind . . . ?"

Young Angel took my impudence in stride.

"Ah, okay, I see how it is, my friend," he said casually. "My bad."

I felt my cheeks begin to flush.

"Thank you," I mumbled.

"No problem, man," he said.

I couldn't ignore a little pang of guilt at my impoliteness as Angel concluded his work silently. I almost apologized. But I didn't want to encourage him, for it was evident he was the garru-lous sort.

Though my quarters remained in a state of perfect order, Angel returned the next day with his rolling supply closet. This time he found me at my puzzling table, where I'd nearly completed my latest 750-piece undertaking, the ancient Roman aqueduct of Segovia, Spain, bathed in footlights set against the night sky.

"I'm back," he said. "Got any messes for me?"

"No," I said. "You can move on to the next room."

"Nah, homie, that's not the way it works. I got a schedule. Every room, every day."

"Overkill, if you ask me," I said.

"Yeah, I don't make the rules, unfortunately."

He'd stationed himself right over my shoulder, practically touch-ing me. To my chagrin, he reached out and snatched a puzzle piece off the tabletop.

"This goes up here," he said, placing it amidst the night sky.

I was furious at this trespass. He'd overstepped a boundary. He had no business touching my personal things or insinuating himself upon my activities.

My ire at this trespass was not lost on him.

"Oh, sorry, dog," he said.

He promptly removed the piece and dropped it back amongst the scrum, mixing them all up as though it would make everything right again. It was too much to take.

"Don't do that!" I said.

"I was just trying to—"

"Get your hands off!" I said.

The young man was clearly shaken by my outburst. He stepped back sheepishly, looking genuinely contrite as the color drained from his face.

"I'm sorry, dog. I didn't realize it was so important that—"

"And stop calling me that, for heaven's sake. I'm not a dog. I don't even like dogs. I'm a cat person."

For once, he was at a loss for words. I'd let all the air right out of him, and now he was left looking somewhat bewildered as he stared at his shoe tops. I knew his shame and embarrassment well, I had lived it countless times, yet still I could not bring myself to extend an olive branch. And so, for the second consecutive day, Angel concluded his work in silence.

By the time he vacated my quarters, I felt terrible. Certainly, he'd done nothing to deserve my wrath. He was obviously a nice kid. God knows, his job couldn't pay much. His familiarity had only been an attempt at friendliness, and I had rebuked it savagely. What was wrong with me? Who was I to admonish friendly advances? I spent a good hour flagellating myself for my cruelty. When had I become such a bitter old man?

So, on the third day, I resolved to be civil.

"I apologize for my rudeness," I said. "It seems I've become one of those cantankerous old men who shakes his fists and tells kids to get off his lawn."

Angel seemed genuinely relieved by this bit of diplomacy, and a smile spread across his face.

"Nah, homie," he said, waving it off. "I get it. I mean, who the heck am I, right? I'm just some cleaner who comes into your personal space and starts invading your privacy. You did the whole puzzle yourself; I understand."

"It's not like that," I said. "I'm just out of practice with people."

"Don't get out much, huh?"

"Hardly at all," I said. "Anyway, I'm sorry. I can't imagine what you must think of me."

"I don't even know you, dog."

This time, I let the dog reference pass.

"Well, I suppose you've heard all about me?" I said.

"A little," he said.

"Surely they told you that I'm a deluded old man who thinks he's a thousand years old."

"Nah, man. They just said you have a vivid imagination."

"It's not true, what they say," I said.

"Whatever, I'm not here to judge you," he said. "I'm just here to empty your wastebasket."

"Don't listen to Wayne, or you'll get the wrong idea about me."

"I make up my own mind about people, so you don't have to worry about that, boss."

"I'm Eugene, by the way," I said.

"Good to meet you, Geno."

Again, I let the pet name pass without comment.

"So, what's it like being so old?" he said.

Many have tried and failed to open me up in recent years, to disarm or erode the formidable defenses I've erected to keep people on the outside. But nothing about Angel's straightforward manner aroused my suspicion.

"Well, imagine being young," I said. "Except you're tired all the time, and you're no longer ambitious, and nothing tastes as good as it used to, and you have to go to the bathroom all the time."

The truth is, physically I'm healthy as an ox. While the ruinous effects of time have taken their toll on my once semi-good looks (I now resemble an elderly chimp with radiation poisoning), my blood work is clean, my ticker is steady, my prostate normal, and my plumbing serviceable.

"You're funny, I like your style," said Angel. "With some of these people around here I feel like I'm talking to a lampshade. It's depressing. But you, you're sharp, Geno."

"That's what they tell me."

The fact is, if I'm being honest, despite my avowed preference for solitude, I was desperate for connection. And there was something naturally disarming about Angel; maybe it was his easy smile. These are the only explanations I can think of as to why I let the young man waltz right through my fortifications and achieve something akin to familiarity so quickly.

The next time I saw Angel, however, he was not the same cheerful presence. There was a distinct air of listlessness about him as he tended to his charge. I allowed him this consolation until a genuine curiosity got the best of me.

"What's got you?" I said.

"I had a fight with my old lady."

"It happens," I said.

"You been in love, right, Geno? Man, you must have been. You're like a hundred years old."

"Hundred and five."

"You had a wife, right? That's her?" he said, indicating the photos on the dresser.

"Yes," I said.

"She looks different in this one," he said of the most recent photo.

"Just older," I said.

"And those are your kids?"

"Those were Gladys's girls, Donna and Nancy, from before I knew her. When she was married to her first husband, Richard."

"What happened to him?"

"He was killed in the war—at Guadalcanal."

"So, you never had your own kids?"

"No."

"You regret it?"

"Sometimes."

"Mm," he said.

Something was still eating Angel, but I didn't want to overstep my boundaries. He pumped some Windex on the TV screen and wiped it down hard enough that the rag took to squeaking.

"I should have handled it better," he muttered.

"Handled what?"

"Aw, nothing," he said. "I'm just thinking out loud. Sometimes I feel like I'm making the same mistakes over and over."

"Believe me, I know the feeling," I said. But what I wanted to say was: "Get used to it."

"You ever fight with your old lady?"

"Not very much," I said. "However, since you mention it, we did sort of fight the first time we met."

"Elana, she just gets these ideas of the way things are gonna be, but she doesn't think about it from my perspective, you know?"

"Perspective is hard," I said. "I wish I could tell you it gets easier. But it doesn't. Even when you've lived as many times as me."

"Whaddaya mean, 'as many times'?"

"Not my first rodeo," I said.

"So, like, past lives?" said Angel.

"Yes," I said.

Sweeping the tile floor, Angel considered the matter; dubious, judging from his knitted brow.

"So, why you, man? Why not me? How come I haven't had any past lives?"

"Maybe you just don't remember them."

"Oh, I'd remember," he said. "I don't forget anything. Maybe you're just dreaming this stuff up."

"Then I'm just as likely dreaming this right now."

"Nah, you ain't dreaming this," said Angel, resuming his wiping. "You really should get some sunshine, man, go out to the yard, it's nice out. You get any whiter and you'll be invisible."

"Thanks for the advice," I said.

"I'm just sayin', man. It ain't healthy."

"Well, I didn't ask your opinion," I said. "Maybe you ought to mind your own business."

"Okay, okay, I got the message. My bad. I was just looking out for you is all."

"I'm a hundred and five years old," I said. "You think I don't know what's right for me?"

"I hear you, Geno," he said. "But it's never too late to learn new stuff, right?"

"Hmph," I said.

He was right, of course; I suppose I just wasn't ready to admit it yet. Still, I didn't want to alienate the young man, whose appearance at Desert Greens had already marked a welcome addition to my otherwise empty evenings.

"You're not wrong," I said. "I probably should get out more."

And while I wasn't compelled toward the out-of-doors immediately, that day was coming.

The Apogee of Knowledge

His third week on the job, Angel, leaning on his broomstick, confessed to me that he hated cleaning my room.

"I'm just going through the motions, dog. What am I even doing here? It's not that I love cleaning or something, I just wanna feel like I'm actually doing something. As far as I know, you never even touch the TV remote, and I clean the dang thing every day. You don't smudge up the mirror, you don't track in dirt on your shoes. You never make a mess, like ever."

He ran a finger across the dresser and showed me when it came up clean.

"See, nothin'," he said. "You can't even make dust, homie."

"I'll try harder," I said.

"I got twenty minutes in here every day and nothing to do, man. I like to stay occupied, you know? The day goes faster that way. Talk to me, homie. Tell me something interesting. I heard you lived in Spain. Tell me about Spain, why don't you?"

"Spain, huh?"

"Yeah, man, I like hearing about other places and other people's lives," he said.

Strange that after so many years, so many decades, of not sharing my past lives for fear of judgment, Angel's invitation was all it
took to break the dam. And thus, I began to tell Angel my story.

You've likely heard how the Muslims and Christians and Jews all
coexisted in relative peace under the Moors. It was not called a
golden age for nothing. But don't believe everything you read. After
the Berbers crossed the Strait of Gibraltar from Tangier, those who
were there before them did not thrive. Me, for instance. I was no
scholar or mathematician. I was neither Jew, nor Arab, nor hardly
what you'd call a Christian, but a lowly Visigoth, the bastard son of
a conquered tribe, who barely knew his mother or father and never
clung to any affiliation nor held any affection for his scattered cabal.
In short, I was born low. And given the cards I'd been dealt, I'd like
to think I did reasonably well with them, though by almost any
measure I did not. In my defense, I was born without love, a child
no more nurtured or cherished than a blind street dog. But beneath
my ragged clothing, behind my sad, gray eyes and my dirty face, I
had poetry in me somewhere. If only ever something or somebody
would unlock it.

My childhood in al-Andalus was a gallery of horrors: abuse, ne-
glect, starvation, you name it. A homeless waif by the age of nine, I
wandered the dusty streets by day and hunkered in the shadows by
night. From my perspective, the age was not so golden. No, it was
an age of stale bread and rancid meat, of fetid water, a few dirty
coins, and a host of glories beyond my reach. I cultivated few allies
along my path to an adolescence that proved to offer little more in
the way of promise.

But it was not entirely without beauty. I can still hear the somber, rhyming verse of the Quran spilling out into the arid streets

of Seville. From the pill-jar sterility of my little room here at the Greens, amongst the blue haired and the forgotten, I can still summon with absolute clarity the entreaties of the young poets upon the square, and the feeling of knowing that I'd never be one of them. As for the machinations of the larger culture around me, the politics of the day and such, I knew very little. I gleaned only what I heard in the streets and the alleyways. I was oblivious to the death of al-Mansur or the destruction of the palace at the hands of the Berbers; these events I only learned in my present life by way of history. The Reconquista at the time was only so much rumbling, largely ineffectual, as it had been for most of three centuries. The Jews and Christians and Muslims still coexisted in relative peace, but make no mistake, the Moors were the ruling class, and don't let any history book tell you otherwise.

My name then was Euric. I was barefoot and ragged, a mass of ungovernable dirty blond hair my only real distinction, trying and mostly failing to sustain a tolerable existence near the turn of the eleventh century. What time had I for poetry, or song, or even religion? My primary concerns were food and shelter. What wouldn't I have done for a hunk of salt fish, or something so exotic as a peach, or a warm place to shelter from the storm? I was hardly better off than an ass.

Not beyond begging, I soon found that my appeals fell on mostly deaf ears, be they Christian, Jew, or Berber.

"You're scaring away business," said the merchants.

"Get a job," said the shoppers.

And so, I heeded their advice and tried to learn an honest trade. I was a highly motivated job candidate and more than willing to apprentice.

"I can't help you," said the blacksmith.

"I'm not looking for anyone," said the stable man.

"Away with you," said the jeweler.

Apparently, not a single merchant or craftsman in all of Seville could see the potential in me. So I became a cutpurse.

"Really, ese? A thief?" said Angel, interrupting my story while dumping the wastebasket.

"You would have done the same in my circumstances."

"Yeah, probably," said Angel. "You just don't seem like the type."

Stomach growling, wary of predation, senses besieged by my ca-cophonous surroundings, I strolled daily through the marketplace, the sights and sounds and smells, from horse dung to saffron, too various to catalog, looking for my next mark—an old woman, a distracted consumer, even a child if such a contingency presented itself. With thievery in mind, I strayed aimlessly about the city at large, drinking from the fountains, admiring the architectural achievements that surrounded me, pining for a little piece of it all that I might one day lay claim to.

Oh, how badly I'd wanted to believe that apogee of knowledge extolled by the Berbers: that with enlightenment one could become exactly what one wished to be in the future. But I was consigned to be a thief, and not a particularly good one. In fact, it was my incom-petence as a criminal that eventually led me to my one true love, the elusive Gaya.

"Who's Gaya?" Angel wanted to know.

"I'm getting to that."

But the truth was, all the sap had run out of me at the very thought of Gaya.

"Well?"

"Perhaps another time," I said.

"Okay, homie. Next time, maybe."

While I was loath to revisit the ordeal, I hated to disappoint Angel, whose companionship was something I'd already dared to count on. I looked forward daily to our exchanges and had come to miss them on his days off—his easy familiarity and his pet names, which I now took as tokens of affection. His weekend replacement was a heavyset gentleman named Jim, perpetually short of breath. That Jim's work was substandard was not the issue. I had endured eleven centuries of misery and insult at the hands of every imaginable tyranny, so surely, I could live with a smudged television screen. However, that Jim was an unrepentant mouth-breather, and a very conspicuous one, was an actuality I found scarcely tenable. It got to where I solicited small talk with Jim solely so I wouldn't have to endure his breathing.

It was always a relief to see Angel's silver-studded nose and faded tattoos on Monday afternoon. Angel had recently coerced me to eat lunch with him out on the green. He called it lunch, but really it was dinnertime given his shift. The two of us sat at a picnic table near sunset, Angel eating his reheated tamales and Tupperware bowl of posole, me my chicken salad croissan'wich and fruit cocktail from the commissary.

Though it was past seven in the evening, the suffocating heat had not quite fled the valley, and a few determined mosquitoes flitted about our food. The desert air was redolent with the odor of sage and creosote and dry grit, the Mojave dust assaulting our nostrils, our ears, any crack or crevice it could find. The desert was insidious and relentless, unstoppable, like life itself.

"So, help me out here," said Angel. "If you're reincarnated, aren't you supposed to go one way or another? Like up or down depending on how good you were? Since you were a thief, wouldn't you come back as like a goat or something?"

"That's more the Hindu conception," I said. "I lived my fullest and most worthy life in the late eighteenth and early nineteenth centuries. At that time, I did more in service to the world than ever before or after."

"And?"

"I came back as a cat."

"No way, a cat? What was it like licking your own testes, homie?"

Actually, relative to some of my other embodiments, my life as a cat wasn't bad at all, at least not those years I spent with Oscar. It was much as you might imagine. I lounged, I stretched, I sunned myself upon the windowsill when there was any sun to be had in Chelsea. I was well-fed and had the lavish attention of Oscar's affections at my disposal. Nothing small, neither winged nor legged, crawled, slinked, scurried, or buzzed about my proximity that I didn't have my way with. And I most assuredly had my way. I had absolute dominion over the flat, and over my Oscar. Beyond grooming myself, and terrorizing insects, and having my chin scratched, had I not possessed the knowledge of my former selves and future aspirations, my life might have been idyllic. The blessing and the curse of my six years with Oscar was that in this morbidly sensitive, oft-misunderstood, fanciful young poet I had at last relocated Gaya. It was her; it was my beloved Gaya re-personified.

Angel snapped off a bite of his tamale, washing it down with a swig of Diet Pepsi.

"A cat, that's a trip, man," he said. "So, after Spain you lived in Italy, huh? What was that like? I think it'd be cool to go to Italy."

"Interminable," I said. "I was lovelorn every minute of every day, saddled with insatiable yearning. I was so hopelessly shackled to the deadweight of my past, and the unendurable absence of Gaya, it was a wonder I didn't take my own life. One's past is what one is. It's the only way by which people should be judged. Oscar said that, not me. But I believe it applies to me."

"What was so special about this Gaya?"

I set my chicken salad croissan'wich aside, picked up my napkin, wiping the flakes from my ravaged lips so I wouldn't look like Herman Billet two doors down. Straightening up, I leaned forward, my rheumy eyes assuming a new focus.

"What was so special about Gaya? To begin with," I said, "everything."

Angel seemed mildly impressed by this declaration.

"She was all that, eh?"

"All that and more, homie," I said, eliciting a grin from Angel. "Imagine you met the most beautiful girl you ever laid eyes on, with a radiance such that when you looked at her, you shone like a moon reflecting her borrowed light."

"Is that Oscar, too?"

"No, that's my own," I said.

"You really fell hard for this girl."

"To fall doesn't even begin to explain it. To soar comes closer. Now, imagine this woman saved your life, you a peasant and a petty thief who had never known love, never even guessed at it."

"For real, she saved your life?"

"With nothing to gain for herself and everything to lose, she saved my life, which up until the moment I met her was unworthy of saving."

"Sounds like a fairy tale, homie."

"Gaya is the truest thing that ever happened to me," I said. "Why do you think I've spent over a thousand years hoping to find her again?"

Oh, but how the act of longing animated you, how it filled up the vacuum of self like a helium balloon, only to leave you emptyhanded and bereft the moment you let go of it.

"You okay, Geno?"

"Yes," I managed to say.

Fighting off this ancient despair, I sat silently with Angel, the desert grit penetrating my nostrils, sandblasting my skin, now grown pale and thin as parchment, though somehow tough as leather. If I sat there long enough, the desert would bury me. And yet I would still go on living. The prospect was too depressing to ponder.

"Elana's pregnant," Angel said out of the blue.

"Congratulations," I said, regathering my composure.

"I dunno, homie. I'm not so sure. I don't know if I'm ready for something like this. I'm twenty-four years old. There's so many things I wanna do. No offense, but I don't want to be a maid the rest of my life. I can barely support us now; how am I supposed to afford a baby? How am I supposed to provide a better life for two people, let alone a baby?"

As badly as I wanted to offer Angel some wisdom or consolation regarding fatherhood, what did I know? Who was I to encourage or dissuade him? Never in all my lifetimes had I been a father. For eleven hundred years, I've been childless. Almost like I'm defective. The fact remains one of the great tragedies of my lives. Perhaps if I'd ever found love after Gaya and produced children, I would have forged that elusive connection to a life force greater than myself, or at least beyond myself, and I wouldn't have to endure being born again and again, only to know the same struggles and heartaches and loneliness. As much as I'd wanted to have children in this life, it was too late by the time I met Gladys.

"Is it the money you're worried about?" I said. "Because if it's just money, I could probably—"

"No, no—"

"Or maybe we could—"

"Nah, man, it's not money, it's everything. It's like the future is coming too fast, you know? And it's not the future I imagined. It's not the future I planned."

"I'm well acquainted with that feeling," I said.

"When Elana told me she was pregnant it was like I couldn't breathe because I was frozen all of a sudden."

"You didn't tell her that you didn't want a baby, did you?"

"Of course not, bro. I'm not that stupid. It's just that I kind of froze, you know? She needed me to be there, and I had a responsibility to be there, but really, I wasn't where any of us needed me to be, and she had to know that. And that made me feel even more trapped, you know? I wanna move forward, I wanna go to SVJC, you know, register for their criminal justice program, which is, okay, I'll admit, sorta ironic considering certain things in my past and where I might have ended up—like dead or in prison. But I wanna get into corrections. Like really correcting, you know. I don't wanna be a prison guard, I wanna be an advocate. Someday I want to reform the whole system, you know? But how can I even think about that when I'm working forty-hour weeks cleaning toothpaste off sinks, and stripping sheets, and all the time looking for a second job because this one's not enough? And then you add a baby to all of that, and I dunno, Geno, I feel like I might explode."

"How can I help?" I said.

"You can't, homie, nobody can. Don't you see? I wanna make more of myself so I can handle more in the future, and that means Elana, and a baby, and maybe even more babies down the road, and my aunt when she gets old. But now just doesn't seem right. How am I supposed to get to where I want to be from here?"

If I could've answered that, I probably wouldn't have wound up anywhere I did—not Italy, not Peru, or Polynesia, or the Oregon Territory, not in Oscar's lap, or here at Desert Greens. If I'd known how to get back to where I wanted to be, I would have been with Gaya.

The First Time

I recalled to Angel every sight and sound, every smell and sensation, of the marketplace on the day I first encountered Gaya, eleven hundred years prior. It was late spring in Seville, and a stultifying humidity permeated the city. The air in the marketplace was acrid with the smoke of cooking fires. Children darted about between stalls. Caged hens clucked incessantly, sheep bleated, merchants haggled in Hebrew and Arabic and Castilian. Somebody upended a cart while chasing a pig.

Hungry and discouraged, with nowhere to go and no one to meet, I worked my way slowly through the crowded square, past the endless rows of stalls and carts, looking halfheartedly for an opportunity to improve my fortune. I say halfheartedly because I had already passed the point of desperation and was nosing steadily toward apathy. I'd arrived at the obvious conclusion that my life was of no consequence. What became of it was irrelevant. The world would go on without me. So why endure all the heartache and struggle?

Maybe it was my indifference that inspired me to take such a foolish risk that day. He was a bigger man than I, especially around the middle, and he wore his purse low. He was a Berber, judging from his djellaba, long and flowing, woven of the finest purple silk. I calculated that he was none too spry, though were he to catch me he would likely wring my neck without too much trouble.

I awaited his approach behind a fruit cart, out of sight. As my heart began to quicken, I attempted, as I invariably did, to rationalize the crooked act I was about to perform. Surely anyone so careless with their money as this man was bound to lose it. If I didn't take it, somebody else would. And besides, he could obviously afford to lose a little money. He hadn't gotten that big belly on a diet of stale bread and dates. That he was a conqueror was reason enough for a conquered mongrel like me to begrudge him.

Just as he passed me, I darted out from behind the cover of the cart and snatched his purse without ever breaking stride. I took flight into the heart of the crowded market, pushing and jostling my way through the throng. I could hear the ruckus behind me, the shouting back and forth, and it was soon apparent that not one man had given chase to me but a handful of men. I hurtled through the horde of merchants and shoppers, my pursuers keeping pace, beginning to spread out in their efforts to apprehend me. At the fountain, I veered to the right abruptly, ducking under the sagging linen awning of a large jewelry stall, where to the outrage of a young mother I upended a child and a display table on my way through to the other side, emerging in yet another row of stalls teeming with shoppers. I raced down the line into the thick of the crowd. I was at a sprint when a determined hand out of nowhere grasped my arm, upsetting my forward momentum, and spun me sideways.

Swinging to face my captor, I fully expected a fist to the face. What I got was something else altogether. A young woman, a Berber if I had to guess; olive skin, silken robe, deep brown eyes that could not disguise some force of kindness and intelligence. She was marked with a little pink mole just below her right nostril, the lone departure from an otherwise perfectly symmetrical face. It was this tiny imperfection that completed her beauty, though I hardly had time to admire it.

"This way," she said. "Quickly."

I did not hesitate to follow as she led me down the crowded row and finally directed me to take cover beneath an inconspicuous cart, skirted with dirty linen. There, I hunched, panting and heaving, as my pursuers fast approached.

"The man that just ran past," came a deep voice. "Which way did he go?"

From behind the dirty linen, I could just discern the fat ankles of my mark.

"I have seen no one run past," said my savior.

"Impossible," he said. "He ran in this direction. You must have seen him."

"I saw nothing."

The big man conferred with several others in a chorus of grumbling.

"And why should we believe you?" he said.

"What reason have you to doubt me?"

"You know my reasons."

"Then perhaps you should know better than to ask me."

Here, the big man let loose a torrent of sharp-tongued Arabic, too fast for me to decipher.

But the woman's response was calm and measured.

"I have no reason to fear you," she said.

"Don't you?" he said. "Your father was an enemy to my people."

"I told you what I know," she said. "I saw no one run past."

Finally, my pursuers dispersed, still grumbling, and after a few moments, I poked my head out for air.

"Thank you," I said.

"Shush," she said.

I began to crawl out from beneath the cart.

"No, stay put," she said, pushing me back. "They will keep look-ing for you, they won't stop before dark."

"But they're long gone now," I said.

"They will circle back around. You do not understand. The man who is looking for you, he is a very important man. He will stop at nothing."

There it was: my death sentence. And I might have resigned my-self to this fate, were it not for this woman, whose very existence compelled me to survive.

"Stay here," she said. "I'll be back."

It felt like hours before she returned to lift my linen cover long enough to thrust a heaped djellaba of dyed cotton upon me.

"Put this on," she said.

To what did I owe such kindness? Cramped beneath the barrow, I managed to wrestle free of my old clothes and slip into the new djellaba.

"Is it safe to come up now?" I said.

"No," she said.

And so I hunched beneath that blasted wagon, the linen skirt obstructing any hope of ventilation, until the traffic of the market-place finally began to wane and the merchants commenced packing their wares, and shuttering their stalls, and wheeling their carts out in droves. Only then did the young woman finally consent to let-ting me crawl out from my stowage, my neck kinked, my extremi-ties numb.

"Thank you," I said, bowing.

"You are not yet safe," she said. "They will be looking for you. And no disguise will render you safe so long as they are making inquiries. You must stay off the streets and lie low for the time being."

I felt myself color and cast my eyes down at the cobbled ground beneath my feet. "The streets are my home," I said.

The observation seemed to trouble her, but only momentarily.

"Then you must come with me," she said.

I would have followed her anywhere, straight into the arms of my captors, into the very fires of hell had I believed in such a place.

"Why are you doing this for me?" I said.

"Climb in the barrow," she said.

"But—"

"Just do it."

"Who are you?" I said.

"I am Gaya. Now get in."

No sooner had I managed to squeeze myself into the hold than she covered me in a wool blanket and began the laborious business of wheeling me through the empty marketplace. I was not at all sure the conveyance would withstand my weight, but I would later come to learn that it could withstand a body bigger than mine.

"Where are you taking me?"

"Home," she said.

Home. Just imagine me, a loveless orphan, a common thief, accompanying this extraordinary woman home. Now you can see why crime was the best thing that ever happened to me. Had I been a scholar, or a prince, or a caliph, I never would have met Gaya, the first person in this world to show me kindness, the first soul in all of Seville to ever see in me something worth saving. Had she never done another thing for me besides hide me under that barrow, I'd still be beholden to her all these years later. But Gaya was not finished with me yet, oh, no.

I fell off talking, and a silence ensued.

"That's it?" said Angel. "You're just gonna leave me hanging?"

Had I been a younger man, had I still believed that in the telling of the story I might get closer to Gaya somehow, I might have had the strength to continue. But as much as I didn't want to disappoint Angel, it had been exhausting revisiting in such detail my one meaningful life.

Bag of Bones

Sunday had become the loneliest day. Until as recently as two months prior, I had all but managed to successfully negate the loneliness that had dogged me through most of my lives. For many years I'd barely kept track of the days. I was an island, inaccessible to the outside world. The bulwark of apathy and indifference I'd managed to erect in the years since my last visitor was practically impenetrable. I didn't want the input of others. So I'd resolved to stand on the sidelines, conscientiously objecting to life.

But it now seemed quite possible that in Angel I had found a friend. A friend! How many lifetimes had passed since I'd fostered a legitimate friendship?

My lifelong friendship with William Clark in the eighteenth century was nothing if not conditional. It is true that Will and I were inseparable playmates from the earliest days of our youth, sleeping under the same roof, eating our meals at the same table, rarely out of earshot of one another, often riding tandem atop the same quarter horse. But at twelve the dynamic shifted, and though we remained near-constant associates through most of our adolescence and into our adult lives, that kinship was not reciprocal. I was, after all, his slave. Will was very good to me, relatively speaking,

just as his father before him had been good to my father. In relation to slavery, you would've had to consider us fortunate. I have no
doubt William trusted me implicitly. Nor do I doubt for one minute
that he loved me in his way. But so long as I remained indentured,
obligated to serve him, how could I call him a friend?

Although my Oscar might have called me a friend, neither was
our relationship reciprocal. While he doted on me at his convenience, I was not only dependent upon him for my very survival in
the flat, I was also fixated on him as the personification of Gaya, so
much so that I had to exercise considerable self-control in order not
to smother him.

It was sheer torture to resist Oscar's magnetism, but I had to, or
my clinginess might have landed me on the street. I developed tools
to distract myself, tic-like habits such as circling the room for hours
on end before taking my rightful place in Oscar's lap or sprawling
upon his writing desk while he fussed over his poems. Only by willing myself not to suffocate him had I managed to become more catlike and aloof, though believe me, such behavior ran contrary to my
instinct to shower him with my attentions. Thus, I could not call
Oscar a friend, strictly speaking. To Oscar, I was a companion at
best, and some days merely an obligation. For it was Oscar who said
famously that cats are only put on this earth to remind us that not
everything has a purpose. If only he could have intuited that my
purpose was singular: loving him wholly and completely.

But once again, I digress.

Without the considerable consolation of Angel on weekends, I
was left with the cold comfort of Jim and his insufferable mouth-
breathing: the hoarse and shallow rasp of it, the perpetual whistling
in the back of his throat like a death rattle.

"Still seventy-nine out there," he said, wheezing like a ruptured
bellows as he stooped to empty the hamper, the uppermost cleft of
his considerable buttocks visible above the waistband of his scrubs.

"Good to know," I said.

"You ought to get some exercise. Walk down the commons or out to the green."

"I ought to," I said. But what I had wanted to say was: "Look who's talking, fatso."

"Well," Jim said, emptying my wastebasket into his rolling trash can, "take 'er easy."

"Take 'er easy, Jim."

A few minutes later, syrupy-sweet Alice with the Southern twang dropped by to deliver my daily doses of simvasta-something-or-other, lisinopril, and two other medications I can never remember. At this point, I honestly don't care what the meds are for. I have little faith in pharmaceuticals, or modern medicine in general, but lately my hope is that in combination they might lengthen my relatively pain-less existence, so I can put off starting all over again.

"Pleasant afternoon, Mr. Miles."

"Afternoon," I mumbled.

"Why, I hope you've ventured out of doors today. It's glorious."

"That's what they tell me," I said.

Alice presented me my little plastic dish of pills, along with a Dixie cup of water, and stood by. They always wait around to make sure I swallow the medication.

"That's it, Mr. Miles, down the hatch. Well done."

I might have wagged my tail at such encouragement had I ever been a dog. After my meds, I climbed out of bed and lowered myself into the aggressively ergonomic office chair stationed at my IKEA drafting table, upon the corner of which Jim had thrice bruised his hip trying to access the window shade. With only my newest jigsaw puzzle to occupy me (a row of colored Victorian houses in old Chel-sea, my former home), I shined the light of my self-reflection not upon the feline trials of Whiskers and his hopeless devotion, but on me, Eugene Miles, this stooping, sagging, wispy-haired bag of bones who outlived his usefulness decades ago.

In this lifetime alone I have seen more technological advances than any of my earlier selves could have ever dared to imagine, from the incandescent lightbulb to the internet, from the ballpoint pen to quantum mechanics, from penicillin to the atom bomb. Yet, for all the discovery and moment of a lifetime that has spanned more than a century, the story of Eugene Miles is the tale of a simple life in two parts: before Gladys, and after Gladys.

I was born in a kitchen in Victorville, California, to Roger and Beatrice Miles in the year 1916, ten years before Route 66 put the town on the map. I was an only child, a condition I was acutely aware of growing up. You'd think that after eleven hundred years of heartbreak and unfulfillment, I might have engineered an invisible friend to bear witness, a companion with whom I could console myself. But I was resigned to my isolation at an early age and have for the most part clung to it ever since despite my yearnings otherwise.

My father owned the first service station in San Bernardino County, back before the original road was even paved. Route 66 was the best thing that ever happened to Roger Miles, or Victorville for that matter. Traffic at Miles Gas and Go multiplied by a factor of twenty once 66 came along and unlocked the desert from San Berdoo to Amarillo. Despite his devotion, and his growing business, my father was hardly a saint. His moods wavered precariously between taciturnity and impatience, a quality his only child seemed to inspire in him to no end.

I was raised in the Christian faith, though I knew as soon as I was old enough to reason that heaven was a pipe dream. Life was not the dress rehearsal for something bigger; it was the courtship, the wedding, and the marriage, over and over and over. Nothing ever went to heaven; it just went somewhere else. It was entirely possible that Jesus of Nazareth was still out there somewhere, working in a coal mine in Kentucky or selling haberdashery in London. For all anyone knew, he was a cat, as I had once been.

My mother was hardly more cheerful in her outlook than my father, though she leaned heavily upon her faith, which acted as her last defense against biting her nails to the quick. She was a preternaturally pragmatic, if not decidedly unsentimental, woman who had grown up hardscrabble on a dirt farm in Idaho. While my father saw to the filling station and garage, my mother tended to the adjoining store and lunch counter. I grew up in that mercantile, playing with my toy soldiers in dusty corners, or in the basement, accompanied by the husks of dead army ants and the ubiquitous prospect of black widows. The sound of the heavy door opening and closing with its cowbell is indelibly printed in my memory, along with the clang of the cumbersome cash register, the unmistakable crunch of car wheels over gravel, the drone of my father's ball games on the radio, and the shafts of dusty morning light that cut through the plate glass windows, dividing the store's interior into alternating wedges of light and darkness, unlike the cellar, which was only darkness.

I was an awkward child and not entirely opposed to this fate. Occupied as they were with their work obligations, my parents gave me plenty of space, as did the little outpost of Victorville, which rarely answered the call of the outside world. Victorville was never a destination but always a stopover on the way to somewhere else, somewhere that wasn't nowhere. Our nearest neighbors were a quarter mile away, a childless older couple. I had little opportunity to engage anybody on a regular basis, and so at an early age I became adept at the art of being alone.

The desert was my playground as a child, and it seemed as if I had the entire Mojave to myself. The dry emptiness and scorched smell of the high desert spoke to me. I embraced the haunted mystery of the place, for what was my very existence if not haunted? I was drawn to the stark finality of bleached bones and the withered snakeskins that disintegrated at the touch of a finger. The desert presented persuasive evidence that life did not always prevail, an idea that offered me solace as a child, and still does now.

My glimpses into the world beyond Victor Valley were few and far between, and nearly always involved distant relatives from Idaho or passers-through. Beyond that, what information I gathered came from the dog-eared pages of the few books I could get my hands on, books read over and over in the dusty light of the store: *Treasure Island, Tarzan, Styrbiorn the Strong,* along with a few old textbooks: *Health Through Science, McCallum's Pathology, General Science for Today,* and *Europe, Then and Now, a Comprehensive History.* Then there were the movie magazines, borrowed surreptitiously from the racks of my parents' mercantile, pored over cautiously by candlelight while my parents slept: *Motion Picture Magazine, Screen Stories, Modern Screen, Photoplay.* Though I had never actually seen a motion picture with my own eyes, I was a veritable almanac of stars and starlets of the day: Gary Cooper and Vivien Leigh, Barbara Stanwyck and James Cagney, Garbo and Robinson and Astaire. Oh, but I was hungry for knowledge of the larger world beyond Victorville. I would have given anything for a companion.

When I was eight years old, a father and son in a red Hatfield coupe stopped at the station to fuel up and water. Before Roger Miles had started pumping the gas, the father of the boy tossed his hat on the driver's seat and climbed out of the car.

"Stretch your legs," he said to the child. "But don't run off."

When his father ducked into the store, the kid climbed down out of the coupe and, perhaps sensing my curiosity, approached me where I was standing in the mouth of the open bay door. He was about my age, I guessed, maybe a year older. But it was clear immediately, from his clothing, his manner, and his every aspect, that he was more confident and worldly than I.

"You wanna race me?" he said.

"Sure, I guess."

"Okay. We'll go from right here to that third fence post. On the count of three, you ready?"

Much to the disappointment of my father, I was not an athletic child. Thus I entertained no expectation of winning a footrace with this boy. But I would've done anything he asked for a few precious minutes of companionship. The other kid got the quicker jump at the count of three and never looked back. I was so impressed with his unorthodox running style, the way his fists punched at the air in front of him as though he were angry at it, that I later emulated his form at length, eventually perfecting it. My father caught me at it once.

"What's wrong with your arms?" he said, wiping his hands down on a rag.

"Nothing."

"Then why are you running like that?"

"Like what?"

"Like you're swimming or something."

"I dunno. I thought it would make me go faster."

"You look like a poof," he said.

I don't begrudge my father for calling me names; he was only trying to help me in his own misguided way.

After the kid beat me in the footrace, we retreated to the store, where I begged my mom for a couple bottles of root beer, but the boy's father insisted on paying for them. We drank them sitting on old tires out back of the garage, while his father chatted up my mother at the counter.

"What's it like living out here?" said the kid. "You must get bored out of your bean."

"It's okay, I guess. Where do you live?" I said.

"Los Angeles."

"What's that like?"

"Big," he said. "A lot more exciting than this place. There's cars just about everywhere you look, and big buildings, and fancy women."

"I'll probably move there someday," I said. And I meant it. God, but I longed to escape the insignificance of Victorville.

I never did get the kid's name, but sadly enough he was about the closest thing I had to a friendly connection before the age of seventeen, and I only knew him twenty minutes.

As a teen, I pumped gas at Miles Gas and Go, and more than ever I began to feel the pull of the outside world, as daily, carloads of young people pulled off Highway 66 to refuel and refresh. College boys and pretty girls in scarves and sunglasses bound for Hollywood or Las Vegas, purchasing sodas and ham salad sandwiches. Invariably, their lives seemed exotic in comparison to my own. Once Wallace Beery himself, whom I recognized immediately from *Silver Screen* and the *Motion Picture Herald*, pulled up in a shiny black Duesenberg with whitewall tires. That car must have been thirty feet long. Mr. Beery ate an egg salad sandwich at the counter and drank two cups of coffee and tipped my mother ten dollars.

More and more as I passed through adolescence, the City of Angels called out to me. I was drawn to the possibility that I could build a life for myself there that could make me forget all the other lives, that I could finally forge a genuine connection with somebody, anybody. More than once it occurred to me to stow away in somebody's trunk. This impulse to flee Victorville said more about the yearning of my teenage self than it said about my immutable self, who already knew from experience that the life of a princess was not necessarily any more fulfilling than the life of a cat.

Eight days before my twentieth birthday, I would indeed manage to escape Victorville and move to Los Angeles with 216 dollars in my pocket, arriving with a leather suitcase that looked like someone had kicked it there from Amarillo. I was wearing my father's old tweed suit, with the wide lapels and the high-rise cuffed trousers, by then a decade out of fashion. My father also gifted me his old '25 Chrysler sedan, which he'd painstakingly restored, though it wasn't much to look at.

I remember vividly the afternoon I drove off, the hot desert wind blasting my face through the open window like a furnace, that tiny seed of possibility taking root in me, the hope that in the great city of Los Angeles I might at last find the satisfaction and inner peace that had been eluding me for so many lifetimes.

A Ghostly Light

In the evenings when Angel came to straighten my quarters, or go through the motions, he urged me to continue my tales of life in Spain. My remembrances seemed to provide the perfect occupation given his lack of anything to do in the way of cleaning.

Each evening, I picked up where I'd left off the previous day, as Angel leaned on his broom, or dusted the dresser to no effect.

Gaya trundled me over the cobbled streets of Seville, up and down the hills for what seemed like miles, the barrow creaking beneath the burden of my weight.

"For heaven's sake, where do you live? Córdoba?"

"Shush," she said.

"Just let me walk on my own."

"Silence," she said.

My God, it was stifling in that cart, cramped beneath the cover of the heavy wool blanket. My extremities were numb in no time, and I needed desperately to pass my water. Yet my chest hummed with something new, a nervous excitement, not because I was in peril, rather because this inexplicably kind woman had taken an interest in me. I had known little of love or kindness in my twenty years, nor had I done anything to earn them. Likewise, I had shown little kindness to others, and love abided on some far horizon beyond my purview. I had lusted. I had coveted. I had yearned. But never had I loved.

When we finally arrived at our destination near dusk, Gaya pulled the blanket back and assisted me out of my cramped hold, and I was confronted by a squat structure of wattle-and-daub lattice, neither crude nor impressive, a dwelling so unexceptional as to be indistinguishable from those flanking it on either side. Immediately, my eyes darted about for a shrub or an alleyway in which to relieve myself.

"Follow me," she said, pushing through the front door.

"But the cart," I said, following her lead.

"The cart will be fine. We must hurry."

"But I have to urinate."

"It can wait," she said.

We ducked into a cellar completely awash in darkness. Somehow, Gaya managed to navigate the impenetrable gloom and light a candle. The entire space undulated in a ghostly luminescence. The mustiness of the cellar suggested an ancient place, a tomb, or a sarcophagus. Crudely constructed shelves lined the back wall, crowded with all manner of miscellany, buckets and hatchets and coils of braided rope. Along the eastern wall was a line of large barrels like wine kegs. Mouse droppings riddled the earthen floor.

"Why bring me here?"

"Because you must remain hidden."

"Surely I'm far enough from the marketplace now that—"

"No," she said. "They will scour the city for you."

"But—"

"Do not underestimate this man. He is the nephew of a caliph from Córdoba. My father once worked for him."

"And?"

"My father is dead," she said, averting her eyes.

"Are you saying this man is responsible for your father's death?"

To this, she offered no reply.

"Is that why you hid me?"

This line of inquiry also met with silence.

"How long must I stay here?" I said.

"Until it is safe for you to leave."

"And what shall determine that?"

"I don't know," she said. "You may never be safe."

The truth was that I didn't care how long I might have to stay. I was ready to occupy that rancid cellar the rest of my days, if only to be near her. What earthly woman would take pity on an idler such as myself, a young man devoid of grace or virtue, a fatherless, motherless vagrant of less value to the world than a three-legged ass?

"Where is the purse?" she said.

"Here," I said, producing the satchel from beneath my robe and thrusting it upon her. "You take it."

"I don't want his money," she said.

"But surely you could use it."

"Only as a last resort."

"You still haven't told me why you're doing all this for me."

"Does it matter?" she said.

"Of course it matters."

"What if I don't know the answer to that?" she said.

"It's because you pity me, isn't it?" I said.

"No," she said. "Not exactly."

"Then why go to all the trouble?"

"Let me think about that," she said. "Are you hungry?"

Before I could answer, there came from up the stairs a thunderous pounding on the door, accompanied by a booming voice. Gaya blew out the candle in an instant.

"Hide behind the barrels," she whispered. "Don't make a sound."

She hurried through the darkness and up the steps, closing the heavy door behind her with a groan. And just when it seemed that it could not possibly get any darker, the room was pure and utter blackness, and the only thing that kept the darkness from swallowing me whole was the furious beating of my heart.

At that juncture, I stopped talking as Angel looked on expectantly.

"Seriously?" he said. "You're gonna leave me hanging again?"

This time it wasn't exhaustion that prompted me to stop. Now I was relishing the audience, the company, the connection, and the best way to preserve it was to pay my story out in measured spoonfuls, to keep Angel wanting more.

The Thousand-Year-Old Toddler

When Angel returned for his Monday shift, his body language bespoke irritability. The jerkiness of his movements suggested he was impatient to make them, and the flare of his pierced nostrils, along with the deep furrowing of his brow, seemed to imply some vexing preoccupation. I was at my drafting table working on a puzzle when he entered as usual with his rolling garbage can, hamper, and tray of cleaning supplies. After an uninspired salutation, he remained stonily silent as he went about his various tasks, emptying the waste pail, wiping down the TV screen, stripping the bed, and stretching over the table to lower the blind.

My immediate instinct was to cheer Angel by offering him distraction. So I regaled him with the story of how Oscar had once thrown a party in his flat in Chelsea with several of his boyfriends, and how after much gin and merrymaking, the boys had decided to have a little fun with me. They fashioned an evening gown and petticoat out of torn drapery and dressed me up as a proper Victorian lady, right down to a bonnet of purple felt cut from the trim of the sofa. Subsequently, and much to my distress, the insufferable deviants proceeded to stand me up on my hind legs and parade me about the flat, putting ribald and most unladylike words into my mouth for their own amusement. Oh, how clever they thought they were, the scoundrels. How pleased with themselves they were! The experience proved to be one of the most humiliating of my feline life, but if my wounded pride could now serve to cheer Angel, then my suffering had not been in vain.

"Aw, Eugene, not today, man," he said. "I just can't take your crazy stories right now."

I'm ashamed to admit how deeply the remark cut me. Despite our growing rapport, I would never have guessed that Angel could've had that effect on me. With one offhanded declaration, Angel had awakened in me feelings of inadequacy that stretched all the way back to Seville, shame and embarrassment that had harassed me through Italy, Peru, Virginia, London, and Victorville. The fact alone that Angel had addressed me formally as Eugene, and not Geno, or homie, or dog, or ese, was enough to send the blood rushing to my face. It seemed obvious that he'd been humoring me all along, and that our burgeoning affection was one-sided, and that I, a doddering old man, had wishfully misread the signals. It was strange how much I felt like a toddler sitting there, as though in front of my father, eyes averted in shame.

Angel must have realized he'd hurt my feelings, because he softened his manner immediately.

"I'm sorry, homie. I'm just in a bad place right now. I didn't mean to be a jerk about it. You know I like your stories, man. I love your stories. You gotta admit, they are a little batshit sometimes, though."

"Do you want to talk about what happened?" I said.

"Nah, not now," he said. "Maybe at lunch. Right now, I just gotta not think about it."

"So, that's an invite to lunch?" I said.

"Sure, why not," he said. "I'll be over myself by then."

But at lunch Angel remained dispirited, barely touching his

steaming posole. After our initial exchange that afternoon I was wary of drawing him out, so we ate mostly in silence out on the green in the dry desert air.

"Aw, man, I really blew it this time," said Angel finally. "I should've kept my big mouth shut, you know? I shouldn't have told Elana I was scared. That's not what she needed to hear. I should have been strong and supportive. She's right, Geno, I'm not a man, I'm a boy."

"What happened?"

"She moved out is what happened, moved in with her mom and her sister up in Victorville."

"Victorville?"

"Yeah, man, it's like twenty miles away."

"I know where it is," I said.

"Oh, I really screwed up this time, Geno."

"About the baby?"

"Yes, man, all of it. This is serious. I've got to get things back on track. I should be up there right now, convincing her."

"Of what?"

"That I'm a man. That I'm ready for this baby, that I'm ready to provide for a family. Somehow, someway, I'll figure it all out. We got almost seven months. But right now, we gotta be together. We gotta plan and prepare. I gotta learn all that Lamaze breathing and the rest of it."

"I think she'll be glad to hear it," I said. "I think if you say to her what you just said to me, everything will turn out okay."

"I hope you're right, homie."

"Bring flowers," I said. "And think of a few baby names, girls and boys."

"Oh, that's good, Geno. Show her that I'm thinking about it. That's really good, bro."

I must say I was rather impressed at my own advice, seeing as how I had zero experience in such matters. Angel's spirits improved immediately, as he started eating his soup in greedy spoonfuls.

"What about Josefina for a girl?" he said between bites.

"It's lovely," I said. "What does it mean?"

"How should I know, bro? I just like the way it sounds."

After our meal, Angel escorted me slowly across the green in the light of sunset. When we were halfway to the cafeteria door, he set his hand upon my shoulder, and something once familiar but far removed stirred in my chest.

To the River

My heart was beating like a scared rabbit's as Gaya swept down the corridor toward the urgent knocking. In the darkness, I groped for a hatchet on the shelf, upending a wooden bucket in the process, wincing as it clattered upon the dirt floor. I froze for an instant, as though the act of stillness might undo the racket. Stowing the stolen purse behind a wooden coffer, I took cover, squatting behind the barrels.

From above came two voices: first Gaya's, calm and composed, then a man's, straight and pointed as an obelisk. By their footfalls upon the creaking floorboards, I followed their progress from room to room, straining to hear their words. But it was not until they descended the basement stairs that I could discern them.

"And what is down here?"

"Storage."

"Storage of what?"

"Dust, mostly. A nest of spiders. Some old tools. See for yourself."

Was she inviting disaster? Was this a bluff? Clutching the hatchet, I tried desperately to quiet my breathing, certain that should my would-be captor burst through the door of the cellar, my heartbeat alone would betray me.

"Open it," said the voice.

If Gaya's invitation had been a bluff, it failed. To my dread, I heard the now familiar groan of the heavy door as a shaft of dusty light flooded in, cutting the room lengthwise in two.

"Flame," said the man.

"I haven't one handy."

"Then find one."

Still hunkered behind the barrels, ears ringing, clutching the hatchet with renewed urgency, I shifted my weight off my heels to the balls of my feet, ready to ambush the interloper should it come to that. I could hear the slight rasp of my enemy's breathing in the darkness, smell his sweat-tinged nearness through the musty air of the cellar.

Gaya was clearly stalling, for she knew precisely where she'd set the candle moments before, yet she fumbled about in the darkness as though searching for it. My adversary cleared his throat and shifted the soles of his leather boots upon the dirt floor, before edging restlessly to the center of the room, where he paused once more, his silhouette framed perfectly in the shaft of light, his back facing me.

I did not reason before I leapt out from behind my cover and struck him once decisively over the head with the blunt end of the hatchet, whereupon he promptly collapsed in a heap. An instant later, the room was quavering in candlelight as Gaya and I stood speechless above the prone body.

"Who is he?"

"I've never seen him before," said Gaya.

"Was I premature?"

"You were decisive," she said. "You did what needed to be done, and you did it without hesitation. That takes nerve."

Whoever he was, he was a good deal larger than me, but lanky, not an imposing figure, and neither was he a soldier, to judge from his plain woolen robe. He lay there motionless, perhaps even dead. When I crouched down to inspect his person closer, I'm ashamed to admit, I patted him down for a purse before I even bothered to check his condition. There were no spoils to be gotten.

Already blood from his head wound was beginning to pool upon the earthen floor. Gaya crouched down beside me and set her hand upon his chest.

"Is he . . . ?" I ventured.

"It is done," she said.

My scalp tightened, and the breath went out of me all at once. What had my depravity wrought now? What new peril had I thrust upon myself? And more important, what dire consequences had I foisted upon this woman whose only transgression was the impulse to protect me?

"What now?" I said.

"We must dispose of him before they come looking."

For all my degenerate ways—sneaking and stealing, lying and cheating and poaching, pinching and pilfering and habitually appropriating that which did not belong to me—never had I crossed such a line as this. For the first time, I had blood on my hands, and the revelation left me numb.

"How do you suggest we do that?" I said.

"We will take him to the river, but not until the city is sleeping."

"And by what means shall we convey him to the river?"

"The same way we secreted you here," she said.

"Apparently it was not so secret after all," I pointed out. "It would appear we were followed."

"It is possible, but I do not think so," she said.

"Then how do you account for our visitor?"

"The man whom you robbed is Assad al-Attar. He has questioned me before in the market about my other activities. He does not trust me, nor should he."

"Why did he kill your father?"

"He was only responsible for reporting my father. But we have no time to speak of such things. Just know that he will find us if we do not act quickly."

I pressed Gaya no further. Without delay, she took leave of the basement and returned moments later, her arms heaped with a large wall tapestry, which she proceeded to spread upon the cellar floor adjacent to the dead man.

"Help me move him," she said.

Once we'd executed the task, we rolled the body up in the tapestry and dragged it to the foot of the cellar steps.

"We would be wise to cover the blood," she said.

It was almost as if she'd done this all before. With the toe of my sandal, then with the hatchet, I obscured the blood spot under fresh dirt, but when my attempts proved insufficient, Gaya waved me aside and proceeded to roll one of the barrels atop the offending patch.

But for the occasional bark of a dog, or the bleating of a sheep in the distance, the city was eerily silent in the cool night air. With considerable effort, we loaded the body into the cart and cajoled it into place, covering it with the heavy wool blanket.

"You're sure about this?" I said.

"We can't leave him," she said. "Assad's men will return, this I know."

I wasn't convinced myself, but already I trusted Gaya's judgment implicitly. I would've done anything she told me to do. I felt strangely alive as we began pushing the heavy cart in tandem, south over the cobbled streets toward the river, the stars, impervious to our dire circumstances, wheeling above.

Flowers

When I arrived in Los Angeles in the summer of 1936, fresh from the teeming metropolis of Victorville, a lean, dopey kid in his father's baggy suit, with little to no life experience in the twentieth century, I spent three nights at a hotel called the Oviatt downtown on Flower Street at a dollar a night. To call these accommodations modest would be a considerable overstatement, even by my own paltry standards. The Oviatt was a hive of squalid activity, clammy, damp, and musty, ripe with the sort of unpleasant odors one would prefer not to contemplate. While downtown Los Angeles was a far cry from Victorville, the privation was familiar.

My room was no bigger than an oversized coat closet, scarcely furnished. But at least it had a window. The wallpaper was blistered and discolored. Other than that, the wall offered no pretense whatsoever, no art or other decorative flourishes. The window was painted shut. Flies circled the room dazedly at all hours, unconcerned by my presence, so much so that they routinely landed on my person, rubbing their forelegs together lazily. My pillow, which had been soundly defeated sometime around the turn of the century, smelled conspicuously of stale Chesterfields and faintly of mold. The mattress springs were shot to hell, issuing a cacophonous protest of creaks and groans every time I so much as moved a muscle, a state of affairs that did not please the adjacent tenant, who pounded on the wall nightly.

"Settle down in there, goddamn it!" he shouted. "I'm trying to sleep."

But worse than the accommodations themselves was the local color, which I found to be garish: winos mostly, grifters, hopheads, and women of questionable repute. Through the wafer-thin walls, they laughed, they shouted, they cried, they moaned in furious ecstasy, while behind my bolted door I tossed and turned the nights away, agonizing about my future and second-guessing my decision to leave Victorville, hellish as it had been.

Despite the rank squalor of the Oviatt, the kid who had beaten me in the footrace in 1924, the kid whose name I never knew or I might have looked him up all those years later for lack of human connection, had not lied to me about Los Angeles: It was big and getting bigger by the hour—big and dirty and busy and noisy, but undeniably glorious in its pageantry. To walk about in the City of Angels was to awaken every sense. Los Angeles was a feast for the eyes and ears and nose, a scintillating buffet of human assortment, a catalog of every sensation from aspiration to desperation, and all that glory and wreckage that lay between. Los Angeles was that rarest of desert flowers, a city rife with opportunity and changing fortunes. Not since the marketplace in Seville had I experienced such cultural dynamism—not in Genoa, or London, or Cuzco.

Upon my second morning in the Oviatt, I made my first acquaintance, a desk clerk named Ed Wozniak, who I came to learn was from Portage, Wisconsin. Ed was a lean, ropy kid a few years older and more worldly than me. What on earth he was doing working the desk at the Oviatt downtown, surrounded by stewbums and harlots, was anybody's guess. As I was crossing the lobby to fetch a newspaper that second morning, Ed looked up from his own newspaper and called out to me.

"You," he said. "What the heck are you doing here? You're way too young for a dump like this."

"I'm looking to rent a room somewhere, but—"

"Well, take my advice, don't look in this neighborhood. Unless you like getting mugged. You got a job?"

"Not yet," I said. "But I'm gonna get one."

"Got any money?"

"Yeah."

"How much?"

Naturally, I was a little wary of answering this question. After all, I hadn't known this guy for sixty seconds, and already he was asking personal questions. He must have registered my reluctance.

"More than fifty dollars?"

"Maybe."

"I know an old lady down the street from my place who might be able to help you with a room, so long as you've got a little money to hold you over. She doesn't want any freeloaders. You're not a musician, are you?"

"No."

"Good," he said. "I'm Ed, by the way. But you can call me Woz."

"Woz?"

"Short for Wozniak."

"Eugene," I said, extending a hand.

Ed shook my hand, then scratched something out on a notepad, tore it loose, and handed it across the desk to me.

"Here's her address," he said.

That was the beginning of my good fortune in Los Angeles. Thanks to Woz, I was able to secure room and board in the house of an old Mexican woman in Boyle Heights named Consuela, who couldn't have been an inch over five foot. And while she was indeed venerable (I would have put her somewhere in her late seventies) and petite (she couldn't have weighed a hundred pounds), Consuela was formidable in her manner, unwavering in her gaze, solid and compact in her construction.

When she met me at the door the first time, she looked me up and down, taking in, amongst my other attributes, my father's baggy suit and fedora.

"You're not a musician, are you?"

"No, ma'am."

"You're sure?"

"Yes, ma'am, I can scarcely carry a tune."

She considered me as though she was still not convinced, peering beyond me to the Chrysler parked at the curb as though to make sure there wasn't a kettledrum hiding in the backseat.

"Are you employed?"

"I just arrived in the city two days ago," I explained. "But I have savings, and it won't be long before I land a job, that I can assure you."

Again, Consuela did not look overly convinced by this declaration.

"Okay, then. Two fifty a week," she said, finally consenting. "Visitors are okay, but no overnight guests. And no musicians."

"Got it. No musicians."

"And I'll need a month in advance."

I drove back downtown to the Oviatt that afternoon and checked out. I stopped by the desk to thank Woz.

"Don't mention it," he said. "I live four doors down, maybe I'll see you around."

Unlike the swampy environs of the Oviatt, my room at Consuela's, a tiny stand-alone studio in the backyard, somehow managed to be airy despite its two hundred square feet. Every morning
without fail, sunlight flooded into the little room, and through the
open window the gentle breeze stirred the lace curtains, smelling
faintly of primrose and sage. It was the smell of promise, the smell
of somewhere, the smell of a place that might help me forget my
loneliness and leave my legacy of yearning behind.

Boyle Heights was a predominantly Mexican neighborhood back
then, quiet in its lack of automobile traffic and construction, and yet
exuberant with the laughter and shouting of children playing in the
neighboring yards and in the streets. Oh, how I might have benefited from all those playmates as a child in Victorville, that sense of
belonging. Who knows how I might have blossomed with a little
company? The families of Boyle Heights were largely poor, but you
wouldn't have known it to watch them live; they laughed, and talked
amongst each other, and cooked outdoors, sometimes three and
four families at a time. The Mexicans had been in California longer
than the Americans, yet somehow they had become outsiders. Still,
I envied their solidarity, at least as it seemed to me. For amongst the
few things I've learned over the course of my ceaseless existence is
that togetherness, that elusive pure togetherness not governed by
intent or motive or design, that togetherness that is not weighed in
pros or cons, nor by convenience, but purely by the desire to connect, is more meaningful than just about anything else. It cannot be
bought or willed into existence. If you should be fortunate enough
to come by this kinship, cling to it with your life for as long as you
possibly can, for when it is gone it leaves a hole that can never be
filled, not in twenty years or twenty lifetimes. Without this connection, death is a reasonable alternative, if you're lucky enough to
find that.

I was lucky I'd met Woz when I did, because four days after I moved into Consuela's, I ran into him on the sidewalk, and he was carrying a suitcase.

"Woz," I said. "Where you headed?"

"Back to Wisconsin. Don't let the sunshine and the palm trees fool you. This place is trying to do us all in."

And that was the end of my would-be friendship with Ed Wozniak. But all these years later I'm still grateful to him for saving me from the Oviatt.

My second week at Consuela's, I landed a job at a filling station on Wilshire, which I managed to convince myself was temporary. I wore a nifty gray coverall with my name stitched upon the breast, and a matching gray cap that said "Union." I worked six days a week, pumping petrol and wiping windshields, checking tires and topping off motor oil, all tasks I could execute in my sleep. Yet pumping petrol along the Miracle Mile was something altogether different. There was never any standing around at Union, not like the Gas and Go, where whole days could pass without any action. Wilshire felt like the center of the universe. Nearly every day I rubbed elbows with the stars, routinely topping off the tank of Clark Gable's convertible coupe, exchanging pleasantries with Ginger Rogers, a Union regular. Robert Taylor once tipped me twenty bucks when I fixed his windshield wiper at no cost. Bogart gave me a tip for the seventh race at Santa Anita, a horse named Balzac's Daughter.

Evenings and Sundays, I taught myself shorthand, which seemed like a reasonable proposition, and a good bet in a world that just kept moving faster and faster. Who had time for entire words or sentences anymore? There were deals to be made and schedules to be met, cases stacking up down at the courthouse. After all, the world was so much more than just a dusty two-lane highway through the desert. I suppose I could have been a mechanic with a little more learning. All those years at Miles Gas and Go had taught me a few things about carburetors, radiators, oil pans, transmissions, and such, though not nearly as much as my father would have liked. Subconsciously, the choice of stenography may well have been an antidote to my everlasting life, an impulse to shorten and abbreviate anything over which I might manage to exercise control.

One did not win Consuela's approval easily, though I paid my rent for the month in advance without fail. I had no visitors, overnight or otherwise. I stayed away from musicians as a matter of course. I was a quiet, considerate, and nearly invisible tenant. Still, in three months' time Consuela had yet to bestow a smile upon me.

Determined to win her over, one Friday afternoon after my shift at Union, while strolling through the Flower District downtown, the thought occurred to me to bring my unflappable landlady gardenias. Pleased with myself the whole walk home, I presented them to her on the front landing, where she was seated upon her wooden bench, surveying the street.

"What's wrong, you haven't got your rent?"

"I just thought these might brighten the place up."

"Hmph," she said.

And while the gesture still did not manage to elicit a smile, it garnered a silent nod of approval. And that was a start.

In the weeks that followed, I made Friday flowers a tradition: agapanthus and bougainvillea, fuchsias and poppies and dahlias, cosmos and zinnias and marigolds, and each time Consuela accepted them matter-of-factly. But I'd be lying if I said that those late afternoon strolls through the Flower District were only to win Consuela's approval. For I loved the color, and the smell, and the vivacity of the neighborhood.

After six months at Consuela's, I still had not managed to establish a career as a stenographer. I kept on at the service station, squirreling my money away to no discernible purpose. When I could make the time, I beat the streets downtown, applying at legal offices. I had no social life, and no real hope of cultivating one, though I was not unhappy. Consider the loneliness of a house cat, and you will begin to understand my capacity for being alone. Sometimes Oscar left the flat for days on end, leaving my food heaped in a bowl for me to ration on my own.

Some Sundays I'd set out early from Boyle Heights and stroll downtown and catch the train and ride it west all the way to Santa Monica. People think Los Angeles and they think automobiles and highways, but in those days, you could ride the streetcar from Pasadena to the ocean. I much preferred it to driving. To be pressed up against all those other lives was a reminder that I was not alone in my endless travels. Surely someone else on the streetcar had also suffered the same fate as me, to live again and again. Maybe it was the old woman in the yellow scarf, the one with the distant eyes. Or maybe the young Black man at the back of the car with the flat expression, he who made eye contact with nobody.

After twenty years in the high desert, the beaches were a revelation, but also an ancient reprise. For the undulating rhythm and pulse of the ocean lived deep inside of me somewhere. Once you have experienced a thing it will never leave you, not ever. I had only to stand ankle-deep in the surf to remember the swaying and swelling of the open water in a wooden canoe at night, my father at the head of the boat, guiding us by the stars. My name was Kiri then; I was but a little girl who never lived past the age of seven. Think of it, a life so brief, nearly a hundred years shorter than my present administration. I had lived two lives before that one, and lived three after, and no matter how long or how short, every one of them endured in the fabric of me somewhere, whether I wanted them to or not. Understand: Life is inexhaustible and undefeatable; try to snuff it out and you're destined to fail. Life will thrive under any circumstances. You will find life three thousand feet below the polar ice caps. Who knows, you might even find yourself down there.

Forever

It took Gaya and me half the night to convey Assad's dead minion to the river, which lay well south of the city. His transport was a grueling and often noisy affair, one that stirred animals and people alike from their slumber as we trundled through the outskirts of Seville, leaving candlelit windows and barking dogs in our wake. But aside from a few grubby night dwellers hunched and muttering in doorways, we encountered scarcely a soul along our way.

"What if the body washes ashore?" I whispered.

"It will eventually. But maybe not before the current carries him clear of the city."

Once again, it seemed as if Gaya had done all of this before. Who was this woman? How had she come by such knowledge?

At the edge of town, after we had breached the broken walls of the city, our course became impassable, and we were forced to abandon the cart and drag the body over the squelchy terrain to the riverbank, where we arrived exhausted.

Never a devout soul, I nonetheless found myself compelled to pray for forgiveness before we rolled the body into the westward current. One never knew.

"And so it ends," I said.

"Doubtful," said Gaya.

We stood side by side upon the muddy bank and watched the dark mass begin its reluctant progress away from the city toward the sea.

"What now?" I said.

"Where is the purse?" said Gaya.

"Hidden behind a trunk in the cellar."

"How much is in it?"

"I never looked."

"We must go back for it," she said.

"I thought you didn't want his money."

"Now things are different," she said. "We may need it."

With that, Gaya turned her back to the river and began slogging through the marsh toward the city. I followed on her heels, troubled every step of the way. It seemed that after a lifetime of thoughtless larceny, I was finally growing a conscience.

It was not long before we arrived at the cart, and I took hold of the handles.

"Leave it," she said.

"But what about your livelihood?"

"What good is a cart when I cannot return to the marketplace?" she said. "Assad will only come for me there. We must retrieve the purse and leave the city at once."

"To where?"

"That we must decide. And soon."

A stolen purse, no different from countless others, or so I'd dared to believe. How was I to know that this one would have such far-reaching consequences?

We trudged along in silence through the darkened streets, the ways of the world suddenly a mystery to me. My fate was now inextricably linked to a woman I had not yet known for a day.

"Who are you?" I said at last.

"I told you already. I am Gaya."

"But who are you?"

"Not who you think I am," she said.

"If not an angel, I haven't the slightest idea who you are."

"I am a lot of things, but I'm no angel," she said.

"What, then?"

"A stranger in my own home," she said. "A bereaved daughter. An asset to the resistance. An imposter."

"Imposter? How so?"

"I'm no more a Berber than I am a Jew," she said. "Gaya is the name my father gave me, though it is not a Christian name. It seems my father had plans for me from the beginning."

"Plans for what?"

"The resistance," said Gaya. "Like my father, I have lived my whole life disguising myself as the enemy, so that I might avoid their suspicion, so that I might undermine and diminish their hold on us. Now you know the truth, just as Assad arrived at the truth."

I could hardly imagine such dedication, such adherence to a belief, such connection to some idea beyond self-interest.

Gaya halted her progress in the darkened street to look me in the eye.

"And what about you, Euric? To what cause are you loyal?"

I averted my eyes in shame. "Only myself."

"And has this proven a worthy cause, Euric?"

"No. Not until this very day."

"And how is today different?"

"Today I met you."

Gaya let loose a laugh, then promptly quieted herself for fear of waking anyone in the darkened houses.

"Why do you laugh?" I said, a rush of blood suffusing my cheeks.

"I laugh at your innocence."

"My innocence? Woman, I'm a criminal. A thief practically since

I was tall enough to reach a purse. And now I'm a murderer, and a conspirator, too."

"And yet you're still innocent," said Gaya.

"How so?"

"You are young," she said. "What do you know of forever? You know nothing of what the future holds."

Little did she know how prescient those words would prove to be.

Life Saver

While I have talked at some length about the staff here at Desert Greens, those who have committed themselves to providing "a secure, comfortable, and nurturing setting while encouraging residents to maintain their own independence and ability," I have neglected thus far to officially describe Wayne, the new resident mental health liaison. Wayne is part of what the brochures call the Wellness Team. No doubt, Wayne is a mental health professional in some capacity, but frankly, I'm not sure about his bona fides. Who knows where he went to college or what exactly his discipline happens to be? Clearly, Wayne Francis is no Sigmund Freud, or he wouldn't be working at an assisted living facility in Lucerne Valley, would he? That is not a knock against Wayne, that's just the way it is. Yet my contempt for Wayne is not unfounded.

Wayne is maybe forty years old, reasonably good-looking if unremarkably so. With his slightly aquiline nose and full lips, he looks a little like me as a younger man, but taller. He doesn't carry a clipboard or wear a lab coat, or scrubs, or anything else that would serve to distinguish him as a healthcare professional. He wears blue jeans and running shoes, and faintly patterned dress shirts with the sleeves rolled halfway to the elbow. I suspect the intended effect of Wayne's unerring flair for the casual is to disarm his subjects. Here at Desert Greens, we are encouraged to think of Wayne as a regular guy, though it's Wayne's job to ask us questions and draw us out, so that he can ascertain our mental wellness. His house calls are invariably unofficial, and he seems to favor the element of surprise. Like last week when I was at my drafting table, absorbed in my cat puzzle. Who knows how long Wayne might have been standing there in the doorway observing me?

"Eugene," he said, startling me. "Can I come in?"

"If you must," I said.

Wayne promptly stationed himself over my left shoulder.

"Ah, cats," he said, stating the obvious, as he often does.

I'd completed that puzzle at least four times, it being amongst my favorites. One thousand pieces; forty cat breeds from Abyssinian to Turkish Van arranged in bordered rows, with varying-colored backgrounds from eggplant to lemon.

"You like cats, don't you?" said Wayne. "You relate to them."

"You could say it comes naturally," I said.

"Always been a dog person, myself."

Wayne abandoned his post over my left shoulder to lean casually against the edge of the bed.

"Tell me, how are you feeling these days, Eugene?"

"About as well as you might expect for a guy who's three years older than the Republic of Austria."

"Is that a fact?"

He produced a roll of candy from his jeans pocket and unfurled the foil wrapper.

"Life Saver?" he said.

"Is that a joke?" I said.

My conversations with Wayne are always a dance. It's obvious he thinks I'm delusional, that any mention of my past lives is the manifestation of some aberrant psychology, the result of isolation, or trauma, or advanced age. And while he is by no means unique in this conviction, I've yet to understand what he hopes to accomplish in persuading me to share my stories. What if I really was just a crazy old man with his fantasies? Would that really be a problem so long as I wasn't scratching the nurses and hurling feces at the walls? I've never hurt anybody with my lack of mortality. The fact is, I hardly discuss my past lives with anyone but Angel, and sometimes Wayne himself, so far as I'm willing to indulge him. So what difference could the veracity of my memories possibly make, especially at this stage of the game?

"Still having your dreams?" Wayne said.

"They're not dreams."

"Oh, right," he said. "Memories."

He popped a yellow Life Saver into his mouth, and I was instantly and painfully reminded that Wayne was an aggressive sucker. Already I could hear the hard candy clashing intermittently with the backs of his teeth. Like mouth-breathing, aggressive sucking is something I can't abide. The slurping and smacking set me on edge. Chances are Wayne also chews ice, yet another quirk that aggravates my sensibilities.

"Tell me, Eugene," said Wayne. "Are they always the same, or do they vary? Your memories, I mean."

"The same. Why would they vary?"

I would state that Wayne seemed to be sucking on the idea, but it was excruciatingly clear that what he was in fact sucking on was a Life Saver, and obnoxiously so. Was it nervous energy, aggression, that caused him to suck so assertively?

"Interesting," said Wayne.

"Is it?" I said. "Why, do your memories vary?"

"Generally not," he said. "But then, I don't claim to have been alive a thousand years ago. How do you feel otherwise?"

"Fine," I said.

"Are you lonely here?"

"Never."

"How's your appetite?"

"Normal."

"Good to hear," said Wayne. "Do you ever feel dizzy or confused?"

"No."

"What about your moods?" he said. "Do you find that they swing abruptly?"

"Hardly at all," I said.

"Are you forgetful?"

"Never."

"Good," said Wayne. "That's good. Tell me, do you ever think about death?"

"Not anymore," I said.

"So, you're not afraid?"

"I didn't say that."

"Do you want to talk about it?" he said.

"No."

"Fair enough," said Wayne. "But if you ever do want to talk about it, I'm here for you."

And with that assurance, Wayne took leave of my quarters, though I swear I could still hear him smacking on that Life Saver halfway down the hallway.

The following day, Angel arrived around four o'clock with his rolling supply closet, looking like he hadn't slept in days.

"How'd it go?"

He shook his head grimly and began stripping the bed.

"Not good, ese. I drove up to Victorville this morning with flowers like you said. I had like six different baby names."

"Did she like any of them?"

"She wouldn't let me in, bro, wouldn't even come to the door. I couldn't get past her mom."

He heaved a sigh and sat down on the edge of the bed.

"I don't know what to do anymore, Geno."

Poor Angel. All but totally defeated, he may as well have been a big white flag sitting there. I wanted to help him, though my previous advice had yielded nothing.

"Keep trying," I said. "Show some grit. What better way to show Elana that you're committed than to keep showing up on her doorstep?"

"I dunno, homie. I'm starting to think she's already made up her mind."

"Don't give up," I said. "She'll come around."

"You don't know Elana, man. She's as hardheaded as they come, just like her mom."

"It always worked with Gladys," I said. "Gladys could be impossibly stubborn. You just need to outlast her, prove to Elana you're not going anywhere and that you're in this thing for the long haul come hell or high water. Think of it as a test."

"I'm terrible at tests," said Angel, slumping perceptibly.

It seems that nobody is quite as resigned to their anguish as the young, nor so quick to throw in the towel regarding the prospect of happiness. Show me an old man, and he's happy he can get out of bed without breaking his hip. Show me a young poet, and he's usually wringing his hands over something. Elana was right. Angel needed some tough love.

"See?" I said. "You're doing it again."

"What?"

"Showing your weakness," I said.

"Easy, homie."

"Don't you understand? Elana wants to see that you'll never give up. You've shown her your doubt, now show her your courage."

"How?"

"By being there."

"What am I supposed to do, buy a florist?"

"If that's what it takes," I said.

"And drive forty miles round trip every day to beg?"

"A thousand miles if necessary."

"What if she never lets me in?" said Angel.

"Then you keep going back," I said. "You stand there the rest of your life."

Yes, my plea was impassioned, perhaps disproportionately so. But how could you blame me? I'd waited more than a thousand years to see my love again, enduring every setback and futility in the book. Think of it: For a thousand years my heart was broken! Empires had emerged and fallen in the interim, whole civilizations had crumbled or disappeared. And all I had was my memories, immutable and unchanging. I would have given anything to show up at Gaya's door every day for all eternity, if only to be rebuked, all so that I might have only heard her voice.

"Okay, Geno," said Angel. "I'll give it a try."

Loyalty or Foolishness

Having traversed the city twice during the night, our shoes still mud caked from the riverbank, Gaya and I were drawing near to her house shortly before dawn when, much to our consternation, we spotted them from the distance of half a block: two soldiers with torches flanking the front door like sentries, and, judging from the light breaching the shuttered windows, possibly others inside.

"Do you think they'll find the purse?" I said.

"They're not looking for the purse, they're looking for us."

"How will we get it?"

"It will have to wait. Perhaps they'll be gone by morning."

"And until then?"

"Follow me," she said.

Though weary of leg, I would've kept walking those streets forever as long as I was following Gaya. We crossed the city a third time, the sun just peeking over the eastern horizon when we arrived at a small home of straw construction on the eastern edge of the city.

"It is my aunt Ostosia's house," she said. "We can rest here."

Ostosia stood straight and tall in the doorway, a raven-haired woman with pale blue eyes. Judging by her fair, smooth skin, she

couldn't have been ten years Gaya's senior, surely too young for wid-
owhood.

"Gaya, my dear girl, you look pale."

"I am only tired, Ostosia," she said. "This is Euric, he is my
friend. May we come in?"

Ostosia appraised me up and down, considering me, and looking
none too impressed. Finally she showed us in and sat us down in her
tiny kitchen, where she fed us bread, and salted fish, and precious
little wine. Inevitably, she inquired as to what occasion she owed
our visit.

"I'm afraid there's been trouble," Gaya said.

"What kind of trouble?" said Ostosia.

"The less you know, the better," said Gaya.

"Are you in danger?"

"Perhaps," Gaya said.

Exhausted, and sensing that Ostosia sought Gaya's confidence,
I left the two women in the kitchen and retreated to the other room,
where I promptly reclined on a wooden bench and closed my eyes
against the offending sunlight.

Perhaps Gaya and Ostosia assumed I was sleeping, or maybe
they wanted me to hear them, because before long they began talking about me as though I were not there.

"Why would you throw away your life for this man you hardly
know?" said Ostosia. "A thief, no less."

"I'm not sure, exactly," said Gaya. "But I was compelled."

"By what?"

"Something about him," she said. "Maybe it's his innocence."

"He's a cutpurse, child," said Ostosia. "You're not thinking
clearly."

"That's just it," Gaya said. "Something about him causes me not
to think clearly."

Ostosia sighed audibly.

"It's even worse than I suspected," she said. "A shock of curly hair, a pair of blue eyes, and you've lost your judgment altogether."

"No," said Gaya. "Ostosia, he is loyal."

"Loyal? You met him yesterday. How can you trust him?"

"It is a fair question," Gaya conceded. "To which I have no persuasive answer. I just know that I trust him, and that he would do anything for me."

"Is that loyalty or foolishness? Perhaps this ruffian's loyalty is owing to your feminine charms, did you think of that? He is, after all, a man. A man will promise you anything, he will promise you the moon, Gaya. But rarely will he make good on his promises."

"This one will," she said.

"Does he know of our plans?"

"Not specifically."

"You told him about the resistance?" said Ostosia.

"Yes."

"A common thief, and you told him?" she said.

"But he could be an asset to our cause," said Gaya. "He is skilled. And clever. He has experience."

"I thought you said he nearly got caught."

"This was a blessing, Ostosia. For otherwise we would not have him on our side."

As I feigned sleep from my place on the bench, my heart thrilled at Gaya's confidence. She considered me a blessing! Skilled and clever! Gaya saw me in a light that had never before shone on me. A day earlier I had been an island unto myself: no family, no friends, no purpose. Now I had a purpose: to be with Gaya. Even if that meant a lifetime of running. Never mind that I was now a murderer, and by association, an enemy of the state. At last, I was connected to something—if not to an ideal, if not to a belief, to a person who had deemed my life worthy of saving.

So full was my heart, so clear was my purpose, that my guilty conscience did not harass me despite the blood on my hands, and I fell asleep with the suggestion of a smile upon my face.

"It's time," whispered Gaya, awaking me gently sometime later. "We must go for the purse."

"I'll go after the purse alone," I said. "You are safer here with Ostosia."

"But what if . . . ? Perhaps it would be more prudent if—"

"Gaya," I said, holding her gaze. "This is what I do."

"Very well," she said. "But first we must disguise you."

In the light of the afternoon, wrapped in a loose-fitting almejía once belonging to Gaya's late father, imama pulled low over my forehead, I skirted the square and stuck to the backstreets, walking with my head down, engaging no one along the way. All my life I'd wandered these streets, a thousand times I'd walked them all, scheming and dreaming and passing the days, but never with such purpose.

I pulled up short of Gaya's house to surveil the situation. There were no soldiers posted out front. The windows remained shuttered. The area all about was relatively quiet but for two boys, maybe six and eight years old, clashing sticks like swords on the north-facing street.

Briskly, I made my way to the back of the house, then slowly crept to the rear window, peering between the shutters. There was no discernible activity in the house. I pulled a shutter back cautiously and took a wider appraisal of the bedroom. The hallway was not visible, let alone the cellar door. I poked my head into the room, turning an ear to the front of the house, where I detected nothing but silence. Satisfied, I clambered through the tiny opening head-first and slithered onto the bedroom floor.

Being that Gaya had promptly stashed me in the cellar upon smuggling me there, I'd never seen her bedroom, and I knew I'd never see it again. Despite the urgency of my charge, I could not help but pause momentarily to exploit the occasion. I'm embarrassed to admit that having snatched her pillow off the pallet, I briefly buried my face in its depths before proceeding to the front of the house. I slunk past the kitchen to the foyer, where I stole down the corridor.

Setting my ear to the cellar door, I registered only silence before pushing it open with its signature groan. I was met with the same tomblike stillness as the previous day. Slowly, I shut the door behind me and descended the stairs. Groping my way toward the rear, I collided with the misplaced barrel, and while I did not topple the vessel, I succeeded in bruising my knee.

That's when the floorboards issued a creak directly above me. Urgently, I felt my way through darkness until I located the coffer on the shelf. Thrusting my hand behind it, I found . . . nothing. With both hands, I fished and fumbled around for the purse with no success, even as the footsteps advanced down the corridor toward the cellar door. Reasoning that the satchel might have slipped off the upper shelf, I scrambled to my hands and knees and groped around on the floor behind the lower shelf. With the footsteps bearing down on me, I was about to give up my search when my fingers happened upon its smooth leather, pinned to the wall. Gathering it up, I clutched it tightly in my hand and turned around just as the cellar door swung open and someone hurried down the stairs until the glare framed the silhouette of a soldier swathed in dusty light.

"Who's that?" he shouted.

I hunkered down and rushed him without even thinking, hitting him just below the waist and toppling him with my momentum. I scrambled over him, up the steps, and down the corridor, bursting out the front door. Darting down the street with the purse in my clutches, I never looked back, though I was nearly certain of his pursuit.

And as I dashed through the streets of Seville once more, dodging women and children, chickens, goats, and beggars, I was more frightened than I'd ever been, or ever shall be. It was not the possibility of violence that terrified me so, nor the thought of capture that harried my breathless pace. No, it was the thought that I'd never make it back to Gaya.

Such Fanciful Yarns

"Eugene? You okay?"

Wayne's voice startled me out of my reverie. He was standing in the doorway holding a half-empty bottle of orange juice from the soda dispenser.

"I'm fine," I said from my place on the bed. "Shipshape."

"You sure about that?"

"I'm sure," I said.

"Looks to me like you've been crying," said Wayne.

Evading his eyes, I looked out the window through the open shade.

"Memories again, huh? Spain? Cathood?"

Considering the source, and the chiding tone, the question warranted no reply, and I continued fixating on the craggy Ord Mountains out the window, scorched gray from the desert heat.

"Maybe you wanna talk about it?" said Wayne.

"No," I said.

"From what I gather, Dr. Stowell liked to talk about it, didn't he?"

The name was like a bucket of cold water across the face. My heart stopped beating for an instant. I'd not heard the name Stowell uttered since 1947.

"How do you know about Dr. Stowell?"

"Sort of a pioneer in the field, you might say."

"Look, I don't know where you're getting your information, but I don't want to talk, Wayne."

"I understand," he said. "But remember, Eugene, any time you want to talk . . ."

"Got it," I said.

Don't think for one minute I didn't know what Wayne was up to. He wanted to expose me for a fraud. He'd been after me since day one. The more I talked, the less anyone believed. As soon as I was old enough to talk in sentences, I began to tell my parents of my past experiences. I think my father was ashamed of what he reasoned to be my overactive imagination, which he considered a sign of weakness. My mother, however, despite the tenets of her Christian faith, and likely bored half to death herself, was tickled by my stories at first, delighted by the details of my bygone lives. *What a vivid imagination he has!* she would say. *So clever! How does he arrive at such fanciful yarns?* At the dinner table, or in the car on our aimless Sunday drives through the high desert, my mother went out of her way to solicit the particulars for her own entertainment. How high were the mosques of Seville? How blue was the Tyrrhenian Sea? Was Sacagawea as beautiful as they say? I was ecstatic to share this knowledge. The more my mother inquired, the more she encouraged me, the more I wished to please her with my memories, regaling her with descriptions of the Andes, their impossibly precipitous peaks and plunging valleys, and the sacred river of Urubamba that had patiently carved them over countess epochs. I told them of my father's travels on the high seas from Tonga to Rotuma, of the great island feasts, and weddings, and ceremonial dances I remembered from my youth, without ever telling her that I did not live to see my eighth birthday, because I did not want to make her sad. My father would grip the wheel until his knuckles turned white, leveling his glare at the desolate landscape out the windshield, as I spoke of the great expedition across the American West, across the prairies and over the divide. I told them of first contact with the Shoshone and the Blackfeet, and how the Native Americans were fascinated by York, the first Black man they had ever seen. I even quoted my Oscar.

"Enough!" said my father.

As I grew older, with each year more distant from my father, who would not abide my storytelling, even my mother began to greet my stories with mounting unease.

When I was nine years old, my parents had me consult with a doctor whom my father summoned from Los Angeles to interview me. His name was Dr. Stowell, and like everything else, I remember him vividly. He was not a young man; I would've put him at about sixty. He wore gray whiskers of an outdated style and spectacles that continually slid down the bridge of his nose. The interview itself was conducted in my bedroom, where Dr. Stowell, notebook open in his lap, sat in a high-backed chair imported from the dining room as I perched nervously on the edge of my bed, my nine-year-old legs not quite reaching the floor.

"Your parents tell me you have quite a colorful imagination, young man. They say you make up the most astonishing stories."

"I don't make them up," I said.

"Oh? Then where do they come from?"

"From my life."

"Ah, I see." Dr. Stowell smiled. "So, you were an Incan princess?"

"Yes."

"And a pickpocket in Spain?"

"Uh-huh."

"Well, it appears you've lived quite a storied life for such a young man. They tell me you were also a cat, is that right?"

"Yeah."

"Are you still a cat?"

"Do I look like a cat?" I said.

"No more than you look like an Incan princess."

"I'm just a boy now, living in this boring town."

"Mm-hmm, yes, interesting," said Dr. Stowell, jotting a line in his notebook. "So, you would characterize your life as boring?"

"No, just the town."

"Would you rather be somewhere else?"

"Anywhere," I said.

"What sorts of things do you do to entertain yourself? Do you read a lot? Is that where you get these stories, from books?"

I could see I'd get nowhere by presenting my case further, that I had nothing to gain by trying to convince anyone, and so I surrendered once and for all. The world would never understand. It was my responsibility to quit vexing everybody.

"Yeah, some of it, I guess," I said. "And the radio. And the movie magazines."

Dr. Stowell smiled and shut his notebook with a satisfied air of finality.

A few minutes later, I could hear from my bedroom as Dr. Stowell conferred with my parents.

"It's my feeling that this is just a stage," he said. "Maybe a plea for attention. At this point, I don't see any real reason for concern."

"I do," said my father. "All he does is read books and daydream. I don't even know where he gets the books."

"What about his moods, do they fluctuate frequently or suddenly? Is he ever despondent for long periods of time?"

"No," said my father. "Gene's just a normal kid on the surface. Except for all the reading and the daydreaming and the made-up stories."

"Well, then I wouldn't worry too much," said Dr. Stowell. "I'd continue to monitor the situation, and I suspect it will pass. Perhaps you should engage the boy more in a variety of physical activities, free him up from his overactive mind. I believe this will yield the desired results."

From that point forward I was forced to play catch and shag balls for an hour every day, though I had little interest in baseball and was never any good at it. This was all the better to my father's way of thinking, because my inability to catch anything not thrown directly into my mitt sent me chasing after the balls every time they whizzed past. It was more like playing fetch than catch. But in theory, anyway, the exercise was diminishing my psychic energy and curbing my delusional propensities.

All I ever wanted was the approval of my parents. Thus, when I saw the lengths they were willing to go to in rendering me what they deemed normal, I learned to pretend, to conform to their wishes. At the dinner table we talked of mundane things, the events of the day. I stopped sharing my pasts. Instead, I began committing them to the page with the rest of my inner life. The activity was a comfort and sated my appetite to share. They might have left me alone had my father not found one of my notebooks.

That's when the routine visits with Dr. Stowell began, and they persisted through the next three and a half years, until I was thirteen. Suffice it to say that the experience soured me on sharing. I made it my policy going forward to close my true self to the world, not to discuss my past with anyone, a practice I scrupulously maintained for the next forty-odd years, until Gladys brought me back around.

A Lot of Us

In Angel it seemed I had finally found somebody I could trust, somebody who believed me. Given his relative youth, he might have seemed an unlikely confidant for 105-year-old me, but there he was, nearly every day, drawing me out of my decrepit shell.

"Hey, Geno, how come you never talk about the war?" he said, wiping the edges of my drafting table while scrupulously avoiding puzzle pieces. "Most old guys, they love to talk about their service time," he said. "I see a group of old farts sitting around Starbucks every Sunday with their matching black caps. They must be almost your age, but they love to talk about the war."

"You like war stories, huh?"

"Yeah, kinda," he said. "So, like, you were in the army?"

"Marine Corps, first division."

"And you earned a medal, right?"

"Purple Heart," I said.

"We don't have to talk about it if you don't want."

"No, no, it's fine."

Angel squirted some Windex on the TV screen.

"So, how old were you when you were drafted?" he said.

"I wasn't drafted. I enlisted at twenty-five."

"So, like, you wanted to go to war?"

"Not exactly. It was more like I was duty-bound."

There was very little holding me in Los Angeles in 1942. Still single and childless, I was working as a stenographer at the courthouse downtown, a job I'd finally secured after five years at the filling station and countless nights of study. By '41, I'd moved on from Consuela's bungalow, though I still brought her flowers on the second Sunday of every month, and we dined on tamales and drank tall glasses of horchata in her sunny kitchen. Amidst a half dozen courthouse acquaintances, grocery clerks and flower girls notwithstanding, Consuela was the only person I could call a friend.

I'd moved into a studio apartment on Third Street, a dreary little place, dark and poorly ventilated, the narrow hallway always smelling of fried onions and disinfectant. I did not lack for company, thanks to the irrepressible roach population. The apartment had none of the sunny, bougainvillea-scented charm of my studio at Consuela's, but it was closer to work, and it was cheap. The flat was 240 square feet tops, and if it looked slightly bigger it was only because it was furnished so sparsely, with nothing but a bed and a desk and a radio, which also served as a nightstand. Not even so much as a sofa on which to entertain. I always meant to buy a bookshelf or two to accommodate the growing piles of history texts stacked willy-nilly along the wall, but I never quite got around to it. I'm embarrassed to admit that in my two years in the apartment, I received not a single visitor, not even my parents.

My landlady was a no-nonsense woman from Cleveland, Ohio, named Doris Gessen, whom I never once in my years in the apartment saw smile. She said she liked me (though you could hardly tell) because I was quiet, I was neat, and I didn't keep a lot of company.

"The lonely types make the best tenants," she once divulged to me.

It is true I was lonely, though the isolation came quite naturally to me. But for all my solitude and self-sufficiency, I yearned to belong to a cause greater than myself. Pearl Harbor was still fresh, and the war was heating up in the Pacific. It was practically all anybody talked about. I was young and healthy; what good was I doing the cause by working in an office all day long, or going home and listening to the radio and eating leftovers? I should have been fighting the evil axis that threatened our way of life. If the great Kirk Douglas was sufficiently moved to serve his country, why not Eugene Miles?

And so, one morning in April of 1942, my mood ping-ponging back and forth between ardency and reluctance, I donned my father's suit, now threadbare and so old that it was almost back in style, and proceeded to the recruitment office downtown, where my fate was sealed. Four days later, I reported to San Diego, where I soon discovered that life as a soldier agreed with me. I was well acquainted with discipline, undaunted by deprivation, and trained by my father in the rigors of subservience. What's more, routine was my natural inclination, for nothing passed the time or soothed my restless spirit like repetition.

In June, my company was deployed from San Francisco, bound for the Solomon Islands.

"Where's that?" said Angel.

"Just east of Papua New Guinea."

"That ain't helping, dog."

"About a thousand nautical miles northeast of Australia."

"What were you doing way down there?"

"The Japanese had taken the Solomons. If we could take them back, we could prevent them from cutting off Australia and New Zealand."

"What's a nautical mile, anyway?"

"It doesn't matter, do you want to hear the story?"

"Hey, I'm still getting my bearings here, homie. Cut me some slack."

The next six weeks were devoted largely to preparation and routine, as we made for the South Pacific aboard the USS *North Carolina*, where I once again proved a natural. I was adept at living in confined spaces, and I was a bona fide stalwart in dealing with monotony.

On the night of August 6, we arrived undetected just off of Savo Island, where the following morning, we were to land at Guadalcanal."

"Guadalcanal? Isn't that where Gladys's first husband was killed?"

"Yes."

"So, was that just a coincidence?"

"There were a lot of us at Guadalcanal. Nearly six thousand in the first division alone."

"Did you know him?"

"No."

"It just seems like a bit of a coincidence."

"Do you want to hear the story or not?"

The first division would split in two. My company was in the smaller transport headed south. We would approach the airfield from both sides of the river. Other than that, we knew little about targets, and even less about our adversaries. The night before landing, we moored out beyond the reef under dense cloud cover and heavy rain, the great vessel rising and falling rhythmically upon the swells. We could no more see Guadalcanal through the weather than we could see South America. But shortly before midnight the clouds scattered and the moon came out, and from the deck we could see the island in silhouette, the beachhead a ribbon of silver delineating the jungle beyond. Aside from a handful of noncommissioned officers, it would be the first action for most of us. Each one of us was sure in his heart that we'd have a bad time getting ashore, and the overriding mood was one of somber resolve. Sleep would not have me, not even for a wink, and I was by no means alone in this regard.

When morning came, I was at once alert but strangely numb, resigned to my fate, whatever it might be. I knew that at least for me, death was only an illusion, and so I feared my earthly demise only insomuch as it meant starting over again. My body was stiff and aching beneath my field khakis as we piled into the boats.

The *Quincy* shelled the beachhead in advance of our landing, the percussion of the shells rattling inside my chest along with a furious heartbeat that may well have belonged to the men pressed fast against me, an audible prayer upon one's lips. The beachhead dipped in and out of sight as the bow of the landing craft rose and fell upon the swells. Every time it rose, the beachhead was a little closer, our fates a little nearer.

A hundred feet from shore, we poured ourselves out like a single organism into the shallows and stormed the beach expecting the worst. I bit my tongue dropping in and could taste the blood and salt water intermingling, smell the miasma of exploded mortar shells assaulting my nostrils.

Much to our surprise, but even more so to our relief, no Japanese forces greeted us there, none that were visible, anyway. Still, we took the prudent course and promptly made for the surrounding jungle. We fought through the thick foliage until we picked up the river along the south bank. Wading past our waists in the chill waters, we progressed toward the airfield, our pace purposeful but deliberate.

God, but it was so eerily quiet under the low gray sky, with only our sloshing progress and ragged breaths punctuating the unsettling silence. Scanning the dense jungle along both banks, I sensed no movement, nothing stirring, and yet I took no comfort at all from this lack of activity because it all felt like a trap.

"Oh, man, this is getting good, homie," Angel interjected. "Almost as good as Spain. But I gotta get back to work. Can we finish this one later?"

"Of course," I said. "By the way, did you go to Victorville yet?"

"Tomorrow morning," he said. "I'm gonna try to catch Elana while her mom's shopping. She always shops on Thursdays."

"Good luck," I said.

"Thanks, dog. And thanks for the story."

"We'll finish it later," I said.

"And Spain, too, man. I gotta find out what's in that purse."

Home Free

I circled back to Ostosia's, darting between houses, then switch-backing up and down the side streets at a dead sprint. As I clutched the rescued purse beneath my baggy robe, the same garment that threatened to trip me at nearly every step, my singular focus was reaching Gaya. Rounding a corner on the ragged edge of town, I was nearly upended by a stray dog, a spindly little cur who refused to give way. When it was clear the little bugger had no intention of moving, I managed to skirt him just in the nick of time without breaking stride. But no sooner had I averted this disaster than I dared to look back over my shoulder, to find my pursuer trailing me by a mere hundred cubits and gaining. I upended a barrow full of pitiful fruit in his path, an obstacle that slowed him for an instant, long enough for me to navigate the next corner at full speed, where I ran headlong into a hunched old woman, who went careening into the street, landing in a heap. I'm not proud of leaving her there, but at that moment it seemed my deliverance. For while the collision barely slowed me, the soldier was forced by conscience to abandon his pursuit long enough to assist the old woman to her feet, shaking his fist and cursing me as I retreated.

The diversion bought me enough time to round the next corner, where I hit the straightaway and doubled my pace, though I was straining for breath. I'd been running all my life, from my father; from authorities, secular and religious; from the unsuspecting victims of my crimes. But never had I run like this, with every shred of will and determination I had in me. I finally had something to run for. Even when it seemed that I was home free, I was unwilling to risk leading anyone back to Gaya, so I dodged for cover into a stable, where I crouched amongst the restless horses, ankle-deep in dung, until darkness fell.

It was in the dim light of the stable, amidst the muck and stench, that I finally dared to inspect the contents of the purse, pouring them out upon the lap of my robe. From the depths of the satchel, beneath several handfuls of sundry coins, some of which I did not recognize, I produced a tiny casket of ivory, intricately engraved with an iconography that was clearly not religious: chivalrous depictions of courtly love, maidens in draping robes and princes in elaborate headdresses, wrapped in amorous embrace upon latticed balconies, their conjoined figures flanked by lions and horses. The lid was affixed with the tiniest of wrought iron hinges. I could not help but marvel at their construction, at once sturdy and impossibly delicate. But even these miracles of metal fabrication did not prepare me for the contents of the coffer. Lined with purple silk, the box housed a single pearl nearly the size of an olive, perfectly round and exquisitely symmetrical.

Plucking the gem from its silky bedding, I held it to the light and turned it slowly between my fingers, inspecting its luster and the perfection of its unblemished surface. Startled by the sudden nicker of my stablemate, I fumbled with the jewel, which shot from my grasp and tumbled into the dung. Even as footsteps approached from the front of the stable, I snatched the pearl from the muck and desperately began stuffing the coins back into the satchel. Barely had I managed to conceal the purse beneath my robe and scramble to my feet when a large figure filled the doorway, blocking my egress.

"Who are you? What are you doing in here?"

A Christian he was, if I had to guess, and not a charitable one.

"I am weary," I said. "I only sought shelter to rest. I will be on my way now."

"My lodgings are not gratis."

"I have no money, I'm afraid."

"What was that you stashed beneath your robe?"

"I stashed nothing."

"The purse, I saw you conceal it in your robe."

"You are mistaken," I said.

The man took a step forward and thrust his hand out.

"You will pay me," he said.

Under no circumstances did I intend on parting with a single dinar, dirham, or daniq of my hard-won spoils.

"I have nothing to offer you."

"But you do," he said, his hand still thrust out in front of him. "Let us inspect the purse."

I had no other recourse but to hunker down for the second time that day and charge headlong at a larger man, this time with less success. Not only did I fail to upend the giant, but he managed to get ahold of my arm, and, clutching me fast against him, he immediately began frisking me for the purse.

I am not proud of the fact that I resorted to biting him, but it seemed my only viable option in the moment, and it was effective, for I left him howling in consternation, and was off and running once more through the streets of Seville. Though my adversary soon gave chase, he was a lumbering sort with no chance of keeping pace. It was only a matter of blocks before I lost him.

Dusk was upon the city by the time I arrived back at Ostosia's house, where I let myself in through the back door.

"Where have you been?" Gaya demanded. "I was worried sick."

"I was only being prudent. Where is your aunt?" I said.

"I sent her out," said Gaya. "I can't risk compromising her. Did you recover the purse?"

"Of course."

Kneeling before her, I emptied the contents of the satchel onto the floor, and Gaya went immediately for the little ivory casket with keen interest.

"Open it," I said.

Gaya lifted the lid and nearly gasped at the spectacle of the pearl.

"Isn't it exquisite?" I said. "Look at the size of it. Who carries such a treasure around in a leather satchel?"

"Somebody to whom it is very dear, probably," she said, closing the lid.

Without further ceremony, she began replacing the coins in the purse.

"Tomorrow we must leave the city," she said.

"For where?"

"North to the mountains. There is a resistance mounting. Small but determined."

"But what of your home?" I said. "You will just leave it?"

"It is my home I am fighting for," she said. "What I leave behind is only a structure. Until we've driven them from this land, we will never—"

But before Gaya could finish, a mighty clatter rocked the house like it was Jericho, and I spun around just in time to see the front door burst open as a pair of soldiers stormed into the room.

Here, I stopped telling the story. Angel appealed urgently to me.

"What? No way," he said. "You are not stopping right there, man. We still got five minutes."

"Sorry," I said. "You'll have to wait, homie."

"And what about World War II?" he said. "You haven't finished that one, either."

"In time, my friend," I said, relishing his enthusiasm.

Oh, what a thrill it was to be wanted, to be anticipated! What a rush it was to entertain and beguile somebody with the stories of my lives.

Not Exactly a Thriving Metropolis

When Angel showed up to clean my room around four thirty the next day, he was out of sorts all over again.

"What happened?" I said. "Did you see Elana?"

"Yeah."

"And?"

"Same as last time. She wouldn't let me in."

"You told her you were sorry again, right?"

"Of course I did, like a hundred times. I told her I loved her, and that I wanted to be with her always, and I wanted to make a family with her, and that if she would just let me in, I was ready to show her how I wasn't a boy, how I was a man. I even brought a bassinet like you said, and a baby monitor from Target, and a bunch of toys, like, you know, one of those baby sharks that sings that annoying song. Not to mention the flowers."

"That didn't appease her?"

"No, bro. She made me leave it all on the porch. Somebody could steal it out there."

"I'm sure they brought it in as soon as you were gone," I offered, a lame consolation, to be sure.

How could I not feel like a heel after I'd given poor Angel that big pep talk and sent him up there all full of purpose to make his case? Not only had the young man done it, but the baby monitor had also been a nice touch. I had encouraged him to go up there and take control of the situation, and he'd come back humiliated. How could Elana turn him away like that? What was I missing?

Perhaps it was only my loyalty to Angel, but I was starting to not like this woman. She seemed hard, and slow to forgive. How could she not give sweet Angel a break?

"Maybe she doesn't deserve you, then," I said.

"Nah, Geno, it's the other way around. You don't even know the beginning of it. She's my savior. I'm the one who screwed this up. This is my kid we're talking about. You think I take that lightly?"

"No," I said. "No, you don't. That seems obvious to me. So, why doesn't Elana see it?"

"You gotta understand, Elana knew me when I wasn't worth a shit, when I was a dumbass making stupid decisions. But maybe she'll come around," said Angel. "Maybe it's like you said, I gotta keep after her, show her I'm committed for the long haul, that I'm not gonna fall back into my old life. Anyone can talk; I gotta show up. But I think I'll give her the weekend to think about it, you know? I spent over a hundred and fifty bucks on that stuff. Anyway, you want me to close the shade? I gotta hit the rest of these rooms."

"No, thanks, leave it open," I said.

"What about the TV screen, you want me to hit it?"

"No, it's fine. I never even watch the thing."

"Okay, then," he said, taking hold of his cart and readying himself to move on.

"Lunch on the green?" I said hopefully.

"Yeah, man, of course. You owe me some stories."

But two hours later, at our usual table under the blighted palms,

a haze of smog butting up against the Ords and the San Bernardi-
nos, eating our respective meals, Angel and I picked up our conversation where we'd left off.

"I think Elana, she just really wants me to think things through.
It's like she's trying to force me to prepare for the idea of a family. I
think the next step is to figure out the insurance and whatever. I
figure if I start handling some of the details, she'll see I mean business. And look, I don't blame her for not letting me off easy, you
know? A real man would have taken the news differently. And I'm
taking it that way now, no bullshit. I'm excited to be a dad. I'll figure the rest out as we go. Sooner or later, if I keep showing up, she'll
see it."

"She'd have to be blind not to," I said.

"You're all right, Geno, you know that? Thanks for letting me
dump on you. And for the advice."

I was thrilled to be of use.

"Why don't you ever leave this place, Geno?" he said.

"And go where?"

"I dunno, anywhere. I figure with all the living you've done, all
the stuff you've seen, you'd get bored as hell cooped up in here."

"Not really," I lied.

Here, I must confess that I've not been entirely honest with you.

For one thing, I still have appetites, albeit diminished ones. I
still yearn for newness on occasion. Some days I look out the window beyond the ancient sprawl of the San Bernardino range toward
the ocean, or gaze east at the desert horizon, and allow myself to entertain the possibility that there is still more living for me to do out
there in the world somewhere, still places to go and people to see.

"They won't let you leave, is that it?" said Angel.

"That's not it. This isn't an asylum. I can come and go as I please."

"So?"

"Well, to begin with, it's not like I have a car, so where am I supposed to go? Nobody's going to pick me up, unless it's Donna or Nancy, and I haven't seen either of them in years. I don't even know if they're still alive. So, where do you propose I would go around here? I suppose there's a Chevron station about six blocks up, and a Shell kitty-corner from that."

"No, man, that's a Texaco now."

"You see my point, though?"

"Yeah, I feel you, man. It's not exactly a thriving metropolis around here. Where would you want to go if you could go somewhere?"

"I can go virtually anywhere I want right up here," I said, indicating my wrinkled cranium. "I can go to Spain, or Peru, or Fiji, I can go over the Rocky Mountains. And I don't even have to get out of my slippers."

"Yeah, homie, but it's not the same, and besides, you already lived it, right, so where's the adventure? You gotta get your skinny ass out there in the world and feel the wind in your face, see the pretty young girls, hear the kids laughing and the horns honking, you know? I know you've got all those places up there in your head, but I'm talking about out there in the real world, ese. This place is deadsville."

Angel was right, of course. But I was 105 years old, hardly my spry young self. I had nobody to visit and no place in particular calling me. So, the question remained: Where would I go? And why would I go? And whom would I go with?

Not the End

Sunday morning, just as I'd nearly resolved to get out of bed and begin the business of puzzling away another day, waiting for a death I assumed would never arrive, Angel surprised me, ducking into my quarters in street clothes, a backward Dodgers cap and a white T-shirt emblazoned with a fist on it that said "I punch Nazis." It was a message I approved of, though it was a departure from Angel's aqua-colored scrubs. He wore madras trousers that ended midway down his shins, where they met the top of his white tube socks.

"What are you doing here?"

"Get dressed, homie, we're going out."

"What do you mean? Where?"

"I thought we'd get some lunch. Maybe drive to LA."

"I can't just get up and . . ."

"Why not?"

I didn't have an answer, of course. My immediate resistance to the idea was mostly out of habit. The fact is, once you get to be my age, even the most trivial outing can be a challenge. For starters, I don't get around particularly well for extended periods of time. Walking to the greens and back is one thing, a few trips to the commissary, sure, but I know what to expect, how to pace myself. And there are no stairs or inclines. Also, I have to go to the bathroom a lot, which presents a different set of problems. Not to mention that I tire easily. Trust me, by the time you hit the century mark, stasis is the path of least resistance. Thus, I lean heavily on my routines to get me through the day; my chicken salad croissan'wich, my puzzles, my naps. Outings beyond the greens are not even a consideration.

"C'mon, homie, let's have an adventure."

"I've had plenty of adventures."

"Yeah, like five hundred years ago. They're just memories now. C'mon, you ain't getting any younger, Geno."

"You don't understand, I . . ."

"What?"

"I have to go to the bathroom a lot."

"So? They've got restrooms for that."

"I get tired easily."

"So, sleep in the car."

He wasn't leaving me much wiggle room.

"I'll go down to the commissary and grab a couple of sandwiches for the road," he said. "You get dressed."

"Could you make mine a—"

"Yeah, yeah, chicken salad," he said.

I must admit, I did experience a certain titillation walking out the double glass doors of Desert Greens and into the sunny parking lot with Angel, feeling the eyes of both Herman Billet and Wayne on my back. I'd be lying if I said it didn't put a little spring in my step. The lot was half-empty, and Angel walked me straight to a black Monte Carlo, glistening like onyx in the desert sun. The car stuck out amongst the blue Priuses and the red Hondas. I would put the vintage of the sedan somewhere in the early 1970s. The chassis was long and sat low to the ground. The paint was perfect and the chrome impeccable.

"Impressive automobile," I said. "They don't make them like this anymore."

"Two hundred and seventy horsepower, and a lotta torque," he said, climbing into the driver's seat. "She's heavy, but she sails."

"She sure rides low," I said, having finally settled into the passenger seat, no easy task for this old bag of bones. "I may need a hand getting out of this thing."

"I love this car," he said. "I've had her for three years, put every extra penny I could scrape up into her—new block, new suspension, new paint. But this is her final voyage, man. I'm selling her to a dude in Pasadena on Monday."

"Why sell it if you love it?"

"Ah, man, Geno, you know I gotta get a family car. This thing doesn't even have seat belts in back. I'm thinking about a Kia Optima. Sexy, right? Anyway, that's part of why I wanted to drive to LA today. Take her for one last run. So, buckle up, homie."

I fastened my seat belt for the first time since the DG shuttle drove me all of two miles to my geriatrician, who made me wait forty-five minutes in the lobby before spending twelve minutes poking and prodding me and giving me the third degree, ultimately informing me (after another twenty-minute wait) that I was in better health than most people half my age. He sent me on my way, and I haven't been back since, and that must have been two years ago.

The heat of the Monte Carlo's interior was oppressive. I could smell the leather seats slowly baking in the sun.

"Roll down your window, homie," said Angel. "You look like you're about to keel over."

I complied with considerable relief as Angel guided us out of the lot and onto the street, proceeding south for four or five blocks.

"You're right," I said, looking out the window. "It is a Texaco now. And that Quiznos is new."

"See, bro, you've been missing out. You comfortable? Gotta go to the bathroom yet?"

"Very funny," I said, settling back into the bucket seat.

"Should only be two hours to LA without traffic," said Angel.

"And where exactly are we going?"

"You tell me, Geno. Anywhere you want," he said. "You used to live there, right?"

"That was a long time ago. My goodness, fifty years ago. I wouldn't know where to begin."

"It don't matter, then," said Angel. "We'll just poke around town, see some sights. If we get really bored, we can go see my cousin in Downey. It's the journey, not the end, right?"

"Ha. The journey has no end," I said.

We picked up the highway north and started toward Apple Valley, the desert sprawl all around us dotted with new development, all of it hemmed in by the broad-shouldered San Gabriels to the west.

"You sure you don't want to stop and see Elana?" I said.

"Nah, man, I told you, I'm taking the weekend off. Besides, I don't wanna go up there until I'm rolling in the Kia. Maybe Tuesday. Only two forty-nine a month, not bad, right? When I sell the Monte on Monday, I can afford it even without a second job, and I'll have a decent chunk of savings, too. We're gonna need that. Plus, you know, I gotta buy a car seat and a bunch of other crap. I'm gonna cover all the bases before I go back to her mom's house. Game, set, match, ese."

I couldn't help but admire Angel's resolve, his ability to pivot and adapt so quickly, his undaunted optimism and belief.

As nice as it was to feel the desert wind blowing hot on my face, it was shocking how much the valley had changed in the past decade, the development spreading out like a rash upon the high desert. Box stores, and strip malls, and warehouses. When I was a boy there had been hardly anything between Lucerne and Apple Valley but a few homesteads. Not even a marked road. Just creosote bushes and empty desert for as far as the eye could see.

"So, how about it?" said Angel. "Pretty nice, right?"

"What?"

"The ride, man, the Monte. She's smooth, right? Glides on air. Man, I'm gonna miss her."

"You know, you don't have to sell her. I've got a little savings stashed away, I could always just lend you the—"

"Nah, Geno, that's nice of you," he said. "But the thing of it is, I do have to sell her, it's time. Seasons, my man, everything has its season. And this season has passed. Kia Optima, here I come."

If only after eleven hundred years I possessed half the wisdom of this twenty-four-year-old. If only I could resolve myself to seasons, but alas, I was a perennial.

"Hey," said Angel. "Tell me one of your stories. Or finish one, or something."

"They're not stories."

"Sure they are."

"They're memories."

"Yeah, but they're still stories, bro."

"Then you believe me? You don't think I'm making it all up?"

Angel looked straight ahead at the road and seemed to consider the matter briefly.

"Yeah, I believe you, man, of course. I don't understand it, and I still don't get why you get to have all these lives and not the rest of us, but I believe you. I mean, how else would you know all this stuff?"

"Well, I was a history teacher," I reminded him.

"History books don't tell you how something feels, homie. There's too many details in your stories. And you're not clever enough to make this stuff up."

Heavily Fortified

The soldiers, one a talkative giant, the other squat and bowlegged, shepherded Gayà and me through the empty marketplace and past the baths, speaking amongst themselves in Arabic, a language I could scarcely comprehend beyond a dozen or so words.

"What are they saying?" I whispered.

"The tall one has asserted that an ass is smarter than a sheep," Gaya explained. "The short one has proposed that either one of them is smarter than a woman. I stopped listening after that."

"What will they do to us?"

"Who knows?" she said.

"I will take full responsibility," I pleaded. "I'm the thief, I stole the purse. You were only being kind."

"Euric," she said, "it's a noble impulse, but this is about more than the purse."

"I don't follow."

"Shush," she said.

Still bantering in Arabic, the soldiers herded us past the mosque and over the terrace before we skirted the darkened gardens.

"This is all my fault," I said.

"Don't overestimate yourself," said Gaya.

Beyond the plaza, they led us to a heavily fortified quadrangular enclosure, the present structure annexed to ancient walls on all sides, as though it had been built upon the ruins of a former edifice. Roman or Visigoth, who could say? What did I know of history then? History was a luxury I could not afford. I spent my entire life thinking only of the immediate future.

Once we'd entered the fortress, we were led through the main chamber and into another large room, where we were confronted by Assad himself, garbed in a fine purple silk robe stitched with golden thread. He looked ten years younger in the dim light of the fortress. We were made to kneel when the first soldier presented Assad with the recovered purse, which he accepted with no visible relief. He neither opened it nor considered its heft, rather set it aside on the desk with no more ceremony than he would a sack of dates.

"So," he said. "A thief and a conspirator."

"Sir," I said, "you must understand. This woman is in no way respo—"

"Silence," he said.

The same man who had seemed like a fat tourist when I'd snatched his satchel in broad daylight, now, in the dim light of the chamber, presented himself in a different aspect: an imposing figure, swathed in shadows.

"I remember when I first met your father," said Assad.

"My father?"

"He's talking to me," said Gaya.

Assad spat out a mouthful of emphatic Arabic, his face flushing with every word, his eyes intent on Gaya throughout the tirade. Perhaps he loved her. What else could account for his irritability?

"What did he say?"

"He demands your silence," said Gaya.

No sooner had I complied than Assad leaned right down into Gaya's face and released another stream of invective that saw his forehead furrow and his dark eyes sharpen to points like daggers. Gaya did not flinch once throughout the onslaught. Jaw set, chin up, she stared right into his pointed eyes. And when Assad ceased talking, like a challenge, she issued only a curt reply in Arabic, one that even I could decipher.

"Never," she said.

Closing his eyes, Assad drew a deep breath and held it in momentarily before paying it out slowly. Calmly, he turned his attention to me.

"And you, thief? How much do you value your freedom?"

All my life I'd been a coward, a miserable, tiptoeing opportunist, concerned only with his own measly gains, all the while cowering in the shadows, acquiescing to every hint of authority. And here I was on my knees again. But next to me was this woman who with a single act of mercy had emboldened me. I looked Assad in the eyes for the first time.

"Who says I'm free? I, who am forced to thieve? I, who must kneel in your presence? I, who was here before you? How is that free?"

"Well, we know you don't pay for anything," he said.

Assad seemed genuinely amused as he turned his attention back to Gaya.

"This is what you're recruiting these days? Laughable."

Gaya glowered defiantly up at him.

"What can you possibly hope to achieve that will make your lives better?" he said. "We grant your people every freedom. You may worship as you please. Under our stewardship you have enjoyed unprecedented abundance. We have beautified your cities, we have educated your people, we've brought you culture. And you thank us with defiance."

As if on cue, Gaya spat on the floor, not a thumb's length from

Assad's sandaled feet. He leaned down and slapped her hard across the face before she could even wince.

"Take them below," he said.

Gaya and I were conducted to the bowels of the fortress, where we were confined to a single cell, an impossibly dark hold, cramped and cool and smelling of earth.

"What did he mean 'recruiting'?"

"He's just trying to be clever. He's fishing for information."

"About what?"

"The inevitable," said Gaya.

Of course, I had no idea what she was talking about.

"What will become of us?" I said.

"We will fight."

"Fight whom?"

"The Berbers," she said.

"But they have armies."

"So do we," she said.

Here, I left off storytelling to gaze out the side window as the desert whizzed past.

"Man," said Angel, arm out the window. "This Gaya chick was a legit badass."

"That, and so much more," I said.

"No wonder you're all broke up over her," said Angel.

"That doesn't even begin to describe it," I said.

Indeed, the ache of losing Gaya was still as fresh as if it had happened yesterday.

"Who knows, man," said Angel hopefully. "Maybe you'll find her again someday. You already found her three times, right?"

"I just wanna die," I said. "Really die."

Angel frowned and shook his head.

"Now, c'mon, Geno, don't talk like that. We're having an adventure here. We're off to see your old stomping ground. And all you wanna do is talk about dying?"

"Don't worry, I've been trying for over eleven hundred years. It hasn't worked yet."

"Look at me, man. No, I'm serious," he said. "I want you to look me in the eye."

I looked him in the bridge of the nose.

"You better not die in my car, Geno, you hear? I gotta sell this thing Monday, and I don't need it smelling like death, you know? And I don't wanna have to explain it to Wayne. Besides, I need you, man. Who else is gonna give me advice? And who else is gonna tell me stories this good?"

City of Angels

Downtown Los Angeles was not at all as I remembered it when I'd seen it last in 1971, a fact that was discernible at ten miles. The modern city center was shockingly vertical, a collision of glass and steel and concrete that seemed to sprout out of the basin like metallic flowers. Practically all that remained of the skyline as I knew it was city hall, once a modern wonder of engineering, now an aged relic dwarfed by its hulking neighbors. Union Bank Plaza, whose five hundred feet had once been a marvel, seemed an afterthought next to the towering monoliths now intent on crowding it out.

"You got anywhere in particular you wanna check out, man?"

"The Oviatt Hotel," I said. "If it's still there."

"Where's that at?"

"Flower Street," I said. "Between Third and Fourth."

"I got you," said Angel.

What a nice kid Angel was to reacquaint me with the great wide world again, to lead me through my past that I might rekindle some of the old spark.

"Hey, old man," he said. "I appreciate you going on this last ride with me."

He was talking about the car, of course, but on the verge of my

106th birthday there was always the chance it could be my last ride, as well.

"The pleasure is mine," I said.

"You wanna drive?"

"Absolutely not."

"I wouldn't let you anyway," he said.

The Oviatt was long gone, of course, not that it was any great tragedy.

"I wonder whatever became of Ed Wozniak?" I said.

"That was the guy that worked at the desk?" said Angel. "The guy that hooked you up with the old lady?"

"Yeah," I said. "I suppose old Woz is probably six feet under by now."

"That, or he's like a hundred years old like you."

"Probably not," I said.

The entire neighborhood was unrecognizable, which shouldn't have come as a surprise, yet somehow it took a little wind out of my sails. Like city hall, I was a relic of a bygone world. The streets of old downtown were cleaner and emptier, a fact that defied convention. All the old businesses had vanished, their hand-painted windows and dusty awnings a thing of the distant past. The Flower District was long gone, gone the young Mexican girls who once graced my Sundays and inspired me to imagine a future for myself. Everything about downtown Los Angeles had seemed to promise something back then. But now, driving through those narrow, gleaming corridors of steel and glass, my eye was drawn upward rather than outward, and that alone seemed like a tragedy. For the pulse and vibrancy of Los Angeles as I recalled it was a palpable life force that surrounded you. Those grubby storefronts and venerable old buildings once swarming with humanity had been replaced by thousand-foot temples, shrines to late capitalism piercing the sky.

It's not that I was totally unprepared for the city's transformation. Five decades had served to soften the blow, for I knew as well as anybody that change was the rule and not the exception. But so much was lost, a fact that became painfully more apparent as the day wore on. Bunker Hill and Chinatown were now hemmed in by superhighways, Boyle Heights now cut off from the city by a tangle of interchanges. Consuela's house was long gone, as well as the four or five adjacent houses, their yards once teeming with children, now but a single drab apartment complex that might have been anywhere. I could no longer hear the laughter of all those families cooking out in their yards.

"So, wait, you were training to be a what?" said Angel.

"A stenographer."

"What's that?"

"Nothing, anymore," I said.

"But I thought you were a teacher."

"That was much later."

"Like after the war?"

"Long after the war."

"Where did you teach?"

"Riverside," I said. "Rubidoux High."

"Never heard of it."

"It's probably gone by now, like everything else. . . ."

"You wanna check? What the heck? It would be on the way back."

"Why not?" I said.

But the truth was I could think of plenty of reasons. After years of my cloistered life at the Greens, all the change was overwhelming. I wasn't sure I could take another disappointment.

At the next light, Angel swung the Monte Carlo around and began piloting us east.

"You want your sandwich, homie?"

"Sure," I said. "As long as it's—"

"Yeah, yeah, man, it's your usual. Bro, you gotta expand your horizons one of these days. On Monday, I'm bringing you tamales from my aunt."

I was fifty-two years old when I started teaching at Rubidoux High in 1968. Teaching was my third career, and the first occupation for which I'd reserved any kind of passion. A hapless prisoner of history myself, what choice did I have but to embrace it as my calling? Why hadn't I thought of it earlier?

I taught world history at Rubidoux, mostly, and sometimes English to juniors and seniors, most of whom I quickly learned did not share my passion for either subject. They were more interested in growing their hair long, and passing around notes, and chattering amongst themselves when they weren't gazing walleyed back at me, their boredom so perceptible that it might have had the effect of gravity on my enthusiasm were I not so single-minded in my mission to edify them. I would not surrender to their indifference and sloth so easily. I soldiered on in the face of their slack-jawed apathy, marching about fervently at the front of the classroom, trying to draw them out, to force their participation.

Gesturing grandly, I would say: "Friends, Romans . . ."

Then I'd wait for their rejoinder. And wait. And wait, as the students, like so many dead chickens, collectively considered my bow-tied visage.

"*Countrymen!*" I said. "Friends, Romans, *countrymen!* Mark Antony, people, upon the burial of Caesar. Really? Nobody?"

Looking out at the classroom, I confronted a prairie of blankness.

"Let's try again. We have nothing to fear but . . . ?"

"Commies?" ventured one pupil, whom I could barely identify as a boy beneath his mop of long hair.

"No! No, man! *Fear itself!* We have nothing to fear but *fear itself*! Did anyone do the reading?"

This is what I had been up against. And while my oratory often fell upon deaf ears, once in a while I'd be graced by a pupil who had some considerable light in her eyes. One such student was Kat Dennis, who wrote me a letter of appreciation in 1989, nearly twenty years after her graduation. The letter remains one of my few cherished possessions. I've committed the document to memory at this point.

> *Dear Mr. Miles,*
>
> *You probably don't remember me, but I took your world history class at RHS in 1970 as a senior, and to this day I still think about it. You'll be interested to know that after Rubidoux I went on to San Francisco State, then UC Berkeley for my graduate work, where I eventually earned my PhD in ancient history. I now teach at Long Beach State, where I find myself commiserating with you often. "Do the reading!" I tell them. History is my life's passion, and I largely have you to thank for it, Mr. Miles. Your revisionist takes on Moorish Spain and the rise of capitalism in the Northern Italian city-states were particularly inspired, and ahead of their time. I often wonder, how did you come by such insight?*
>
> *All of this to say thank you, Mr. Miles. I now know firsthand that teaching young people can be a thankless job, but somehow, in the face of indifference, you always managed to retain your zeal for history, a page of which, as you know, is worth a pound of wisdom.*
>
> *Sincerely yours,*
> *Dr. Katherine Dennis*

Amongst my younger, more progressive colleagues, I was a bit of an odd duck with my sweater vests and bow ties, and history jokes, which never quite succeeded in amusing the faculty or the student body. *A Roman walks into a bar. He holds up two fingers and says, "Five beers, please!"*

While I was not renowned for my social graces, my reputation as an educator and my perceived expertise as a historian were impeccable. Where matters of curriculum were concerned, my judgment was practically beyond reproach amongst my peers.

It was near the conclusion of my fifth year at Rubidoux when I was summoned one afternoon to the principal's office, much to my surprise, where I was greeted by the lean, bespectacled visage of Principal Maxwell himself, along with his associate, a frog-eyed man, squat and officious as a county courthouse, and not unfamiliar to me as the district's new administrator, a Mr. Spencer.

It seemed to me that whatever occasioned this impromptu meeting, it was unlikely to be a good development.

"I suppose you're probably wondering why we called you here, Eugene?" Maxwell said, lowering himself into his seat.

"Actually, yes," I said.

"Eugene, you know Fred Spencer, our administrator."

"Of course," I said, extending a hand.

"Eugene," said Maxwell. "I've been observing you for what, three years now?"

"Five, sir."

"At any rate," said Maxwell, "long enough to have developed a feel for your . . . unique style."

"Sir?"

"I'm speaking mostly of your tall tales."

"Tall tales, sir?"

"The colorful stories," he said. "Your first-person accounts of certain historical events."

Here it came, I thought. They were going to shut me down. I'd made myself too comfortable within the subject of history. In shar-

ing my personal impressions and insights regarding the world, ancient, Victorian, and otherwise, I'd crossed some ethical line. They
thought I was a loose cannon. I braced myself for what was sure to
be some form of disciplinary action, at the very least a warning.

"Personally, I think it's a brilliant approach," croaked Spencer.
"These kids are so hard to get through to these days. This speaking
in first person shtick is . . . well, so immediate, so theatrical. I can
see why it would be effective in holding their attention."

"Some days more than others," I said.

"I did fourteen years in the classroom myself," Spencer observed.
"So I'm more than just a pencil pusher. I commend you for embrac-
ing the unorthodox. If there's one thing these kids aren't interested
in, it's the status quo. Well done, Miles."

I was never very graceful at receiving compliments, but then, I'd
had so little experience at it. My ears were burning from the flattery.

"Apparently, Fred is not the only one who has taken notice of
your groundbreaking approach," said Maxwell.

"Oh?"

"In fact, one of your peers—whom, I cannot say—has seen fit to
nominate you for this year's California Educator of the Year Award.
Now, what do you think of that, Eugene?"

I was dumbstruck by the development. Not since the war had I
been distinguished in such a manner.

"You look surprised," said Maxwell.

"Indeed, I am," I said.

"Well, you shouldn't be," he said.

"Congratulations, Eugene," said Spencer. "You're a finalist for
the CEYA, Rubidoux's first."

I was stunned by this news. When had fortune ever smiled upon
Eugene Miles or any of his incarnations? I hardly knew what to do
with the news, so I kept it to myself and didn't tell a soul. But such
was the pride of Maxwell that the entire faculty soon learned of my

distinction, which made me a bit of a celebrity for the better part of a month. I invariably downplayed the attention, for I found it uncomfortable. But rest assured, inwardly I was pleased with myself.

I didn't win the award in the end—it went to an English teacher in Chico—but just to be a finalist was the pinnacle of my teaching career and, with the exception of my Purple Heart, the greatest honor ever bestowed upon me.

Still, the academic esteem of my peers did not quite amount to social acceptance. There were whispers amongst staff that I was a homosexual. An unmarried man in his fifties, childless, reserved—it all seemed to add up. It wasn't true. But I was, as ever, an outsider. My only friends were my coworkers, whom I rarely if ever saw outside of school. The office secretary, Barb Sandoval, a woman of roughly my vintage, took pity on me. I suppose she probably imagined me at home every night in my one-bedroom apartment, eating TV dinners and watching the late movie by myself, which wasn't far from the truth, though I rarely watched television, or stayed up late.

"Eugene," she said to me one afternoon when we were alone in the teacher's lounge. "May I ask you a personal question?"

"Certainly," I said.

"You're sure I won't be prying?"

"I've got nothing to hide," I said.

"I was wondering, are you seeing anyone currently?"

"No," I said. "Not for some time. But as a rule, I don't think it's a good policy to date work assoc—"

"Not me, silly," she protested. "I've been married for twenty-eight years. But would you be interested perhaps in meeting someone, a friend of mine? She's a widow, around your age if I'm not being presumptuous. Quite a nice-looking woman."

"Well, I suppose I . . . that is, if . . ."

"I think you'd get a real kick out of her. She might even laugh at your jokes, she's a real history buff."

"Oh?" I said.

"I believe she studied history in college."

"Really?"

"What do you say?" said Barb. "Can I set something up?"

"Well, okay, sure," I said.

"Oh, good," she said. "I think you're going to get a real kick out of Gladys."

When Angel's Monte Carlo pulled to the curb, it was a small moral victory to find that Rubidoux High was still in operation, though updated nearly beyond recognition.

"So this is it, eh, homie?" said Angel, idling at the curb. "You want to get out, peek in some windows or something? Maybe we can walk the hallways."

"Nah," I said. "It's enough to know something I remember is still standing."

"Anywhere else you wanna check out?"

"How about West Covina?"

"Sure, man, whatever you want, Geno. What's in West Covina?"

I arranged to meet Gladys at King George's Smorgasbord in West Covina. Perhaps not the classiest restaurant in town, but a favorite of mine for the roast turkey and mashed potatoes, and exceptionally reasonable pricewise. During all my visits I was never able to establish for which King George the buffet was named. Likely not George of the Hellenes or George of Bohemia. The stylized, vaguely Tudor décor seemed to suggest King George of Saxony, though it might just as easily have been any one of the Georges of the United Kingdom, or even one of the Hanover Georges.

I arrived at the royal buffet ten minutes early and found a quiet table toward the back of the dining room, though not so far back that I wouldn't be visible to Gladys upon her arrival. I wore a sweater-vest and khakis for the occasion, with no bow tie, which I deemed too formal. Was I nervous? Oddly, not very. Despite my relative isolation, I was not a misanthrope. People did not make me nervous, nor was I lacking in self-confidence. My social exchanges did not feel awkward or labored, at least not to me. While I may not have been remarkable in any way, I was sufficiently comfortable in my own skin to engage socially when I felt the call, which was rare.

When Gladys walked through the door, she waved like she'd known me forever and proceeded straight to the table. The first thing I noticed besides the fact she was at least three inches taller than me, before I'd even registered the liveliness and intelligence in her dark eyes, or her high cheekbones, or her full lips, was the little red mole just below her right nostril.

"Eugene," she said. "Barb has told me all about you. You teach history! That's incredible. My favorite subject!"

"And mine," I said.

I sensed a palpable tension immediately, an unknown potentiality that occupied the space between us like a magnetic field, a force that could just as easily repel as attract. She started to sit down the instant I began to stand up. Then she started to stand up again, and I began to sit down.

"What do you think?" I said. "Should we . . . ?"

"Oh, yeah, right, of course," she said. "Why wait?"

Side by side, we walked to the buffet, where we collected our orange trays, our plates, our silverware, and our green cloth napkins.

"The cloth is a regal touch," she said.

"Polyester," I said. "The fabric of kings."

"So, what do you think, George the Sixth?" said Gladys. "Are we to assume this is his smorgasbord?"

"What makes you think so?"

"Oh, I don't know," she said. "He's the most recent King George that comes to mind. Probably the most well-known George at this point."

"True. But then, why not call the place King George the Sixth's Smorgasbord?"

"Too long maybe? Also, kind of a tongue twister."

"I think you're right," I said.

Here was a perceptive woman who looked the world straight in the eye, curiously and confidently, a woman undaunted by new experiences.

Gladys went straight for the Brussels sprouts. I didn't begrudge her this choice, though I never could abide Brussels sprouts myself. They tasted like farts. I was holding out for the green bean casserole, if Gladys would hurry up and make up her mind about the pasta.

"What is this?" she said.

"Some kind of macaroni, it looks like."

"But what are these here, the shiny, sweaty things?"

"Meatballs, I believe."

"They're not exactly round."

"Not exactly," I said. "That's part of the charm."

"What kind of meat, do you suppose?"

"Beef would be my guess."

"Not lamb?"

"Possibly lamb," I said. "Shall I ask?"

"No, no. Just curious," she said, passing on the meatballs.

We worked our way through the remainder of the line before resuming our seats, plates loaded.

"So, tell me," Gladys said. "Do you have a favorite period, a certain time in history that fascinates you?"

"As a matter of fact, I do," I said. "That would be the Moorish occupation of Spain, in particular the turn of the eleventh century."

"Really?" she said. "What a fascinating epoch. All those cultures blending together, all that scholarship. A golden era for the intellectual."

"And rampant conquest," I said. "Let's call it what it was: precolonialism."

"Colonialism? In the eleventh century? I don't think so. Colonialism didn't begin until the Portuguese in the sixteenth century."

"With all due respect, are you serious?" I asked. "And what about the Phoenicians and the Greeks and the Romans? Were they not colonial? Colonialism, as I view it, goes back much further than the sixteenth century."

"Well, I don't see the Moorish occupation of Spain as colonialism at all," she said, a little stridently. "The Moors brought culture to Spain."

"They ruined the Visigoths."

"They elevated the Visigoths!"

"Oh? And how is that?"

"By educating them! By freeing them from feudalism," said Gladys.

"No, no, no," I insisted, an edge of annoyance creeping into my voice. "That's not how it was at all. The Moors didn't cross the Strait of Gibraltar to save the Visigoths! The Christians, the Jews, nobody asked the Moors to come grace them with their culture."

"But that's just it," said Gladys, her voice reaching a new pitch. "There was no culture before the Moors!"

"Oh, ho, ho," I said. "Is that a fact? No culture? Gothic culture was not culture? Visigothic law was not law? What about all the basilican architecture that survives to this day?"

"The Moors brought science," she said. "They brought art. They encouraged diversity."

"Ha! They tolerated diversity, there's a difference."

"No, they encouraged it," she said. "The Moors enlightened

Spain. The Moors didn't erase anyone, they didn't shove their culture down anyone's throat."

"But they did in an everyday sense," I said. "They made you feel like less."

"And how would you know?" she said. "Were you there?"

The room started spinning slowly counterclockwise as I realized I had to tell this woman my long-held secret.

"Yes," I said. "As a matter of fact, I was there. What about you?"

She rolled her eyes at me. Oh, but what eyes in which to get lost! Her big irises seemed to pulse in the center as though her heart were beating behind them. Suddenly I was weightless in those pulsing eyes, floating in what I can only describe as a profound state of recognition, pure and unassailable. How had she found me? Or had I found her?

"Gaya?" I said. "Is it you?"

"Excuse me?"

"It's you, it's really you, isn't it?"

"I'm afraid I don't know what you're talking about, Eugene. Is this some kind of gag?"

Inexplicably, impossibly, there we were, my Gaya and me after ten centuries, reunited at the King George's buffet in West Covina.

"Wait," said Angel, pulling to the curb in front of what was once King George's Smorgasbord and was now a Little Caesars pizzeria and a nail salon. "I'm confused. How could you be so sure that Gladys was Gaya?"

"I just knew. The eyes, the mole, all of it."

"But she said all that good stuff about Moors. Why would she do that when she was part of the resistance?"

"She had no memory of it at that point. She was only espousing the old chestnuts she'd been taught in her history classes. The golden age mythos. I could hardly hold it against her that she was a romantic."

"I don't know, Geno. No offense, but it doesn't quite add up. How did you know it was really her?"

"I told you, I just knew."

"But, I mean, how?"

"How does a newborn know its own mother without ever having laid its eyes on her?"

"It just came out of her!" Angel countered. "Look, homie, I'm not saying I don't believe you, it just seems like a bit of a leap."

"Her eyes," I said. "I saw it in her eyes."

"I dunno, dog."

"Forget it," I said.

"C'mon, don't be that way, Geno. I just wanna know how you knew. It's kinda confusing."

"You wouldn't understand," I said, waving him off.

"Well, maybe if you explain it."

"I'm tired," I said. "Please, I wanna go home."

With that, I put my face to the side window and began to sulk for the long drive back to Desert Greens.

Cloudy Skies

Monday morning, I was back to business as usual. I awoke early and set to work on my puzzle, a Charles Marion Russell rendering in watercolor of Lewis and Clark on the lower Columbia, months before our crossing at the mouth of the river. Will, with his red hair, stands in the canoe, a flintlock rifle cradled in his arms, as Sacagawea, our Shoshone guide, communicates with a group of Columbia River Indians, Chinooks, I believe they were. There I am in the boat, right behind Sacagawea, the gold hoop through my left earlobe just barely visible.

I was struggling with the most troublesome portion of the puzzle, the blasted gray-brown bluff in the background, partially obscured by wisps of cloud, when I was startled by a voice.

"I hear you took an outing with Angel."

It was Wayne, as always disturbing my peace from his place in the open doorway, where he was employing his fastidiously cultivated air of casualness.

"So, how was that?"

"Fine," I said.

"The big city, huh?"

"That's right."

"Well, that's great," said Wayne. "So glad to see you opening up socially again."

Again? When had I ever opened up socially in the first place? My entire life had been a clinic in disassociation.

"So, any adventures to share?" said Wayne.

"We ate sandwiches and drove around."

"You go by the old facility?"

"And what facility would that be?" I said.

"Not ready to talk about that, huh? That's okay. What about Riverside? You visit the high school?"

"Yes."

"How was that?"

"It was fine, Wayne, just fine."

I closed my eyes, hoping that when I opened them again, Wayne would be gone. But no such luck.

"You and Angel have really taken a shine to each other," he said.

I tried the eye trick again for good measure, but there was Wayne, still leaning in the doorway.

"I hear you guys eat lunch together out on the green quite a bit."

I neither confirmed nor denied this rumor.

"So, how's that?" he said.

Ignoring him was useless.

"About how you'd imagine, Wayne. Two guys eating lunch."

"What do you guys talk about?"

"A variety of subjects," I said with an edge of annoyance.

"Do you tell him about Gladys? Your past lives? Your life in Los Angeles? The war?"

"And what business is that of yours?"

"Actually, your well-being is very much my business, Eugene. I'm simply asking about your life. This recent uptick in your social activity sounds like a positive development."

"Am I being assessed? Is that what's happening? I'm a hundred

and five years old, what exactly do you hope to accomplish by analyzing me, Wayne?"

"Am I analyzing?"

"It sure feels like it."

"Just curious, is all," he said. "What does Angel think about your
past lives?"

Here, my patience finally gave out.

"Damn it, Wayne, why don't you ask him yourself?"

"I'm sensing some hostility, Eugene."

"Good. I was beginning to wonder if you ever listen."

"Of course I listen," he said.

"Then I'm asking you: Kindly leave me alone."

"Okey dokey," said Wayne.

"And please shut the door behind you."

Finally, Wayne acquiesced. Why was I being such a jerk to the
man? Besides the fact that he'd been grating on my nerves with his
antics and his noisy Life Savers since the day he arrived, hectoring
me with his incessant questions, bombarding me with his continu-
ing campaign of analysis, probing and prying and soliciting personal information at every turn, I have trouble trusting mental health
professionals in general. And why would I? Besides Dr. Stowell,
they have never listened to me, let alone believed me, though until
recently I've always been forthcoming, candid, and invariably coop-
erative with their investigations. I've answered the same questions a
hundred times. But they only hear what they want to hear. I am not
a psychological curiosity. I have no reason to lie to these people. Is
it my fault if they lack imagination, if they cannot think beyond the
formal constraints of their fledgling science, if they cannot conceive
that the world is full of alternative explanations to their diagnosis?

Later that afternoon, when Angel popped in to service my quarters for the first time since our trip to LA, I was still irritable.

"How's it hangin', ese?"

"Hmph," I said.

"You're still sore at me about the Gladys stuff, is that it? Look, all I was saying was that—"

"Close the shade, will you?" I said. "The glare is giving me a headache."

"Hey, I brought you something for lunch today, homie. Tamales from my aunt Olivia."

"Not big on spicy food," I said.

"Naw, man, it ain't spicy, bro," said Angel.

"I'm gonna pass."

"Okay, I see how it is," he said.

"No offense," I said.

"Whatever you say, Geno. But it's pretty cold in here, if you know what I mean. You want the AC off?"

"Leave it on," I said.

I am not proud of how I snubbed Angel on that occasion. He'd shown me nothing but kindness and companionship in the weeks I'd known him. But inevitably, like everybody else, it seemed like he'd begun to doubt me of late, and that smarted a little, for in Angel I'd thought I'd finally found a believer.

Optimal

Try as I might, I could not begrudge Angel for long. I'd come to depend on his companionship, his sympathetic ear, and his news of the outside world. As Oscar famously said, "The bond of all companionship is conversation." Thus, when Angel made his appearance the following day, I played a different tune.

"Angel!" I said, setting aside my puzzle piece. "How goes it, homie?"

"Feelin' better today, huh, old man?"

"Considerably."

"That's good."

"And I apologize for my rudeness," I said.

"No worries," he said. "Hey, man, I brought tamales again. At lunch you oughta come check out the Optima."

"Let me check my schedule," I said. "I might have to shuffle a few things around."

Angel flashed his warm grin, and it was a relief to have him in my confidence again.

"It's a date, then," he said. "I'll swing by in a couple hours."

As promised, Angel retrieved me on his lunch hour, Tupperware of tamales in hand, and walked me slowly down the corridor and out the back door, where we cut across the green to the parking lot. The Optima, though not nearly so conspicuous as the black Monte Carlo, which may as well have been a hearse, was still the sportiest car in a lot full of hybrids and economy cars.

"It ain't so bad, right? I'm not crazy about white, I wanted black like the Monte Carlo, but I didn't want it to get too hot for the baby."

"Good thinking," I said.

"Can I show you something else?"

"I love surprises," I lied.

Angel fished the key fob from the pocket of his scrubs and unlocked the Optima's doors with a squawk. He ducked into the car momentarily and reemerged with a small black coffer.

"I don't know what I was thinking, bro. No wonder Elana and her mom won't let me in the house. I'm so stupid. The second Elana told me she was pregnant I was supposed to get down on my knee. Duh. But I was so freaked out about the baby, I missed my cue completely."

He opened the coffer to reveal a ring, nothing extravagant, a slender band of gold with a single inset diamond of maybe half a carat.

"It belonged to my mother," he said. "My aunt gave it to me."

"It's beautiful," I said. "When are you gonna ask her?"

"Sunday. We're going to brunch in San Berdoo."

"Congratulations."

"Thanks, Geno."

Angel stashed the ring back in the console, shut the door, and activated the fob with another squawk. Moments later we were beneath the ragged palms, eating tamales.

"Not bad," I said.

"I should have nuked them for a minute or two."

"I rather like them cold," I said. "A little dry, maybe, but not bad. Compliments to your aunt."

If ever a more wholesome, salt-of-the-earth food was devised than the tamale, I don't know what it is, and I've been around an awful long time. I couldn't help but recall Consuela's kitchen vividly, though it was some eight decades removed.

"Before Spain, you gonna tell me what happened with the airstrip?" said Angel.

"Airstrip?"

"The war. Whatchamacallit canal or whatever. Where Gladys's first husband died."

"Guadalcanal," I said.

We slogged waist-deep against the current through the steepbanked Ilu River toward the target, hectored by insects every step of the way, our nerves frayed from both the faint rumble of a distant firefight and the ominous silence of our immediate surroundings. The kid next to me was named Brooks, Johnny Brooks, a rifleman from South Carolina. He was a good egg, Johnny Brooks, polite and conscientious. The kind of kid who helped old ladies cross the street.

"I don't like this," Brooks whispered, scanning the high bank on both sides, his rifle poised above the lazy dark current. "I don't like it one bit."

"I heard they fled west," I said.

"Don't suppose the damn Japs are gonna just give away an airstrip, do you?"

We waded on in silence, fighting off the bugs, exhausted but alert.

"I always wanted to be a professional ballplayer, and goddang if I didn't come close," said Brooks.

"Yeah?"

"I was a hell of a third baseman. Not a goddamn error senior year, and I hit .467. Signed a contract with the Cards last October. The St. Louis Cardinals, can you imagine? Daffy, the Big Cat, the rookie Musial. A man named Freedlander came to our house all the way from St. Louis. Gave me a real nice bone-handled jackknife as a gift. Still got it right here in my pocket. Four thousand bucks they were gonna pay me! Can you imagine? For playing baseball? Heck, I was a hero in Camden. Even posed with my dad for a picture on the front page of the *Chronicle*."

"Not bad," I said.

"I was supposed to report to Miami Beach, third week of February," he said. "Miami Beach!"

"You'll get your shot," I said.

"The hell I will. I'm a realist, Miles. I don't expect to get out of here alive, let alone fully intact."

"You're just spooked," I said. "Look around, Brooks. Word from upstairs is we've got them outnumbered four to one."

"That don't mean a dang thing," he said.

Brooks was right in the end. He was killed five weeks later, along with 446 other men in the first major action at Henderson, the name US leadership conferred on the airstrip after we took it. I was amongst those who reclaimed the dead, and it was me who found Johnny Brooks. That's how I wound up with his bone-handled jack-knife, a token of our brief friendship, lifted from his front pocket.

"So, you took the airstrip?" interjected Angel.

"We took it twelve hours later with help from the fifth division."

"I knew it," said Angel. "I knew you were setting me up with all that ominous-silence stuff. So, you took the airstrip, then what happened?"

"Then the real hell began."

Death wore many faces on that cursed island: disease, malnutri-

tion, and not the least of them enemy fire. Amidst clouds of ma-
larial mosquitoes, our stomachs feeding on themselves, we readied
ourselves for attack at any moment. If the constant threat of bom-
bardment weren't enough, the humidity and heat were relentless.
We were sorely undersupplied. After a brutal defeat at Savo, most
of our supplies were withdrawn. Those rations we carried with us
were exhausted in a matter of days. Soon, we lived solely on the rice
we'd seized from the Japanese stores. Either we picked the maggots
out, or we ate them.

"That's harsh, dog."

"Worms, too," I said. "It was like the rice was actually alive,
squirming on our spoons."

"Ech," said Angel, setting down the last of his tamale with a
grimace. "Stop. That's all I can handle for today. I think I like Spain
better. Even the cat."

He gathered our corn husks and stuffed them in the empty
Tupperware.

"Sometimes you're just too damn vivid, Geno," he said, replacing
the lid. "At least for lunch talk."

"You think it's my imagination? Is that what you mean by
'vivid'?"

"Nah, man, I didn't say that. I just mean your memory is sharp.
I've seen the medals; I know you were there. And nobody makes up
the maggots. C'mon, I'll walk you back in."

Angel lent me a hand getting up from the picnic bench, then
slowly began escorting me across the green in the twilight, endlessly
patient with my sluggish pace. As we walked shoulder to shoulder,
it was almost as though Angel was holding my hand.

In the foyer, we passed Wayne, whom I was surprised to see at
that time of the evening. Usually he was gone by the time Angel
and I took our late "lunchtime" repast. Wayne was talking to a
woman of fifty-five or sixty years of age, presumably the daughter

of a resident. I saw him take notice of our passing, and I could feel his eyes on my back as we proceeded down the corridor.

When we arrived at my room, I paused in the doorway.

"Elana better say yes," I said.

"You're telling me," said Angel.

"For the brunch, make sure you get a table in back, or outside, or somewhere private," I said.

"I'll feel it out when we get there," he said.

"No. Call first. Don't leave anything to chance," I said. "Trust me, you want everything to be just right. Have you thought about what you're gonna say?"

"Yeah, I've thought about it."

"And?"

"I'm gonna explain myself, like I told you. About how I blew it the first time around, how I was freaked out about the baby, and I wasn't thinking straight, and how even before that happened, I'd been thinking—"

"No," I said. "Talk about the first time you met her. Don't make this about the pregnancy."

Angel smiled and shook his head in apparent wonderment.

"Man, you're good, Geno. Real good."

"I ought to be after all this time."

"I'll let you know how it goes, dog."

We exchanged a fist bump before parting ways.

No sooner had Angel taken leave of me, however, than Wayne intercepted him in the corridor.

"Mr. Torres, hey, hello. I was wondering if I might have a chat with you?"

"Uh, yeah, sure," said Angel. "You mean now, or . . . ?"

"Just drop by my office at your convenience. You know where that is, right?"

"Yeah."

"Any time before seven thirty would be great."

"Okay," said Angel.

The exchange, innocuous as it may have sounded on the surface, left me uneasy as I retired to my room, shutting the door behind me. Heavy of bone, and more tired than I can remember, I sprawled out on the bed, feeling every bit of my eleven hundred years.

Shadow World

Though it was nearly impossible to mark time in the dim depths of our subterranean hold, I would estimate that Gaya and I spent five days in captivity, during which we were provided water and bare sustenance, a thin gruel of unknown origins, utterly tasteless and served cold, along with a large ceramic bowl to be utilized in lieu of a latrine, the vessel being emptied daily by a sentry, who came and went at intervals. Beyond these brief interludes, we were left with the darkness, an amorphous shadow world to which our eyes eventually adjusted well enough to see each other at arm's length.

Assad never beckoned us. It seemed his plan was to let us rot down there. When we were not sleeping shoulder to shoulder, Gaya and I passed the interminable hours by talking, or not talking. It was useless to plot an escape, even if we could somehow breach our barred cell, for there was only one way out, a corridor guarded on either side of the heavy door.

"How long will he leave us down here?" I wondered aloud.

"Who knows?" she said.

Had I been sequestered down there alone, confronted with such deprivation, I'm quite sure I would have unwound mentally in a mat-

ter of days, but with Gaya next to me, I could have endured anything. Alone I was nothing, void of humanity, but beside her even
my suffering had meaning. While Gaya did not reciprocate my
adoration, at least not conspicuously, and I was powerless to guess
at the boundaries of her devotion, neither did she rebuff my affections. I spent untold hours in the musty darkness trying to devise
ways to make her laugh. I spelled out for Gaya my most comical
tribulations, failures, and humiliations as a thief and a beggar. Being clubbed senseless by an old woman with a leg of lamb. Nearly
having my hand gnawed off by a toddler while attempting to filch
the purse tucked snugly in the folds of his leather conveyance. Trip-
ping headlong into a manure cart on a botched retreat. Every time
I succeeded in eliciting her amusement, whether the gentle burble
of her laughter or her smile that lit up the darkness, I was over-
whelmed by a sense of well-being the likes of which I had never
known and have not known since. Oh, how I might have entertained her had I access then to the seven lifetimes' worth of folly
and fiasco I would one day possess! I might have regaled Gaya with
tales of Oscar or York or Eugene! But as it was, all I could give her
was the roguish misadventures of Euric, because they were all I had.

At one point during our interminable ordeal, day or night I could
not say, I awakened in the darkness to the sound of Gaya's muf-
fled sobs.

I reached out for her, but she was not fast beside me, rather on
the opposite side of the cell. Sidling toward her, I took hold of her
by the wrist.

"What is it?" I said.

"It is nothing," she said.

Though I knew better than to press her for an answer, I dared to
move nearer and drape my arm about her shoulder. When she did
not shrink from the gesture, I pulled her in closer and offered Gaya

the very words I longed to hear from her every day for the rest of my life.

"I am here," I said.

And though she tendered no reply, she nestled closer to me as her sobs began to subside, her head resting firmly upon my shoulder. And with her left hand she reached out and took mine and held it fast in the darkness.

After an indeterminate interval of days, Assad finally beckoned us from our hold, at which point we were escorted back to the chamber where Assad had greeted us upon our arrival. Though the room was lit murkily at best, we squinted against the brilliance of the lantern as we were forced to kneel once more.

"Refreshed, are we?" said Assad, to his own amusement.

"You've got your purse back," said Gaya. "What use could you possibly have for us now?"

"Very little," he said. "In fact, should you disappear altogether, I would hardly notice."

"Is that a threat?" she said.

"Merely an observation," said Assad. "Silent, you are useless to us."

"Why did you summon us here?" I ventured.

"It is just as your companion guessed—your companion is exceedingly clever, if you hadn't noticed. We have no use for you. And being that the purse is accounted for, I should think you've suffered sufficiently for your transgressions. It is time to end that suffering."

"You're going to kill us?" I said.

Assad let the question hang in the air for an intolerable duration. In that brief silence, I resigned myself to dying. I wanted desperately to reach out and grasp Gaya's hand in that moment, but for reasons I could not account for, I did not dare. It was as if my hands were bound behind my back.

"He won't kill us," said Gaya.

"Won't I?"

"No," she said.

Assad smiled as though at a perceptive child.

"You see?" he said to me. "Very clever she is, your companion. Always one step ahead."

"Then what will you do with us?" I demanded.

"I will do nothing to you," he said. "You are free to go."

Of all the probabilities jockeying for position amidst my riotous thoughts, freedom was somewhere near the back of the mob. So far removed from any expectation was this news that it was akin to being granted life anew.

"Thank you," I said, from my knees.

"Don't grovel," said Gaya.

"Rise," said Assad. Then, to the guard: "See them out."

Resuming my feet, I swore I would never again resort to thievery, at least not for my own benefit.

"Steer clear of trouble," said Assad, as though he could hear my thoughts.

We were escorted out of doors and beyond the walls of the complex, where we were released unceremoniously into the blinding sunlight. Shielding our eyes from the offending glare, drawn to the shadows, we proceeded briskly away from the fortress, lest our captors have occasion to change their minds.

"Why did he let us go?" I said, my head pounding from the glare.

"Because," she said in a low voice, "Assad believes I will lead him to the resistance."

"But he just acknowledged you were a step ahead of him, did he not? So why would he expect you to lead him knowing his intent?"

"Because he is patient," she said. "Until he's not. He thinks if he waits long enough, I will make a mistake. But I will not."

"What happens now?" I said. "Do we leave the city as planned?"

Here she halted her progress and turned to face me, taking hold of both my hands.

"You can do whatever you want, Euric," she said. "You did not ask to join the resistance. And I was wrong to implicate you. You just fell into my lap."

"But I fell for a reason," I entreated.

"Go back to your normal life," she said.

"I have no normal life. I'm nothing, I'm nobody. And what about you? What will you do?"

"The same."

"But you no longer have a cart."

"I will make do," she said.

I was seized by an unfamiliar panic; my whole life seemed to hang suddenly in the balance. Here I was about to lose everything, and yet I'd possessed none of it a week prior. I could not let Gaya escape me.

"What if I did ask to join the resistance?" I said. "You said it yourself, I could be useful."

"Do you even profess to be a Christian?"

"Now I do."

"Then we shall see," she said. "I will find you when I need you."

"But how? How will you find me?"

"I found you once, didn't I?"

Angel, leaning on his broom, was not satisfied with this outcome.

"So, that's it? She just ditched you?" he said.

"Not exactly," I said. "She was just protecting the cause."

"I dunno, dog. After what you guys had been through, that seems pretty cold, her knowing you had nowhere to go and all."

"The story's not over," I said.

"Okay, then, what happened?" he said.

"You'll have to wait until Monday."

"Monday?" he said. "Come on, ese, that's not cool."

But Angel knew by now that this was my way, to leave him hanging. You can't overestimate having something to look forward to, so long as you know it's actually coming.

Sunday, Sunday

No sooner had Jim trundled his custodial cart into my peaceful quarters on Sunday than I could hear the infernal rasp of his mouth-breathing, much to my discomfort. As he stooped over and took hold of my wastebasket, exposing his ample butt cleft, I braced myself for the inane conversation that would inevitably follow. Jim was quick to oblige.

"You a Dodger fan?" he said out of the blue, emptying the trash.

"No."

"Angels, huh?"

"Nobody," I said, hoping to end the conversation.

I deplored baseball, which I associated with my father, his endless radio broadcasts, and those compulsory ball-tossing sessions, the sole aim of which was to deplete my overactive imagination.

"Nobody, huh? That's too bad," Jim said.

"Oh?"

"C'mon, you gotta love the great game, right? Me, I like the radio best—theater of the imagination. You just close your eyes and imagine being there. Breathe in the fresh air, smell the hot dogs, feel the sun on your face. You ought to give it a try. Good way to kill some hours."

"I manage to keep myself pretty busy," I said. "But thanks."

"Gotcha," he said. "Giants, today, though, just sayin'. Great rivalry. First pitch in about four minutes. Five seventy on your AM dial, in case you decide to check it out."

Why was it that everyone sought to improve my life somehow, to foist newness upon me, to fill my days with activity? What did they expect from me? I'd lived a full life—seven full lives! After centuries of being tossed about at the whim of fate, couldn't they accept that I had chosen this life for myself?

"You can pull the shade down," I said.

"Gotcha, chief."

No sooner had Jim lowered the shade and taken leave of my quarters than another unwanted visitor appeared in the doorway, his Life Saver clattering against the back of his teeth.

"Eugene," said Wayne. "You ought to get some light in here."

"Mm" was all I said.

Undaunted by this chilly reception, Wayne chose to interpret my listless response as an invitation to enter my quarters, where he leaned casually against the dresser, obstructing my reading light.

"Reading about the war again, eh?" he said.

"Boy, you don't miss a thing," I said.

"I'm paid to observe, after all."

"Well, I'm not paying to be observed," I said. "I came here to live in peace, not answer questions all day long. Your predecessor never interrogated me. Every day is like the Inquisition with you."

Wayne shook his head and grinned. "Another Spain reference. Man, I hope I have half your salt when I'm ninety-two," he said.

"I'm a hundred and five," I said. "We've been over that."

"Ahhh, right," said Wayne. "Whatever you say. So, I had a little chat with Angel Torres the other day after work."

"Good for you."

"Solid kid," he said. "Quite the . . . interesting past. Nice of him to take an interest in you. You don't see that too often in healthcare anymore. Technically, it's not something I should encourage, and yet it seems harmless enough. Is it?"

"What are you implying?" I said.

"Nothing at all," said Wayne.

"You think he's trying to exploit me, to get his hooks in my coffers, to weasel his way into my will, is that it?"

"Heavens, no," said Wayne. "It's just good to see you open up to somebody."

Exasperated, I set my book down on the desk and spun around deliberately in my office chair to face him.

"What do you want from me, Wayne?"

"I just want to talk."

"Why?"

"It's my job, Eugene. Making sure that everybody around here is okay, that they're thriving, that's what I do."

"I don't need a savior, Wayne. I'm a hundred and five years old. How is talking to you gonna make me okay? I'm not lonely. I don't feel isolated. I have nothing to get off my chest. And I'm not afraid of dying, if that's what this is about."

"Let's talk about death," said Wayne.

"Why?"

"You brought it up," he said.

"There's nothing to talk about," I said.

"The thought of death doesn't unsettle you at all?"

"Why should it? It's an illusion."

"You keep saying that. But where's your proof?"

"I have nothing to prove," I said.

"Angel mentioned that you told him about Consuela," said Wayne.

"That's right, so? We went by the old neighborhood," I said.

"Ahh," he said.

"Just say it, Wayne."

"Say what?"

"I'm a liar. That's what you think."

"That's not true," Wayne said.

"You haven't believed me from day one. Just like my parents, and every set of foster parents I ever had, and every shrink I ever talked to."

"Besides Stowell," he said.

"You're just like everybody else around here. You think I'm a psychological aberration, a freak."

"Actually, I think you're one of the most fascinating people I've ever met," said Wayne.

"Well, I wish I could say the same," I said, swiveling back around in my chair, where I promptly resumed my book. "Now, could you please get out of my reading light?"

"Oh, yeah, sorry about that," he said. "Anyway, good talk. I gotta make my rounds."

"You do that, Wayne."

By the time I'd managed to get rid of him, my concentration was already shot. Impelled by a sudden irritability, I set my book aside and began tapping my foot on the floor reflexively. I considered the half-completed puzzle on the desk momentarily but could muster neither the focus nor the patience requisite for the task. Wheeling my office chair to the nightstand, I turned on the clock radio and, with some trepidation, set it for AM 570 just in time for the first pitch.

Bosh

When Angel showed up on Monday, he could barely contain his enthusiasm. Grinning ear to ear as he entered with his custodial cart, he opened the shade and let the late afternoon sunlight flood the room. But I was not feeling sunny.

"She said yes!" Angel announced. "She didn't even make me squirm!"

"Mm," I said.

Obviously, my reaction to this news was not what Angel had anticipated. His thousand-watt grin dimmed in an instant.

"What's wrong?" he said.

"Nothing is wrong."

"Didn't you hear me? Elana said yes, bro! I did what you said: I called ahead of time and got the best table on the patio. I even arranged for a bouquet of flowers. Then, before they even brought the menus, I popped the question on her. Bro, I was so scared she'd say no, like maybe I'd missed my chance, you know? But she said yes, homie!"

"Congratulations," I said flatly.

This response was equally deflating to Angel.

"Yeah, okay, thanks," he said, fishing his bucket and rag off the cart. "It's like this again, huh?"

He worked in silence for several minutes, wiping down the immaculate dresser and spraying the window.

"So, I hear you've been talking with Wayne," I said.

"Yeah, he's a pretty interesting dude, actually," Angel said.

"He's insufferable," I said.

"Ah, man, he ain't that bad, Geno."

I wanted to be happy for Angel about his engagement, I really did. But his consorting with Wayne felt like a betrayal to me. How could I trust Angel again if he was discussing me behind my back?

"And what did Wayne have to say?"

"Not much," said Angel.

"I find that hard to believe considering he solicited the conversation with you in his office."

"Okay," Angel said. "Let's see. Well, one thing he told me was that you're the reason he came here."

"Me? Did he?" I said. "And why on earth would he say that?"

"I don't know, he said you were fascinating. And that he first learned about your case when he was at UCLA. He said he'd read about you in journals a long time ago."

I could feel the blood rushing to my face as I evaded Angel's eyes, frowning.

"What?" he said, registering my disapproval.

"What did he tell you about Stowell?"

"Nothing," said Angel.

"He's trying to turn you against me," I said.

"What?"

"He's gaslighting me."

"Wait, what? That just sounds paranoid, dog. Why would he do that?"

"Did he imply that I was delusional? Did he tell you that I made it all up—Spain, Italy, Oscar?"

Now Angel evaded my eyes and didn't respond straightaway. Instead, he replaced his bucket and rag on the cart and set his attention to stripping the bed.

"Well?" I said. "Did he?"

"Okay, maybe a little," said Angel.

"And you concur with this diagnosis?"

Angel donned a pained expression and looked away once more.

"Look," he said. "It doesn't matter to me one way or another, homie."

"So, you believe him?"

"I didn't say that, Geno. But why did you lie to me, bro?"

"Lie to you?"

"Wayne said you're only ninety-two."

"Nonsense," I said. "I'll be a hundred and six in August."

"He says it's on your birth certificate. Nineteen twenty-nine."

"Bosh," I said, waving it off. "He's just slandering me."

"Who's Consuela?" said Angel.

"I told you who Consuela was."

"Who is she really?"

"What do you mean?" I said.

"You never told me about Metropolitan."

"Well, listen," I said. "I don't know what Wayne has been telling you, but—"

"What about Gladys?" said Angel. "What's the real story with her? Wayne said there's a lot more to it."

"Gladys? And how would he propose to know that?"

"He didn't say," said Angel.

"Well, whatever he says he's read about me, or knows about me, I've only known the man for eight months. So, he hardly knows the first thing about me."

"He says Gladys isn't who you told me she is. He says that you were never married to her."

There it was. I'd been exposed. A sudden tightness gripped my chest, and I was seized by a shortness of breath. I saw a single red flash before I was overcome by an abrupt light-headedness.

"Whoa, Geno, you okay?"

Dully, I sensed myself sliding from my chair. As the light drained from the room all at once, I was weightless. For the briefest instant I thought I was dying, actually dying, and I wasn't afraid.

But not this time, alas.

When I came to groggily, I was flat on my mattress with no less than four people hovering at my bedside, looking down upon my prostrate form with grave concern. Amongst them was a female nurse, midfifties, vaguely familiar, and a male orderly whom I did not recognize, along with Wayne, and Angel, who had presumably alerted them all to the event.

"You gave us quite a scare," said the nurse.

"It was nothing," I assured her. "I tried to stand up too quickly. Probably dehydrated."

I began to push myself upright in bed, but the nurse gently dissuaded me, easing me back down.

"Lie back," she said.

A moment later, a physician entered the room. Young and generically handsome, he looked like a doctor on a soap opera, like his name should've been Dr. Travis Sinclair. I caught the nurse staring surreptitiously at him as he checked my vitals.

"I'm Dr. Talbot, Eugene. I'm just gonna give you a quick once-over and ask you a few questions, is that okay?"

"I'm fine," I said.

"You're probably right," said Talbot. "But we're gonna look you over, just in case. Is this the first time this has happened?"

"Yes," I said.

He shined his light directly in my eyes, and I could all but feel my pupils constricting as I squinted against the glare.

"How have you been feeling generally of late? Any trouble breathing? Any headaches, any pain or discomfort I should know about?"

"No."

"Have you been losing weight?"

"Not that I can tell."

"How about your appetite?"

"The same as always."

"Can you say *ah* for me?" said Talbot. "Real wide, now."

Talbot peered down into my throat with his light.

"May I ask how old you are, Eugene?"

"I'm a hundred and five," I said, frowning directly at Wayne.

"He's ninety-two," said Wayne.

"Which is it?" said Talbot.

"A hundred and five," I insisted.

Wayne appealed to Talbot with a roll of his eyes. "His birth certificate says ninety-two," he said.

"Either way," said Talbot, "I gotta hand it to you, Eugene, you're an impressive physical specimen. Vitals look pretty good, blood pressure is a little low, but not too bad. Any chronic conditions I should know about?"

"Just living," I said, a witticism that was all but wasted on him.

"And how are you feeling now?"

"Normal," I said.

I attempted to sit up again, but this time Talbot deterred me gently.

"Not quite yet, buddy. Right now I want you to get some rest, okay? But a little later, I'd like to run a few labs, if that's all right."

"Fine," I said.

"Nurse Fahey, if you could monitor him in the meantime? Mr. Francis," he said to Wayne, "if I might have a word with you?"

"Of course," said Wayne.

Talbot and Wayne retreated to the corridor, where they began consulting quietly.

"Geez, homie," said Angel. "You really freaked me out. I thought you . . . well, you know. . . ."

"I should be so lucky," I said.

"I'm sorry if I upset you, bro," he said.

"Don't give it another thought," I said. "So, did you two pick a date?"

"We're thinking August twentieth. But it's not set in stone yet. We gotta see what's available for venues. You gotta be there, man."

"We'll see," I said. "I'm gonna need to check my schedule."

"Hey, about the other thing, really, I shouldn't have said anything, Geno. Screw what Wayne says, I know who you are, dog. Forgive me, man. I feel like this was all my fault."

I read genuine anguish on the face of the young man, and I realized in that moment that I loved him, that he was literally like some kind of guardian angel looking after me, and I was powerless to begrudge him whatever he chose to believe about me, so long as he was there.

One True Light

All I've ever wanted in any of my incarnations was to connect with another wholly and authentically. Deprived of meaningful connection, we are ciphers at best, and at worst invisible. To be seen, to be accepted, warts and all, that has been my greatest aspiration for over a thousand years. To be adored for my flaws. To be loved unconditionally. And with Oscar, I came so close.

"Oh, Whiskers," he would say, scratching behind my ear in a moment of abstraction, fountain pen poised above the empty page, a dab of blue ink beading upon the tip. "My precious. How simple your life must be, you rascal. How easy to manage your emotions, your expectations, to govern your desires and simply act on them without judgment or consequence!"

Of course, Oscar had no idea, but that was immaterial so far as my immediate objective was concerned. Despite our star-crossed physical manifestations, setting aside those cursed feline limitations that would not allow me to sing my plaintive song in a tongue that Oscar might fully comprehend, I was still Oscar's muse! For a brief period, anyway, I was the apple of Oscar's eye.

You must understand that I was selfish in love, that once I had

captured Oscar's affections, I was constitutionally incapable of sharing them with another. For I was determined to be his one and only
for all my days in Chelsea. And I was almost there. Oscar doted on
me, confessed his innermost fears to me, scratched the underside
of my chin, my belly, called me his precious. Sometimes, when I
sensed his temper was agreeable, I dared to demand his attention,
even preened if the mood was right, strutting across his ink-strewn
pages until he gathered me up in his arms.

"Whiskers, my precious," he would say, guiding his long, delicate
fingers down my spine. "Does there exist a more magnificent crea-
ture than you? Oh, but don't think I don't see it: You are a vapid and
vain little devil, who cares not a whit for anything beyond his own
comfort and convenience, but you are magnificent, and that nobody
can deny."

Of course, Oscar had me all wrong, and he might have been
projecting a little bit. If I was vain, it was only to win his attention.
If I seemed vapid, it was only his inability to grasp the depths of my
emotions. My singular focus in life was Oscar, and Oscar alone, but
what did I care if he misunderstood me, so long as I was his precious? Many a night I slept curled beside his pillow, listening to him
mutter and murmur in his sleep, hoping to hear my name.

I was not by a stretch Oscar's only suitor. There were many. But
I could contend with my human competitors, for Oscar was dishon-
est with them. He did not trust them the way he trusted me. How
could he, when the little harlots were loyal to no one? Only with
me was Oscar ever truly honest, truly vulnerable. Thus, I tolerated
my human rivals, even employed my cloying charms on them if I
thought it would get me a spot on the bed between them.

It was a good life, until everything fell apart.

He was a plug-ugly tom, big and ungainly, a homely shade of
gray, speckled with black, with dead green eyes and a long, regal

striped tail, which comprised his only real attribute. And boy, did he flaunt it, whipping that thing around like a boa, hoisting it magnanimously in his wake, curling it elegantly upon the windowsill, furling and unfurling it as the sun hit his ugly face just so, even sweeping the useless appendage gently across Oscar's face. Imagine! So average, so utterly unextraordinary, was he! A worthless lump where pest control was concerned. I once watched a roach scurry right over his tail, and the scoundrel did not so much as budge from his place on the settee. The tom was torpid in his daily routine, careless in his hygiene, altogether unworthy of affection, let alone affections so delicate and sublime as Oscar's.

But the greatest insult of all was the name that Oscar bestowed upon this interloper he'd brought home: Precious, he called him, Precious! My pet name! My rightful and preferred name, as I never favored the moniker Whiskers, which was so cliché, so frivolous. Precious, the name Oscar summoned upon those wistful occasions when he found himself stymied by his literary endeavors, the name he lavished upon me as I lay beside him in bed, purring to my heart's content.

"Precious wescious, wittle wover," he would say to the big clod, who would invariably advance with his graceless plod and make a show of that useless tail of his, swishing and wagging it in Oscar's face, sounding that ugly guttural purr, blunt and indelicate as a steam locomotive.

My manner was incorrigible toward the tom when I acknowledged him at all. I hissed at his nearness and brandished my claws should he dare to cross my path. Oscar took his side more often than not, and that caused my hatred to burn hotter still.

"Whiskers, you incorrigible puss. Make nice!" he scolded me.

But of course, I dared to ignore these decrees, for never would I confer anything but contempt upon my rival. By all rights, the tom might have bullied me, the big lout, but he didn't. He might have

begrudged me my dwindling share of Oscar's affections, but he
didn't. He might have lorded his supremacy over me at every juncture. But instead, he was a portrait of aloofness. He was no more
threatened or intrigued by me than by the moth that wavered with
impudence in front of his face. And for this, I hated him most of all.

That Oscar would ever take in that graceless simpleton, that
lumbering clodpoll, that he should presume to name the beast Precious, well, suffice it to say that I had never lived to know such betrayal. And yet, I was powerless. I had no choice but to forgive
Oscar. Worse, I loved him more with every perceived slight, every
failure to notice me, so hopelessly compelled was I to be his, or
anyone else's, one true light.

Work Around

I'm going to be completely transparent: I rather enjoyed the attention of the nurses and orderlies resulting from my recent fainting spell. They each seemed to approach me with a certain curiosity and awe, as if by surviving such a swoon at my advanced age I'd somehow managed to extricate myself from the jaws of death. Maybe they'd witnessed such an event before with different results. Eight months ago, the woman in 213, Mrs. Elinore Casper, a name that suited her perfectly with her wisps of ghostly white hair and her skin as thin and cadaverous as medieval parchment, dropped dead suddenly in the commons in front of half the staff. Maybe they'd all thought I was a goner.

About a half hour after the episode, Dr. Talbot returned to check on me, arriving at my bedside with his winsome smile and perfect hair.

"How are you feeling, Eugene?"

"Fine."

"No light-headedness?"

"Nope."

"No numbness?"

"No more than usual."

"Good, good," he said. "Listen, I'd like to move you over to Valley Med. Strictly as a precautionary measure. Run some labs over there. Work up a CBC panel, pretty routine stuff."

It wasn't that I was frightened, more that I was comfortable, and the thought of all the energy it would take to go somewhere else was daunting. As much as I'd begrudged my existence at Desert Greens all these years, recent events had softened my perception of the place considerably. I didn't want to leave. I suppose I was afraid that if I did, I'd never be back.

"I'd really rather not," I said, anticipating pushback.

But Talbot absorbed my trepidation with no apparent reservation.

"Okay, that's fine," he said. "I get it. We can work around that. Tell you what, we'll just do the blood work here. Sound good?"

"Yes," I said. "I'd much prefer that."

In my thousand-odd years of experience, I've come to expect little in the way of thoughtfulness or delicacy from handsome men beyond Oscar. Perhaps it was just jealousy, but too much seemed to come too easily to them, while an unextraordinary lump of flesh like me had to fight for every scrap of attention or adoration he could get. I had to be smart or funny, or like Euric, courageous and loyal and enduring, while the superior physical specimen just had to be tall and square-jawed and symmetrical. But in Talbot, I had finally found a man to challenge this assumption.

"Do you have any questions, concerns?" he said.

"No," I lied.

"This must be a little unnerving."

"Not really."

"You're a braver man than I," said Talbot. "Stay put and I'll be back shortly for a blood draw. Don't go anywhere."

As if I could.

Moments after Talbot took his leave, Angel dropped back in to check on me, wheeling his cart in front of him.

"How goes it, ese?"

"Not bad," I said.

"Listen," said Angel. "I've been thinking about everything Wayne told me, and the rest of it, and—"

"I'm sorry I lied to you," I said. "You must think I'm a fraud."

"Nah," he said, setting a hand on my shoulder and giving it a little squeeze. "I'm sure you have your reasons, Geno. Whatever works, bro. I'm just glad you didn't keel over on me."

Dear Angel, so genuine, so quick to accept and forgive. I didn't want to let him down completely.

"I swear to you, the rest is true," I said. "My other lives. I'm not making them up. Spain, Oscar, it's all true."

"Whatever you say, Geno, it doesn't matter."

"It matters to me," I said. "All my life I've been called a liar."

"Well, in all fairness, dog, didn't you bring some of that on yourself?"

"Yes, okay, maybe. But I'm not lying about Gaya, or Spain, or Chelsea. No matter what Wayne says."

"I believe you," said Angel.

"Can I ask you something?" I said.

"Of course, dog."

"It's about your past," I said.

"Aw, man, do we have to?" he said.

"If you don't want to, I'll understand."

"Look, I was young," he said. "I was involved in some bad stuff, with the wrong people. I didn't exactly grow up in Beverly Hills, you know? People convinced me that if I wanted to make anything of myself, it was the only way. They were wrong."

"Why didn't you ever tell me?" I said.

"You never asked."

Here, I wanted to press him for more information, but Talbot returned in that instant, effectively ending our conversation.

Angel gave my shoulder a final pat.

"Okay, homie, you take it easy, okay?"

"I need you to believe me," I said.

"I believe you," he said.

But I could see in his eyes he wasn't convinced.

And how could he be?

I'd lied about Consuela, about young Ed Wozniak befriending me, about Gladys, about the war. I'd no more been at Guadalcanal than I'd been to the moon. I was twelve years old in 1942. I found the medals in a box at St. Vincent de Paul, just as I'd found the photo of the woman and the two girls tucked between the pages of a dog-eared copy of *De Profundis,* which I chanced upon in 1991 amidst the stacks at the Goodwill in Burbank. The letter from my former student was a fraud, a pathetic attempt to imbue myself with some meaningful legacy, typed by my own hand on an old Underwood. I was never a teacher, but a janitor of eighteen years at Immaculate Heart, wheeling a garbage barrel around like Angel, cleaning up graffiti, and unclogging toilets. Most everything I'd told Angel about my life had been a fabrication, or a perversion of some small truth, and Angel had believed it.

On top of that, I had told Angel nothing of Metropolitan or Dr. Stowell, nor had I any clue what Wayne might have told him. Eventually, I would have to tell him the truth if he didn't know it already, and that was a dreaded prospect indeed. For, as my beloved Oscar noted, "the truth is rarely pure and never simple."

II

An Unfamiliar Pride

Without Gaya or her cause to lend purpose to my life, I promptly reverted to my squalid ways. Except for the thieving—that I'd sworn off unless the cause demanded it. I swallowed my pride and resorted to begging in the streets of Seville. The results were predictable.

"Get a job," they said.

"Off the sidewalk, you dirty dog."

I spent weeks scouring the city for Gaya, though I'd vowed not to call on her under any circumstances. I was to treat this directive as my sworn duty to the resistance. But I was powerless against the magnetism of Gaya. I ventured near her house daily looking for signs of her comings or goings. Some nights I crouched in the shadows and kept vigil, hoping for a glimpse of her silhouette as she passed by the lamplit window. But the house remained dark. Likewise, I cased her aunt's house with the same results.

By day in the plaza, amidst the dizzying chatter, I kept my ears ceaselessly alert for any news of the resistance, anything that might hint at Gaya's whereabouts or well-being. Perhaps she had fled north for the mountains to join the gathering resistance. Maybe she was lying low in some far-flung corner of the city. Alas, I heard not so much as a whisper.

After a fortnight of largely unsuccessful begging, my self-respect got the better of me and I resumed the search for gainful employment that I'd abandoned years ago. Just as I had in my younger days, I beat the street looking for an opportunity, soliciting butchers and bakers and, yes, candlestick makers. I appealed to smiths and masons and cobblers.

"You?" they said. "Ha!"

"Get lost, you dirty scoundrel!"

Stomach protesting, sandals in tatters, discouraged beyond all reassurances, I was on the verge of recommencing my criminal endeavors when I finally caught a break.

He was an old tanner named Perero who couldn't have been a hair over five foot, with skin so leathery and worked it might have undergone tanning itself. Not a man of gregarious temper, rather a terse and joyless persona, though not wholly without sympathy, or he would not have distinguished himself as the only man in Seville willing to employ me.

"Are you strong?" he said, sizing me up doubtfully. "You're certainly not big."

"Ahem," I said, looking down on him. "With due respect, sir."

"Hmm, yes, you've got a point there."

Mine was the filthiest of jobs. First, I was tasked with scraping the blood and manure off the hides. I hefted them into a cart until they were heaped well over my head. Then, consumed in a cloud of flies, trailing a miasma of putrefaction, I wheeled them halfway across Seville to the nearest viable waterway, the partial remains of a Roman aqueduct. How could I not recall hauling Assad's dead minion to the river as I conveyed the barrow over the cobbled streets? My whole life seemed to consist of dirty work, whether it was honest or not.

Worse than rinsing the hides, though, was getting rid of the hair, soaking the skins generously with urine, mine or anyone else's, never in short supply, then massaging it into the roots. By the end of the day, my hands were chafed to a rosy red and I smelled like the seediest of back alleys.

For all the unglamorous tasks associated with the job, I was learning an honest trade for the first time in my life, a knowledge that imbued me with an unfamiliar sense of accomplishment. If only Gaya could have witnessed my turnaround, then she would've seen that she had been right to believe in me. I was more than just a lowborn Visigoth castoff with larceny in his heart. I was an upright man, even if I did stink of urine, somebody she could rely on, a man who could bring more to her resistance than mere thievery. I could bring character and integrity and strength. Ah, but when would the day come that I could show her?

One afternoon, guiding my mountain of stinking hides toward the old aqueduct for the fiftieth time, the ubiquitous swarm of flies a nuisance I scarcely noticed anymore, I was trundling along, nodding my head at faces now familiar, old women and children, the wheelwright and the butcher, the miller, and the beggar, when I paused to relieve myself in an alleyway. I had just begun my business when I was suddenly seized from behind. My captor spun me around to face him, and I immediately recognized him as one of Assad's soldiers, specifically the talkative giant.

"What's this?" I demanded.

"Silence," he said.

"There's no law against urinating!"

He spun me back around and began binding my hands behind my back.

"You can't just pick me up any time you feel like it. I've done nothing wrong! Let me go!"

Ignoring my plea, he conducted me impolitely out of the alley and into the street.

"What about my cart? My hides?"

Looking wistfully back over my shoulder at the heaping conveyance, I knew that my only chance at an honest life had escaped me.

The soldier shoved me through the streets from whence I came, my shame visible to the butcher and the wheelwright, the miller and the beggar.

"I did nothing!" I assured them.

Emboldened by this injustice, I attempted to free myself from the giant with no success, twisting and tugging. When my physical attempts proved futile, I resorted to verbal abuse.

"Release me, you witless brute! Don't think you can strong-arm us! We were here before you!"

But neither the butcher, nor the baker, nor the candlestick maker, nor even the beggar, was moved to action by my pleas.

Through the marketplace and past the plaza to the walled fortress the giant pushed me, oblivious to my protests.

Moments later I found myself in Assad's chamber, where I was forced to my knees to wait while the man himself was beckoned to greet me. He soon appeared in a flowing silk robe, sky blue, his manner composed.

"And so, the thief hath returned," he said.

"I am no thief. Nor have I returned. You had me dragged here by this imbecilic titan."

"The result is the same," said Assad.

"What do you want with me?" I demanded.

"Where is she?" he said.

"I have no idea. I haven't seen her since you released us."

"You're lying."

"I'm not."

"You follow her around like a stray dog. You've been to her house a dozen times, as well as the residence of her aunt."

"Maybe I'm looking for her, too," I said. "Did you ever think of that?"

A mirthless grin spread across Assad's face.

"If I believed that," he said, "I'd have left you on the street until you led me to her. But I suspect that is not the case." Here, his grin wilted. "In fact," he said, "I'm beginning to think you're willfully leading me away from her."

He gazed straight into my eyes as though trying to locate the truth there. I met his gaze unflinchingly, until I could no longer hold it and cast my eyes down.

"I'm going to ask you one more time," Assad said. "Where is she?"

"I told you I don't know."

"You also told me you're not a thief," he said. "And yet I recall you stole my purse."

"Not anymore, I'm not. I've given it up."

"You're a changed man, are you?"

"Yes."

"Nonsense," he said. "Be true to your nature, boy, be an opportunist. Tell me where she is, and I will release you without further inconvenience. But if you continue to defy me, you will most certainly regret it."

"How can I tell you what I do not know?"

"And if you knew, am I to presume that you would tell me?" he said.

That's when I made a grave error of pride.

"Never," I said.

Assad smiled again. "See, you are not changed, you are still a fool, as well as a liar. But the good news is that I have the power to change you. I can make you tell the truth."

"I do not possess the truth you wish to hear," I said. "I know nothing of her whereabouts."

"We shall see," said Assad. "Given the right circumstances, you might reconsider—many before you have. Maybe some time to think is what you need. I will give you as much time as it takes. Eventually, you will make the reasonable choice. Take him away," he said to the giant.

Assad's goon jerked me back onto my feet and led me out of the chamber, then along the length of the long, dim corridor and down the steps to the pitch-black bowels of the fortress, where I was locked once more in seclusion, this time without the comfort of Gaya to share in my suffering.

"Don't forget to put out the torch, you big ass!" I called after the giant.

Who was I anymore? The old Euric would never in a lifetime have dared to goad a larger man than himself, nor boldly defy a person of influence. The old Euric was a gutless malingerer who tiptoed in the shadows, who neither heard, nor saw, nor said a thing that might implicate him in anything of consequence. My only motives had been to profit unseen and exist undetected. I had taught myself not to shine. Defiance, provocation, these qualities had been beyond my capacity, along with courage and grace and integrity. But now I had something to fight for, someone to protect. Yet, how could I protect Gaya knowing nothing of her whereabouts or her affairs? For all my newfound purpose, I was useless to Gaya's cause, no matter how convinced Assad may have been otherwise.

My whole life a willful misanthrope, I still would have given both my eyes for a shred of companionship down there. If not my beloved Gaya, then at least a mouse, a cricket, a dung beetle, anyone or anything to serve as a reminder that I was in fact living and not dead. Allied, I might have endured, but alone I was damned. Left to myself in the darkness, it was a matter of a day before my spirits began to flag. It seemed I was consigned to this hellish existence for the rest of my days, that I would rot there amidst the deafening silence and implacable darkness, and the stink of my own excrement.

My fears were not unfounded. For during the days and weeks to follow, I was denied so much as a plate of gruel, or a bucket into which I might empty my bowels. I was granted only water, and just enough to keep me alive. Eventually, I was afforded a meager portion of mush. When the guard appeared daily with this pitiful sustenance, he would not speak to me, nor even acknowledge my existence. But his mere presence there in the darkness, the slight grate of his breathing, the bitter scent of his flesh, was sufficient, just barely, for me to convince myself I still existed. But every day it got harder. My thoughts grew foggier and more distant until they were scarcely comprehensible. When I could harness the focus to reason at all, I attempted to devise a way out of my hold, but there was no way out I could see save death.

"Bro, you were in deep," said Angel, holding a forkful of reheated lasagna.

He was dining that evening at my drafting table, atop the unfinished puzzle, careful not to disturb it, while I lay on my back in bed, resting per Dr. Talbot's instructions.

"That Assad was merciless," said Angel.

"Not true," I said. "His mercy was just conditional. He believed in his cause as much as Gaya believed in ours. Remember, he was taking orders. A thousand years later, history has yet to decide one way or the other whose cause was the more just. It's true that the butcher and the baker were not persuaded by my plight, perhaps because they were in agreement with Assad that their lives were indeed better under al-Andalus, be they Jews, Christians, or Muslims. Each man chooses his own truth. But to call him merciless is to misunderstand his perspective. He might have tortured or killed me at any time, but he didn't."

"You're a lot more forgiving than me, homie."

"Make no mistake," I said. "I shall never forgive him, but I can understand his position."

"You sure you don't want me to run down to the commissary and get you a sandwich?"

"I'm sure."

"How long until you'll know anything?"

"They had to send my blood across town, so who knows?" I said.

Angel wiped his face and began packing away the remnants of his lunch.

"Keep me posted, ese. I'm sure you're fine."

"Of course," I said. "I'm always fine."

Even more than usual, I hated to see Angel go. In his absence, my mind sought distraction with little success. Despite Angel and everybody else's assurances, and though I had little reason to believe my blood work would return anything out of the ordinary for a man of my vintage, I could not shake the creeping certainty that one way or another, my life, this life, all of my lives, were winding down.

Things to Come

The following day began with a visit from Wayne. I should have recognized this unwelcome development for what it was, a harbinger of things to come. As was his custom, Wayne invited himself into my quarters and leaned against the dresser, peering down at my current puzzle, upon which I was halfheartedly at work: the Alcázar of Seville, its striking red walkways lined with greenery, its arches, its white banisters.

Mercifully, Wayne was not sucking a Life Saver as he peered over my shoulder, or I may have snapped.

"Lisbon?" he said.

"Seville," I said.

"Ah, I see," he said. "And does the palace look familiar?"

"I had no occasion to visit it in my day, if that's what you mean. Only from the outside."

"Mm," said Wayne. "Amazing you remember it all after all this time. So, how are you feeling after your event?"

"Is that what we're calling it, an event?" I said. "I'm fine."

"Nervous?"

"About what?"

"The test results," said Wayne. "It's okay to be nervous, you know?"

"Thanks for the permission, Wayne. I'll keep that in mind," I said. "Do you think I'm afraid to die, is that what this is? Well, probably not gonna happen. I might be checking out of this mortal coil temporarily, but I'll be back before long—you can bank on it."

"I see," said Wayne. "Can I ask you something?"

"Can I stop you?"

"How can you be so certain you've actually had these experiences? Did you ever have any past-life regression or hypnotherapy?"

"No."

"Not even at Metropolitan?" he said.

The mere mention of Metropolitan put me on edge.

"No," I said.

"How do you know these memories, as you call them, are not delusions?" said Wayne. "Because Dr. Stowell said so?"

As usual, I was running out of patience for Wayne. God, how I resented his entire manner, the way he executed his endless interrogations as though they were innocuous, the expression of some innocent curiosity that just happened to cross his mind, when they were actually part of an extended campaign to undermine my credibility. Why, I still had no idea.

"What is it with you, Wayne? You're relentless. What exactly is it about me you find so fascinating? Angel said you came here because of me. What the heck is he talking about?"

"I've been interested in you for quite a long time," said Wayne.

"Why?"

"Like I said before, you're a fascinating case. Isn't that what Dr. Stowell thought, too?"

"Leave him out of it."

"Why so touchy about Dr. Stowell?" he said.

"What do you want from me, Wayne?"

Wayne plucked a framed photo off the dresser and presented it to me as though I hadn't seen it before ten thousand times. It was the picture of Gladys and me seated at King George's Smorgasbord, wineglasses half-full, Gladys looking a little stunned.

"Who is the woman in this photo?"

"My wife, Gladys," I said.

"Yes, it is Gladys," said Wayne. "Gladys Van Buren. But she was not your wife."

"How do you know her last name?" I said.

"Because it's my grandmother's first married name," he said. "Your Gladys is my grandmother, Eugene. I'm Nancy's son."

My scalp tightened. The ramifications were too various to process all at once.

"That's it, Eugene?" he said. "Nothing to say for yourself?"

Indeed, I was struck dumb.

"Whatever you may have told Angel or anyone else," said Wayne, "I know the real story. Some of it, anyway."

"How did you find me here?" I said.

"A former colleague of mine works with your geriatrician."

"So, you're stalking me?"

"I'd hardly call it that," he said. "I just wanted to meet you."

"Taking a job just to meet someone seems like a little much, doesn't it, Wayne?"

"I was tired of LA, and the opportunity presented itself."

"Well, you've met me, congratulations," I said.

"Did you know my grandmother kept journals?" he said.

"Is that so?" I said. "Very interesting. What does this have to do with—"

"Journals about you," said Wayne.

Irritably, I turned my attention back to my puzzle, but I could feel Wayne's eyes boring holes in me.

"Are you ready to talk about it?" he said.

"No."

"Why not?"

"Because I don't see the use in dredging up ancient history?" I said.

"And yet, you do it all the time," said Wayne. "I want to know why you abandoned my mother, Eugene."

"I didn't abandon your mother!" I said.

"But it didn't end there," said Wayne. "You couldn't just let Gran Gladys move on with her life. Thirty years later, you had to come back and—"

"Stop it!" I said.

Before he could press me any further, I attempted to stand in a huff, but the ground dissolved beneath my feet. Staggering, I managed, with the steadying arm of Wayne, to resituate myself in the chair, where I bowed my head.

"You okay?" he said.

"Yes," I said.

But it couldn't have been further from the truth. All the vitality, what little I had left, had run out of me. Slumping at my desk, I buried my head in my folded arms.

Wayne set a hand on my shoulder and gave it a squeeze. Only then did I begin to weep like I hadn't wept in fifty years.

"There, there," said Wayne sheepishly.

I hated him more than ever at that moment, yet if he had offered me a reassuring hug, I would have gladly accepted it.

"It wasn't how you make it sound," I offered weakly. "I hardly knew Nancy. I didn't meet her until Gladys—"

"I know all about Metropolitan," said Wayne. "I know about your outings. I know about the Oviatt."

A new wave of anguish washed over me.

Wayne patted me on the shoulder once more, and it was then I turned in my chair and grabbed him around the waist and hugged him.

"We don't have to talk about it anymore, Eugene," he said, gently extricating himself from my awkward embrace. "Not until you're ready."

"Thank you," I said.

Suddenly, it seemed that my life was crumbling at the foundation. Everything I'd worked so hard to build, paltry though it might've been, everything I'd constructed, thankless and pathetic as that might've seemed, was slipping away below my feet, and once again I was falling, but this time only mentally and emotionally.

As if my ordeal with Wayne were not enough to tax my limited resources, it was only a matter of hours before Dr. Talbot appeared at my door, looking a little haggard, but handsomely so, his unkempt hair still falling just right near the end of the day.

"May I come in?" he said.

"Of course."

"Madrid?" he said, indicating the puzzle.

"Seville," I said.

"Always wanted to go," said Talbot. "I hear the food is incredible."

"I wouldn't know," I said. "It's been a long time for me. When I was there, I didn't eat so well."

"Listen, I won't beat around the bush," he said. "The lab ran your panels, and the results came back."

"And?"

"And we found some abnormalities that are a little concerning," he said.

"Abnormalities?"

"Your blood counts are out of whack," he said.

"What does that mean?"

"It means your body is almost certainly fighting something."

"Like what?"

"That isn't clear yet," said Talbot. "We need to run more labs. Get some imaging, a biopsy if need be. But I'm not really equipped here, Eugene. I'd like to send you to a hematologist. I put in an urgent referral to a doc in San Bernardino. His name is Max Wexler. We were together at UCLA. He's the best heme/onc in the county."

"But I don't want to go anywhere," I said.

"I'm afraid you're gonna have to, Eugene, if we're gonna get to the bottom of this."

"What are we talking about here, Doc? How bad could this be?"

"Look, I don't want to speculate until we've run more tests," he said.

"Worst-case scenario?"

"You sure you wanna do this?" he said.

"Give it to me," I said.

"We could be looking at leukemia," said Talbot.

My ears started ringing.

"I thought leukemia was a young person's disease."

"Not necessarily, not if it's chronic. And again, I said 'could.' Let's not jump to any conclusions here. You asked me for the worst-case scenario, and that's it. It could also just be an infection, something easily treatable. We just don't know until we get you over to Max. Okay?"

"Okay."

"How are you otherwise? You comfortable?"

"Isn't that a question you ask someone who's dying?"

"No more dizziness?" he said.

"No," I lied.

"Good," he said. "I'm going to see to it Max gets you in stat, so we can get some answers. In the meantime, relax. Don't worry. This could be a cakewalk, Eugene. We just need to stay on top of it."

This time it was Dr. Talbot patting me on the shoulder, and it was all I could do to stop myself from hugging him, too.

I remained at my drafting table for several hours after my consultation with Talbot, hardly touching my puzzle, afraid to stand up for fear I might collapse again. I reached for my book and tried to read for a while, but I kept reading the same sentence over and over until I finally abandoned the endeavor. Captive in my chair, I wished I'd asked Wayne or somebody else to open the shade, so I could see out, and perhaps find some solace in the changeless, rockbound face of the Ords.

I was still sitting there late that afternoon when Angel popped into my quarters cheerfully. Having just arrived for his shift, he was still in jeans and a T-shirt. Right away, however, I noticed something else different about his appearance, but I couldn't quite put a finger on it.

"You get a haircut?"

"Nah."

"Shave your sideburns?"

"Nah, man, it's my nose ring. I eighty-sixed it."

"Ah," I said. "You look taller without it."

Indeed, as little sense as it made, he did look taller somehow. Leaner, less bull-like.

Angel laughed. "Okay, Geno, whatever you say."

"Why'd you do it?" I said.

"I dunno," he said. "So many changes lately, I figured, why not? I'll look more like a dad, you know? Any news from the doc?" he said.

"No," I lied.

"Then you're probably all good, homie."

"Probably so."

"No news is good news, right?"

I shouldn't have lied to him. How could I expect to earn his trust when I continually misled him, first about my fabricated life, now about my seemingly imminent death? I just didn't want to let Angel down, I suppose, any more than I wanted to feel the air go out of the room upon sharing the grim news. Eventually, I'd have to level with him about a lot of things, and I wasn't looking forward to that inevitability.

Nobody to Anybody

I'll confess that I've been less than completely transparent about my past. But understand: I am not delusional, which is to say, I do not believe my own fabrications. I've suffered only one delusion in this lifetime, and that was a passing manifestation in young adulthood, which followed the cessation of my foster care and marked the beginning of a very difficult transition. Beyond that lone delusion, which we shall address at another juncture, I am guilty only of embellishment. And who could blame me for wanting to be something more? Young Eugene Miles was nobody to anybody, not even himself. The same could be said of middle-aged Eugene and elderly Eugene. This is not an apology, not an excuse, simply an explanation. I do not wish at this time to revisit the horrific circumstances precipitating my expropriation from my parents' household in Victorville at the age of twelve, nor do I wish to elucidate at any length on my nightmarish tenure as a ward of the state foster care system, which only served to destabilize my already precarious psychological equilibrium. But the least I can do is correct a few articles of disinformation and provide a cursory background of my real life. And we may as well start with my arrival in Los Angeles.

While it is true that I found myself in Los Angeles as a young man, my arrival there was not what I've given you to believe. I was no wholesome innocent when I arrived in the City of Angels in my father's outdated suit, no starry-eyed hopeful, nor future war hero for that matter. I arrived in Los Angeles from foster care in San Bernardino, a morbidly depressed and psychologically ravaged adolescent.

In order of appearance, Moe, Jacobson, Fernelli, Zharnov, Hall, Blasingame, and Guidry were the names of my custodial guardians between the ages of twelve and sixteen. Simple math will tell you that I never stuck anywhere long, but math alone does not tell the whole story. Suffice it to say that this mistreatment far outweighed any benefits conferred upon me as a ward. I was not defiant, or even irreverent, merely damaged. While I may not have been an adorable child, or gifted, or in any way distinguished, it is my belief that I was worthy of love, or at the very least some modicum of protection, which I was never fortunate enough to receive. It was hard not to take this deficit personally, though I'd like to think I bore it all courageously.

As appalling as my wardship may have been, the worst was yet to come. At sixteen I was placed in a boys' group home, which was to mark the final chapter of my gruesome journey through state foster care. My time at Home of the Guardian Angel was, in a word, hellish. So bad, in fact, that public school was a relief. At school, I was bullied, but nothing like the way I was bullied at the boys' home, where I was beaten, and hectored almost daily by the proprietors and the other boys alike. Gene the Unclean, they called me, no matter how frequently I bathed. Vaseline Gene, because they claimed I was a serial masturbator. Gene the Queen, because they decided I was homosexual. For my litany of perceived flaws, I was locked in closets, had my head submersed in toilet water both clean and dirty, was pinched, punched, and spat upon. The other boys harangued me for my silence, for my awkwardness, for my stature,

my posture, my pallor, my acne, and for the simple offense of reading voraciously, my lone escape from the waking nightmare of my
life at HGA. I didn't dare tell a soul about my past lives for fear of
what might have been done to me.

Nothing I could do or say seemed to help my cause at Home of
the Guardian Angel. For reasons I fail to understand to this day, I
had not the benefit of a single ally amongst the adults assigned to my
charge. In my experience, the proprietors were, to a person, willfully cruel, and in several instances sadistic. What I would have
given for a true guardian angel! But surrounded by devils, I withdrew to such an extent that at times I felt detached from my own
actions, my own feelings, sensations, and even thoughts. I discovered within myself, or should I say revisited within myself, a recess
deep enough that the pinching and punching and harassment could
hardly reach me there.

By the time the young caseworker arrived at HGA to assess my
situation, I was largely uncommunicative.

"Hello, Eugene," he said, extending a hand. "My name is Ed
Wozniak, and I've been assigned to your case."

Wozniak left his hand out there for a long moment, finally clearing his throat as my cue. When at last I reached out to shake his
hand limply, he registered the bruising up and down my arms.

"Where did all those marks come from?" he said.

"Nowhere," I said.

"Did somebody do this to you?"

"No," I said, looking at the floor.

"How did you get the bruises?" Wozniak insisted.

"I did it myself," I said.

Clearly, Mr. Wozniak was not buying this explanation.

"Is there anything you want to tell me, Eugene?"

"No," I said.

"Why would you bruise your own arms?"

"I don't know. I was bored, I guess."

Wozniak looked at me knowingly.

"I find that hard to believe, Eugene."

"Well, it's true," I said.

"Who are you protecting?" he said.

The answer, of course, was myself, but instead I said nothing and continued staring at my shoes, feeling the heat of Mr. Wozniak's gaze.

"You can trust me, Eugene," he said. "I'm here as your advocate. That's my job. Whatever you share with me is in strict confidence. It is only in your best interest that I ask you to share with me. Do you like it here?"

"It's okay, I guess."

"You guess?"

"Yeah," I said. "Sure, it's fine."

"You can tell me the truth, Eugene."

There was no way on earth I was going to snitch. If I divulged my abusers or disclosed the details of my mistreatment to this man, and the others caught wind of it, there was no telling what they might do to me. Thus, I defaulted once more to silence, until Wozniak was forced to press.

"I need you to tell me about the bruises, Eugene."

"I told you already."

"The truth, Eugene. How did you get them?"

"I fell."

Wozniak regarded me sympathetically, and I glimpsed great kindness and vulnerability in his eyes. So much so that I began to feel sorry for him. Vulnerability couldn't serve him well in his profession, it seemed.

"Eugene," he said. "I can't help you unless you tell me the truth, do you understand? I want to help you."

"I don't need help," I said.

He looked me directly in the eye once more and held my gaze.

"I think you do, Eugene. Please. Talk to me."

Finally, Wozniak wore me down with his kindness and determination, and I submitted. I told him everything, a compendium of my entire legacy of abuse the past eight months at the hands of Donny Esposito and everyone else. Once I began, I could not stop. I divulged every detail, though I'd be lying if I said I did so without fear of consequence. Wozniak was visibly disturbed throughout my testimony. When I lifted my shirt to show him the extent of the bruising recently bestowed upon me by Esposito, Wozniak gasped. I swear, I thought he was going to cry.

"I'm going to get you out of this place, Eugene, I promise," he said. "Do you understand?"

"Now?" I said.

"I don't have the authority at this instant. But very soon," he said.

As badly as I wanted to, I didn't believe him, and even if I'd elected to do so, I would have assumed that "very soon" meant weeks or months, and that "out of this place" only equated to relocation in some equally dreadful place, for that was the pattern experience had taught me. Thus, the moment Wozniak departed I was filled with dread. That night I slept in fits, fearing for my future.

But the following day, Ed Wozniak made good on his promise. He showed up at Home of the Guardian Angel first thing in the morning, served my discharge orders, and delivered me personally in his beat-up Chrysler sedan to my new foster home in Boyle Heights.

Knowing what I now know about the wheels of bureaucracy, it's hard to fathom how Wozniak executed my rescue so expediently. On our way out, he let the administrators know in no uncertain terms that there would be consequences for their dereliction of duty. Wozniak gave them an earful, God bless him.

"There's nothing wrong with you, Eugene. You don't deserve to be treated like that," he told me as we sputtered along through the basin, the Chrysler shuddering at thirty-five miles per hour, misfiring every quarter mile. "Nobody does. If everybody got the care and attention they needed as human beings, such places wouldn't exist."

A lovely ideal, but impossible, I thought. Who amongst us ever really got what they needed in this life? Born against our wills into a world we didn't ask for, a world that seemed to begrudge our very existence, we were lucky if anybody was paying attention at all. If we were really lucky, we found love, or something resembling it; we found purpose, even if it didn't amount to much. But in my experience, these were the exceptions, not the rule. Still, Ed Wozniak was out there doing his damnedest to save people, and he didn't need to do that. Even if the world was a horrific place, it was a little less so with Ed Wozniak in it.

"You'll be safe where I'm taking you," he said. "You need fear nothing. You can be yourself."

Whoever that was. I hardly had a thought in my life beyond self-preservation, and yet I had no sense of self. I didn't even know what to yearn for. I was whatever the world decided to make me, usually a target.

"No matter what anybody has told you, you are worthy, Eugene. Don't forget that," Ed said, as though he could hear my thoughts. "What you have endured is not your fault."

That day when he dropped me off in Boyle Heights was the last time I ever saw Ed Wozniak, but I'm still beholden to him for his kindness. He brought me to a better place, even if it was destined not to last.

I boarded with an old widow named Consuela Perez, who lived in a two-bedroom cottage, squeezed between two larger houses on a predominantly Mexican block. She couldn't have been five feet tall, but what she lacked in stature she made up in bearing. Consuela had the unflappable demeanor of a royal guardsman. One might have clapped one's hands three inches in front of her face without warning and Consuela would not have flinched. Threaten her at gunpoint, and you'd better be prepared to pull the trigger.

"You'll be in the back bedroom," she told me as we stood in the kitchen. "It's sunny in the morning, so you might want to use the shade. Edward tells me you like books. You'll find some on the desk. Are you hungry?" she said.

"No, ma'am."

"You're lying. I know what hungry looks like. Sit down," she said.

I lowered myself into a chair at a small table constituting the dining area. Without a word, Consuela cracked two brown eggs and scrambled them in a small iron skillet upon the stovetop, then nestled them on a plate, slightly blackened from the grease, beside a stack of corn tortillas.

"Eat," she said.

And I did, voraciously, while Consuela sat across from me, watching on silently.

"I will not hurt you," she said finally. "And you will not hurt me. Is this understood?"

"Yes, ma'am."

"You will not smoke or drink in this house."

"No, ma'am."

"And no music."

"Understood, ma'am. May I ask why no music?" I ventured.

"I don't trust it," she said. "My late husband, Felix, was a musician. He was also an abusador, an adúltero, and a borracho, until he got hit by a streetcar. May God rest his soul. But I doubt it."

Here, she began making the sign of the cross over her chest before waving it off.

"Edward tells me you are unwell in your mind. What does he mean?" she said.

For this I had no answer.

"He tells me you've been hurt."

I said nothing.

"The world hurts you, over and over," she said, patting my hand. "Here, you will heal."

Sitting at that sunny kitchen table with my eggs and tortillas, I wanted desperately to believe Consuela. But as badly as I wanted to lean into her assurances, I just couldn't seem to see past my trauma.

That first night my sleep was so tortured that I awoke screaming in the darkness. Before I could gather my bearings, Consuela was at my bedside.

"It's okay," she said. "You just had a bad dream."

"It wasn't a dream," I said. "It was a memory."

Despite the discomfort of my first night, life at Consuela's quickly assumed a consistent quality. School was out of session for summer, so to keep me occupied and on the path to healing, Consuela implemented a rigorous campaign of daily routine. Each day began with the preparation of breakfast, Consuela watching on as I cracked the eggs and scrambled them myself in the little skillet, while she set the plates out and warmed the tortillas, wrapping them in a cloth. Midmornings, I worked alongside Consuela in the garden, weeding, watering, and displacing snails mostly. After lunch each day, I embarked solo on an afternoon stroll from the heights to the flats and back again, always pursuing an identical path, walking with my head down, alone with my thoughts and distractions, never quite awake to the possibilities surrounding me, which was just how I wanted it, or supposed I wanted it.

Every other Thursday, we walked and bused together back and forth to the downtown library, weighed down considerably with books upon our return. In the evenings, I consumed books ravenously. I read history and psychology, mostly. Rarely did I read novels, not even Oscar's, for the stories seemed like frivolous constructions, imitations of life, hewn and shaped from the muck of existence into something conveniently comprehensible. The whole enterprise seemed disingenuous. And yet, I loved my motion pictures for their fictional stories. Nearly every Sunday that summer, Consuela and I rode the Red Cars into Hollywood, where we took in matinees at the El Capitan, or Hollywood Music Hall, or westerns at the Hitching Post. While the picture shows were even more frivolous and conveniently comprehensible than novels, they transported me back to one of my few childhood comforts, movie magazines. Amongst the pictures we saw that summer were *Tomorrow Is Forever* and *A Stolen Life*. At the picture shows I could exist outside of my body, and that was an experience to savor.

Despite the kindness of Consuela, or Ed Wozniak, or anyone else, I could barely stand my own life. In bed at night with the lights out, I summoned the lives of Euric and Whiskers and the others, all the lives I dared not speak of, clinging to these antiquities that they might eclipse the insufferable glare of my present life. But it didn't work. The night terrors only got worse. I grew increasingly agitated, pacing the house as though I were angry at the floor, muttering under my breath, clenching and unclenching my fists, my mind skipping like a phonograph record.

My temperament grew steadily more volatile as the days wore on, my behavior more unpredictable. Consuela managed these fluctuations better than any mental health professional I'd yet to encounter, but she was powerless to deter them. She could not unwrite my story. Almost daily, I began to throw tantrums triggered by the slightest wrinkle or dysfunction in my routine, an unwanted fragment of eggshell in the frying pan, the severed root of a dandelion. When the mood overcame me, I was unreachable, a sparking live wire skipping across the blacktop, searing anything in its wake. One afternoon, amidst such a fit, I inadvertently blackened Consuela's eye when she tried to restrain me. It was purely accidental, and I feel horrible to this day. I was only trying to break free of her clutches as she attempted to comfort me. But my intentions hardly mattered, as the force of the blow sent her reeling halfway across the kitchen. Even as she recovered from the impact, Consuela did not panic, but calmly consoled me at a distance of six or seven feet.

"Everything is okay, Eugene," she said. "You are safe here."

Eventually, her calming influence prevailed, but the damage was already done.

Two days later, a caseworker arrived unannounced to assess my situation. I can say with near certainty that the caseworker was not called there by Consuela, that their appearance was mere coincidence, a matter of bureaucratic course. This time, it was not Ed Wozniak, however, but a middle-aged woman, who sat across from us at the kitchen table, my substantial file spread open in front of her. She was a detail-oriented person who exuded an air of competence and good judgment but was clearly not given to frivolity. This I could glean from her wardrobe choices, a modest gray skirt, perfectly tailored, and a matching gray jacket, buttoned to the top. The efficiency of her movements suggested to me she was somebody who liked to get straight to the point.

"My name is Doris Gessen," she announced. "I've been assigned to your case."

I was looking at my feet, sure she could discern my guilt.

"My goodness, what happened to your eye?" she said to Consuela.

Consuela smiled, feigning embarrassment. "I'm a clumsy old woman," she said. "I walked straight into the refrigerator door."

Doris Gessen looked immediately back at me, still staring at my feet, then once again at Consuela, doubtfully.

"Show me," said Doris Gessen.

The directive caught Consuela by surprise.

"You mean . . . now?"

"Please," said Doris.

Consuela stood up and walked across the kitchen and opened the refrigerator door.

"It was dark," she said.

"Show me how you hit it," said Doris Gessen.

"But this has nothing to do with—"

"Please, show me."

The dramatization that followed proved to be a hopeless charade. Doris Gessen did not believe the story for an instant. Indeed, she soon attempted to disprove it, after several passes demonstrating that the injury was inconsistent with the purported circumstances of the collision. Given Consuela's height, her angle of approach, regardless of the darkness, there was simply no way that Miss Gessen could envision the scenario. I might have saved everybody a lot of time with a confession, had I been so inclined. But I was desperate to stay at Consuela's, where I was seen, and heard, and treated with a dignity to which I was unaccustomed. Had I managed to hold myself together, to control my impulses, to present myself in a more flattering light in order that I might prolong my stay at Consuela's, I might have turned a corner. But it seemed I had no self to gather.

Saviors

I did not leave Consuela's house willingly. The fact is, I went kicking and screaming as two orderlies led me from the house to the curb, where a green van awaited me. They persuaded me less than gently into the back of the vehicle, where they placed me in leather restraints. Poor Consuela with her blackened eye stood on the porch watching, beside herself with what I could only imagine to be unwarranted grief and guilt. As the van pulled away from the curb, I saw through the rear window her tiny figure standing there forlornly, executing the sign of the cross over her heart. And that is how I came to Metropolitan State Hospital, the very facility Wayne once alluded to.

My first six months at MSH, I hardly ever got out of bed. The staff had to force me to eat, and even then, it was a task I would only perform in the isolation of my room, and only enough to keep them off my case. Situated on the ground floor in the northeast corner of the facility, my quarters comprised a room, ten feet by twelve with a single bed, an overhead light, and a small dresser painted the same dreary egg white as the walls. The room had one window facing east toward the San Jacintos and was at turns bleak or sunny depending on the time of day, though my outlook was hardly susceptible to such variables. Light and dark were just equal parts of the gray area in which I existed.

For weeks on end, I bunched myself up like a fist, gazing dully at the shiny surface of the plaster wall, whose every imperfection, every crack, paint drip, and fissure, I came to know intimately. My body felt like an imposter, an unfamiliar shell as rigid as iron, perpetually bracing itself for impact, muscles aching from unrelenting tension. This shell was the unwitting repository for a maelstrom of emotions I had no use for, nor any language to express. Thus, these sensations had no names, such as shame or fear or despondency, nor had they any context attending them. They lived beneath the surface of me like parasites, scratching at the underside of my skin, impossible to reach. I had only one emotion I could catalog, and that was dread, dark and all-consuming. For I knew that existence beyond that stingy mattress and those noisy bedsprings was a hopeless proposition fraught with peril, and no orderly or nurse was going to convince me otherwise. Hypervigilant in my distrust, I spoke to no one those first months. I had seemingly lost any ability I might have ever possessed to connect with others. And yet, somewhere deep down, I still yearned for a savior.

In the spirit of transparency, it is now incumbent upon me to rectify another half-truth, this one involving Dr. Frank Stowell. Previously, I told you that Dr. Stowell had begun interviewing me as a child in Victorville at the behest of my parents. However, it was in fact at Metropolitan State Hospital where I became acquainted with Dr. Stowell, who was not an older gentleman, as I previously portrayed him, rather a young man, driven by intense curiosity and ambition.

Though I was initially put off by what I perceived to be his arrogance, Dr. Stowell earned my trust gradually as I began to recognize his confidence for what it really was, professional drive and intense commitment to his work, which he believed to be of utmost importance.

"If we can understand human behavior, we can predict it," he was fond of saying. "If we can predict it, we can influence it positively."

The senior staff, Drs. Maxwell and Spencer, seemed to want little to do with me, whom they deemed insane, and even less, it seemed, to do with Dr. Stowell, whom they considered an undisciplined upstart and a charlatan. It should be noted that Dr. Stowell did not immediately adopt me as his prized patient or the culmination of his career aspirations. It was more personal than that at first. Stowell seemed to understand the crude bulwark of my defenses and was respectful of my physical boundaries. He knew better than to touch me unexpectedly or startle me with quick movements. While the rest of the staff at Metropolitan were intent on infantilizing me, Stowell spoke to me as an equal. Were it not for Stowell's encouragement, I might have died in that bed at MSH. Stowell helped me see my situation clearly.

"Trauma lives in the body," he told me. "Not the mind. You can't outsmart it, Eugene, no matter how hard you try. You can't finesse it or reason with it. Trauma does exactly what it wants."

"What does it want?" I said.

"It wants to reenact itself again and again. It wants to tell its story."

"What does this have to do with me?" I said.

"You need to tell your own stories, Eugene. All of them."

After seventeen years, someone had finally granted me license to tell my life stories freely, to reveal my truth without fear of disbelief or shame. Dr. Stowell would eventually distinguish himself as the first, and arguably only, person to accept the veracity of my former incarnations, from a tenth-century cutpurse to a nineteenth-century cat. Maxwell and Spencer by contrast would not entertain what they considered my delusions. Trust me, however, when I tell you that even Dr. Stowell's acceptance was not easily won. Dr. Stowell was a skeptic by nature who had many, many questions. I spent countless hours alone in his presence, and I'd be lying if I said I did not for the most part relish Dr. Stowell's attention. While I had been the frequent object of derision, to be the object of another's fascination was a thrill to which I was unaccustomed. Thus, I was more than happy to participate in Stowell's investigations.

Sometimes Dr. Stowell and I would walk the hallways together, while other times we'd stroll the outdoor perimeter of the hospital under the relentless sunshine, where I would regale him with tales of my former lives. But most often we convened in private amidst the sterile confines of my quarters, where I sat on the edge of my mattress and he upon a straight-backed chair directly in front of me. Here, Stowell committed endless notes to his yellow legal pads throughout our sessions, consultations that resembled nothing so much as interrogations.

"Describe to me once again the marketplace the day you met Gaya," he said.

"It was late spring," I said. "Almost summer. The humidity was unbearable. The air in the marketplace smelled of cooking fires. Children darted about between stalls. Caged hens clucked incessantly, sheep bleated, merchants haggled in Hebrew and Arabic and Castilian. I remember shortly before our meeting somebody up-ended a cart while chasing a pig."

"Mm-hmm," he said, jotting a note. "And where was Ostosia's house relative to the market?"

"Northwest. But we didn't go to Ostosia's until—"

"What about Gaya's house? Where was that relative to the market?"

"South," I said.

"What time of day was it when the soldiers seized you?"

"Which time?"

"The first time."

"It was evening," I said. "Shortly before dusk. It was after dark by the time we reached the fortress."

"Describe Oscar's apartment to me once more," said Stowell.

"I thought you wanted to hear about Spain."

"Please indulge me," he said. "Oscar's apartment."

"It was a large flat, in Chelsea," I said. "Lots of sunlight. Three bedrooms, two bathrooms."

"And the floors?"

"He was on the second floor."

"I mean the floors you walked upon, the surface."

"They were painted wood, except for the rugs, which were four, one in each bedroom and one in the living room."

"What was the view out Oscar's bedroom window?"

"The neighboring flat."

"And who lived there?" he said.

"An old woman who had a dog whom I tortured frequently through the window."

"What kind of dog?" said Stowell.

"A bulldog, a brutish-looking thing with an oversized head and an acute underbite. I took pleasure in sitting in the window and watching him across the way, knowing he could never get to me."

"What did he do?"

"He had fits, snarling and circling, and barking his phlegmy discontent, all but throwing himself at the window until the glass was glazed in slobber."

"In which hand did Oscar hold his pen?" asked Stowell.

"His right. The same one in which he held his blasted cigarillos. Oh, but they stank. The smell of them clung to every surface."

"Where did he keep his papers?" said Stowell.

"In a basket on a shelf beside the desk."

"How many cushions were on the sofa?"

"There was but one cushion," I said.

"Who was taller, Lewis or Clark?"

"They were roughly the same height. I'd put them around six feet."

"In which state did you begin the expedition?"

"Missouri," I said.

"What was the exact date?"

"That, I can't recall. Dates have never been important to me. It was spring. Sometime near the middle of May I would guess. But in truth, the expedition began in the fall of 1803, when Lewis came down the Ohio River to Louisville with nine men from Kentucky, where Will, me, and seven other men awaited their arrival at the falls. I can still smell the silt of the river bend east of the falls."

"How is it you can remember precise smells but not dates?" said Stowell.

"Numbers are largely meaningless in the big picture. Sensations abide, particularly smells."

Stowell might easily have been a prosecuting attorney. He'd ask me the same questions two and three times, sometimes weeks apart, always jotting down my responses. Subsequently, he would try to lead me with questions specifically designed to expose contradictions or inconsistencies in my recollections. He even went as far as coercion.

"Making up these stories could be a way of getting attention, could it not?" he said.

"I suppose it could," I said.

"It might validate you, distinguish you as somebody worth listening to, somebody with a wealth of experience."

"Yes," I said. "It might. It does. It's doing that right now, no?"

"How do I know you're not trying to get attention?" he said. "You admitted yourself that you felt like nobody, yes?"

"I only volunteer this information when you ask for it," I said. "I should think if I wanted attention, I'd just keep having fits. Or throw my feces about or jump up and down screaming *fire*."

"You've said you've often felt invisible, isn't that right?"

"Not as often as I've wished it," I said.

Such leading statements I would confirm only so long as they were truthful. Others I would correct.

"Now, if I recall, the plaza was on the south side of the fortress, correct? And the baths were to the north, yes?"

"No," I would say. "Both the plaza and the baths were west of the fortress."

"You're sure about that?"

"I'm certain."

"So far as you could tell, beneath his robe, Assad was a thin man, was he not?"

"He was not. He was thick around the middle. His ankles were ample, he was jowly about the chin."

If it is not already apparent, one of Dr. Stowell's favorite tactics was to toggle between my lives as though to catch me off guard.

"You said Oscar kept his papers in a desk drawer, yes?"

"No," I said. "He kept them in a basket upon a shelf, just to the right of his desk. Atop the shelf there was a woven runner with tassels at which I would frequently claw, to Oscar's consternation."

"What color was the runner?"

"That I cannot say with any certainty. I was effectively color-blind. If I had to guess I would say green."

"And Gaya's cell was to the left of yours?" said Stowell.

"My left, looking forward, yes. But the first time we shared a cell."

"And how many cushions upon Oscar's sofa?"

"One."

"And when Clark came down the river from Kentucky—"

"Lewis," I interjected.

"Very well," said Stowell. "When Lewis came down the river with seven men, he—"

"It was nine, not seven," I said. "And we were nine, those who were there to greet them."

So, you see, Stowell was unremitting in his campaign to discredit my recollections. But I was telling the truth at every turn. Thus, I had no need to withhold information or evade questioning, no fear of being exposed as a liar or a fraud. But do not think for one moment that Dr. Stowell gave me the benefit of the doubt. Not those initial months. His inquisitiveness was exceeded only by his skepticism. He was nothing if not scientific in his methodology. It was only after exhaustive cross-examination that he finally concluded my recollections were too specific and well informed, too consistently recalled, to be mere delusions or contrivances.

Did I feel vindicated by this conclusion? Alas, no. Well, perhaps, but only slightly. I knew better than to expect as much from the rest of the world. Thus, it was no surprise that nobody beyond Dr. Stowell believed me. In fact, whispers were that his conclusions regarding the veracity of my claims were widely scorned amongst his peers.

It has been suggested that in accepting my past lives as true, Dr. Stowell was exercising a confirmation bias, that he simply wanted to believe, perhaps as a means of coping with his own fear of death. More recently it has been proposed that my "delusional" past lives were the result of something akin to cryptamnesia, extensions of hidden traumas cobbled together without context in an attempt at emotional and psychological continuity. Even Wayne Francis, Desert Greens' own anointed psychological authority, has hypothesized that my past-life memories are the result of a "source monitoring error," which is to say that the "monitoring mechanism" of the source has been damaged at some point, thus names and places and events have been memorized, in my case, but the source and timing of these acquisitions have been lost. According to Wayne, this is a survival mechanism that allows me "to construct possible futures and anticipate those events so that I can be adaptive to new environments."

All these conclusions share one thing in common: They all run contrary to the law of parsimony, that is, their plurality is posited without necessity. Dr. Stowell saw that the truth was much simpler than all that. Given the information right in front of him, he reasoned correctly that I had in fact lived before.

Poor Fool

After a string of days, the number of which I could hardly guess at, the guard finally came to retrieve me from the bowels of the fortress. Hands bound, I was led to Assad's chamber once more, where I was forced as always to kneel before him. As before, the dim light of the chamber was blinding to my unaccustomed eyes.

"And how are you finding your accommodations? They tell me it's quite dark down there. May I offer you some refreshment?"

"No," I said.

"Perhaps now that you've had some time to consider the matter, you're ready to discuss the whereabouts of your associate?"

"I know nothing of her whereabouts," I said. "I've told you as much already. Why are you holding me here?"

"Because you're a liar," he said.

"I'm not," I insisted. "I've told you the truth."

Assad shook his head in discouragement.

"You possess a stronger will than I supposed," he said. "Generally, I'd say that's a good quality, but I'm afraid an unfortunate one in this instance."

"What do you want with her, anyway? She poses no threat to you. She's a common merchant."

"We both know better than that," he said. "Your friend is an agitator and a sworn enemy of al-Andalus. Though I will admit she is quite comely."

"Your eyes are unworthy of her," I said.

Assad only laughed.

"How did I not see it before? I must be blind. You love her," he said. "Now it all makes sense. You poor fool. She's blinded you with her considerable charms."

"You're wrong," I said.

"And you probably think you're the first."

"Do not speak ill of her," I warned.

"Or what?"

"You'll pay for this."

"Highly unlikely," he said. "I pay only for what I want. Supposing I was willing to pay you? Maybe that would refresh your memory. Why didn't I think of it before? Surely a few dinars would persuade you to talk?"

"I don't want your money."

"And yet, you stole my purse. Perhaps we should try a different method."

"You can torture me, but I can't tell you what I don't know."

"What do you know?" said Assad. "What has she told you about me?"

"That you were somehow responsible for the death of her father."

Assad smiled. "Her father? Ha. That useless beggar? What makes her think I had anything to do with his demise? He was a drunkard. He drowned in the river. What of it? And what of our man they dredged from the river south of the city? That was no accident, not with his head stove in. I suppose you and your lover had nothing to do with that?"

"She's not my lover."

"Then you're even more foolish than I supposed to protect her for nothing. You're so pitiful, I haven't the stomach to look upon you. Put him back down," said Assad. "And leave him there."

I believed this to be my death sentence. And though I was resigned to it, I can say in hindsight that I had no conception of how bad it would be.

The coming weeks saw my already meager rations cut in half. My cheeks grew sallow, my ribs began to protrude, and my shoulders, once broad, were reduced to sinew and knob. But my spirit was the first to leave me, a psychic release of life force steady and deliberate as the draining of blood. And in its stead, the crushing deadweight of apathy suffused every fiber of my being. My mental acuity was not far behind. Starving and desiccated from lack of water, my mind began to betray me in the darkness. Thoughts not of my own conception began to impose themselves upon my wayward consciousness. I shuffled about my cell ceaselessly in the dark, trying to ward off these foreign thoughts, gesticulating and muttering, pulling at the roots of my hair until it began falling out in clumps.

At some point, even madness ceased serving as an impetus to move, and I abandoned my pacing, consigning myself to a corner, where I curled up as though against the cold. Forced to breathe my own putridity without reprieve, I retched frequently, the retches graduating to coughs, the coughing escalating into paroxysms that racked my entire body. And soon a malevolent presence, formless but palpable, seemed to occupy my squalid cell with me. If I believed as much, I'd say it was the devil himself.

I am certain I was close to death on the day the guard descended the steps leading a second prisoner down the dim corridor. I clambered to my feet for the first time in days, pressing myself fast against the cold iron bars to observe their approach. In the dancing torchlight, I could only make out their figures at first, one tall and straight, whom I soon recognized to be the giant, and the other smaller, frailer, and looking at the ground. As they drew nearer it became clear that the captive was none other than Gaya, head bowed, arms bound behind her back. She stared fiercely at the ground as she passed, retching at the rancid stench emanating from my cell. Even in the half-light, I could discern that her face was battered and swollen, her bottom lip split, one eye half-closed.

I tried to utter her name, but when I opened my mouth to speak, I found that I no longer commanded a voice. Nothing escaped me but a single breath, strangled and impotent. I reached out to her desperately through the bars, but the guard promptly beat my arm with his club.

"Back!" he commanded.

Gaya never looked up, but had she deigned to do so, it is unlikely she would have recognized the hollow-eyed, wasted sack of bones reaching out to her, wrapped in a filthy robe hanging in tatters. The guard led her to the cell just beyond mine, pushing her in forcefully. I heard her cry out as she hit the dirt floor.

Such was the extent of my mental deterioration that I thought I might be dreaming it all. In recent days, one state had become virtually indiscernible from the other. But Gaya was so close I could hear her breathing in the next cell, and hear, too, when she began to sob in the darkness. When I finally found my voice, I no longer recognized it as my own; it was dry and brittle as a husk, and so weak it was hardly more than a whisper.

"Is it really you?" I said.

"Who's that?"

"It's me, Euric. Are you really here?"

"You're talking to me, aren't you?"

"Forgive me," I said. "I've been down here so long that I . . . are you okay? What have they done to you?"

She fell conspicuously silent for a moment.

"It is best we don't talk," she said at last. "They'll only think we're conspiring."

"But—"

"Better that we never met," she said.

"I was nothing before you," I said.

"And what are you now, Euric?"

This time, it was I who retreated into silence.

"It was never my intention to involve you," she said. "Our alliance was pure happenstance. But now that you're involved, understand that you owe me nothing. You are not obligated to protect me. Save yourself."

"I could never betray you," I said.

But she didn't say another word.

The next day, my rations and water were inexplicably doubled. My pot was emptied. I was even granted a candle. Gaya, meanwhile, was left to linger in the adjoining cell, receiving nothing in the way of sustenance. Assad did not beckon her, nor did the guard so much as acknowledge her when he came with my provisions. If only I could have given them to her. I would have given anything to save Gaya. But I couldn't see her, couldn't touch her, and still she refused to speak to me for reasons I failed to comprehend. To hear her groaning in the darkness, I thought I would die of powerlessness.

This lasted for days, during which I received two meals and two cups of water daily, as well as a clean bedpan. But not Gaya, who withered away in her hold, receiving only enough water to keep her alive. I tried to comfort her in the darkness, but my words seemed to fall upon deaf ears. Each day as I grew stronger, Gaya grew weaker.

On perhaps the sixth day, the guard came for me and led me to Assad's chamber once again, delivering me like a sack of rice at his feet.

"How are you feeling?" he said. "More vigorous, I hope?"

"She'll starve down there," I said. "You can't just let her die."

"Oh?" he said. "And why not?"

I would've leapt up and strangled him on the spot had my hands not been bound.

"You're despicable," I said.

"I must seem so to you," he said. "But I have my orders and my loyalty. You just happen to be on the wrong side. You know what you want, and I know what I want. We each have our own truth."

"And what is my truth?"

"Her," he said.

My ears rang in the ensuing silence. Assad was correct, and there was no denying this truth. He took a step toward me and squatted down until he was at eye level, and looked at me meaningfully, setting a hand upon my shoulder.

"What if you could save her?" he said.

"How?"

"It's quite simple. She trusts you, no?"

"She trusts no one."

"Perhaps not," he said. "But she's confided in you before, has she not? So, bring me information, and I'll bring her food."

"She won't talk to me," I said.

"Give her time," said Assad. "Perhaps were she given to know, directly or indirectly, that you lobbied on her behalf, that she was being fed because of you . . . well, you can see how that might soften her."

"You underestimate her," I said.

"Or perhaps I overestimate you," said Assad.

I had no intention of betraying her, but I knew she must have nourishment or her days on this earth were numbered.

"Start feeding her now," I demanded. "This instant. And bring her plenty of water."

"Very well," said Assad. "It's settled then."

But nothing was settled. Chances were that Gaya would still not talk to me, let alone confide in me. But, I had to try something; her time was running out.

Back in my cell, I could hear Gaya retching and groaning in the darkness. It was only a short time before the guard came with food and water. But Gaya refused it. I should have known.

"I'd rather starve," she said.

Still, it was a relief to hear her speak.

"As you wish," said the guard.

"No, leave it!" I pleaded. "Gaya, you must!"

"Take it away," she said.

And without further ceremony, the guard retreated down the corridor with the provisions.

"Gaya, what are you doing?" I said. "You'll perish."

"So be it," she said. "I have no wish to prolong this."

"But I do," I said. "What about the . . . ? What about . . . well . . . about . . . us?"

The question was met with silence. The longer it lasted, the more I agonized. I felt like a fool, a hopeless idiot, and yet, no less determined to make Gaya mine.

"I'm sorry," she said at last. "Perhaps in another life."

How Many Lifetimes?

I had been at MSH for eight months when the new orderly arrived. I recognized her immediately, though she looked virtually nothing like her former incarnation in stature, complexion, or otherwise, but for the little pink mole below her right nostril. When I saw the mole, I knew it was positively, unequivocally her. While I admit that this intuition defied explanation, I've never been so certain of anything in all my lives. Somehow, someway, it was her. Why the universe saw fit to make me wait for over a thousand years before bringing her back to me fully realized, I cannot say.

She was clearing a table, clutching a stack of pea-green food trays by the window in the southeast corner of the cafeteria, dappled in morning sunlight, when I approached her from nearby. Startled by my sudden appearance, she stiffened.

"Gaya," I said.

"Excuse me?" she said.

"It's you, it's really you."

"Do I know you?" she said.

"It's me, Euric," I said. Surely the name Eugene would mean nothing to her, for she had known me only in my medieval guise.

"Euric," she said politely. "What an interesting name. Hello, Euric."

How many lifetimes had I endured in vain to arrive at this moment? The revelation awakened every nerve in my body.

"Gaya, it's me," I said.

The young woman smiled, but it was uneasiness rather than recognition that shone in her eyes.

"Actually, my name is Gladys," she said. "But close."

"It's really you," I said, my eyes dewy.

"Have we met before?" she said.

"Of course," I said. "Long ago. How could you forget?"

She inspected me closer but still registered nothing familiar.

"Did you go to Inglewood High?" she ventured.

"No," I said. "Much further back than that."

"First Presbyterian?"

"Keep going," I said. "Way back."

"I'm afraid I . . . well, I'm not placing you."

"Spain!" I said.

"Spain?" she said, tilting her head curiously. "I've never been to Spain."

"Under the Moors," I said.

This explanation only served to escalate her confusion.

"You mean Charlie and Janet Moore?"

"No, the Moors, from history!"

I took hold of her wrist gently and looked her directly in the eye.

"Gaya, it's me," I said.

The trays slipped from her grasp and landed on the tabletop with a clatter, her disquiet edging toward fear as her eyes darted about the cafeteria for help.

"What is it?" I said. "What's wrong?"

"I'm afraid you've mistaken me for someone else," she said, extricating her wrist. "I've never seen you before in my life."

"Not in this life," I said. "But certainly you must—"

"Please," she said. "I don't know what you're talking about."

Visibly shaken, Gladys beat a swift retreat across the cafeteria, where she promptly conferred with another orderly, both of them staring at me from across the room as Gladys recounted our exchange.

Shortly thereafter, I was reprimanded by senior staff members, as well as Dr. Stowell, for making physical contact with a hospital employee. Yet I was only mildly disheartened by this debacle. I couldn't very well expect her to remember me right away, but I knew—that is, I hoped—she'd come around. It was only a matter of time and patience. I could lead her there eventually.

Two days later in the commons, amongst the muttering half-wits, I was careful to maintain a comfortable distance when I made my apology to Gladys. That she might feel less threatened, I took the additional precaution of doing so in the presence of Dr. Stowell, who was making his rounds.

"I'm truly sorry," I said. "I was certain you were somebody else."

A lie, of course, but a necessary one, as clearly Gladys was not yet prepared for the truth. The idea would take some getting used to. Thankfully, Stowell was on hand to assist me in disarming her.

"I can assure you, Eugene is harmless," Dr. Stowell observed.

Gladys seemed to accept this reassurance. "I'm sorry to have disappointed you," she said to me.

Oh, but wasn't she lovely? So gracious, so quick to forgive! She couldn't have been twenty-two years old, my elder by a mere handful of years, yet she possessed such poise.

"Sometimes Eugene's impulses get the better of him," Dr. Stowell explained. "Isn't that right, Eugene?"

"It's true," I said. "I'm working on it."

While beholden to Stowell for his faith in me, and for coming to my defense, I can't say that his speaking on my behalf didn't arouse a certain uneasiness.

"But I'm also quite charming, if you get to know me," I said.

"He is a charmer, that's a fact," concurred Dr. Stowell.

Still unsure, Gladys hinted at a grin but didn't quite commit, and I thought I saw the slightest glimmer of recognition there.

"Well," she said, "I'd better get back to my duties."

Just like that, my life had meaning, a purpose, a cause. I managed to convince myself it was better that Gaya was slow to recognize me. We hadn't enjoyed much of a courtship in Spain, and here was my opportunity to win her affections all over again. Soon enough she would see beyond the muddled guise of my current incarnation and recognize the man she had come to trust and confide in, the man whom she had all but predicted she would meet again in another life.

Ironically, my biggest obstacle to achieving this vital connection with Gladys came in the person of my biggest ally, none other than Dr. Stowell, who, in the confidential bounds of my quarters, cautioned me against the dangers of such an enterprise.

"This is a hospital, Eugene. Boundaries are the rule, not the exception. Your interest in Gladys could be construed as unhealthy. In fact, in all likelihood, that is exactly how it will be construed by the staff, particularly if Gladys should have any objection to your . . . advances."

"Advances? You make it sound unseemly," I said.

"Which is precisely how it will seem to anyone who is unaware of your shared history."

"So, you're saying you believe me? It's really her?"

Here, Dr. Stowell was noncommittal, clasping his hands and considering the matter at length.

"Let's just say that I'm intrigued by the possibility," he said at last. "Though there exist a great number of variables—a great, great number—about which I remain skeptical."

"Such as?"

"The probability, for starters. What are the odds?"

"Probability implies that our reunion is not by design," I said.

"And you believe it is?" he said.

"Of course it is. You said it yourself. The odds are astronomical."

"Whose design, then?" said Stowell.

"Providence," I said.

"I'm a scientist, Eugene. Providence cannot be demonstrated, therefore I cannot accept it as a cause."

"Unless she recognizes me," I said. "Unless she can tell you all the same stories that I told you: Assad's fat ankles, the smell of the dungeon, our first meeting."

"Who's to say you haven't informed her of these details and planted the memories?" said Stowell. "If this connection is as vital as you suggest, then best to let her arrive at the conclusion herself, correct?"

"But what if she doesn't?" I said.

"Then it wasn't to be," he said. "It was you who conjectured providence."

"But . . ."

"Eugene, I can't compromise my reputation further than I already have on something as indemonstrable as providence. Unless I can document this alleged connection somehow, I—"

"You're jealous," I said.

"Nonsense," said Stowell. "I'm protecting you, and I'm protecting her. Let this serve as a warning, Eugene. If you don't exercise good boundaries, we both stand to lose everything we've worked for."

What choice did I have but to comply with Stowell? He was my one believer, my lone advocate. And yet, it was clear that he, too, was compelled by the prospect of Gladys. The prudent course of action was to be friendly but not familiar with Gladys. I would be Eugene from Victorville, she would be Gladys from Inglewood, and Euric and Gaya and all that we were in Spain would remain beyond the scope of our association until such time as she acknowledged these connections of her own volition. That was the plan, anyway.

And so, I stayed between the lines and kept to the immediate and observable. The weather, the food, and the news of the day, mostly. Gradually, I disarmed Gladys in this manner, until after several weeks we had developed something of a rapport.

"Good morning, Eugene," she said brightly.

"Good morning, Gladys."

"How are you feeling?"

"Old," I said.

"How can that be?" said Gladys. "You're only a young man."

"You might be shocked to learn the breadth of Eugene's experience," said Dr. Stowell.

Stowell had become ubiquitous, attending his prized patient like a shadow, always interjecting, putting words in my mouth, insinuating himself into our conversations at the first sign of intimacy, protecting his reputation.

"Is that so?" said Gladys.

"Oh, yes. Vast experience," said Stowell. "Eugene is a fascinating case. One for the books, as they say. Eugene's case could potentially change the course of human psychology. And that's no exaggeration."

After all my restraint, all my careful observance of boundaries, it was Stowell, not me, who pressed matters with Gladys, a development that might have been hard to account for had he not entertained the possibilities himself. The fact was, his ego and ambition may have been clouding his judgment. Moreover, his candor seemed grossly unprofessional, defying the sacred tenet of confidentiality.

I should have cut him off then and there, but Gladys seemed mildly impressed by the distinction of my case, so I let Stowell maintain the floor.

"Imagine," he said, "having lived before many times and being able to recall each life as vividly as if it happened yesterday. Eugene can remember Northern Italy in the fifteenth century the way you might remember your high school graduation. He can recall his life in tenth-century Spain as though he were still living it. I've managed to mine from Eugene the stuff of living history."

Now he was just bragging. There I was on the cusp of rekindling an ancient connection, and Stowell was determined to claim proprietorship of my experience.

"Don't you have somewhere else to be?" I said.

Though even Gladys seemed taken aback by the forwardness of the suggestion, Stowell actually took a hint for once.

"You're absolutely right," he said. "Here I am taking credit for what really amounts to your work. I'll leave the two of you to your conversation and attend to other business."

"He treats me like his pet," I said when Stowell was gone.

"He certainly advocates for you," she said.

"Is that what he's doing?"

Gladys looked at me curiously for a long moment, until her face began to color with the realization. "You're jealous, aren't you?"

I cast my eyes down at the tile floor.

"Oh, Eugene," she said kindly. "I could . . . we could never . . . I work here, this is my job. You're just a boy."

"But I'm not," I said.

All the trust I'd managed to earn was spiraling down the drain in an instant. I was losing Gladys before I'd ever won her, losing Gaya, losing any hope for connection. It was clear that I had to change my tactics immediately.

"Wait," I said. "You don't think I . . . ? Ha! Gladys, I think you've got the wrong idea."

Her relief was considerable, a sentiment that might have broken me had it not soured on my tongue and washed bitterly down my throat.

"Oh, good," she said. "I thought that . . ."

I'm not proud of my petulance, but when it comes to matters of the heart, convention often flies out the window. I was hurt and ashamed.

"You must think pretty highly of yourself," I said.

"Eugene, I—"

"Just because you're a few years older, you think I'm a boy? I've had the experience of a half dozen men."

"Oh, I've embarrassed you, haven't I?" she said kindly.

"Me? I don't think so. If anyone, I'd say you've embarrassed yourself," I said, heat suffusing my face.

"Eugene, I didn't mean . . . I just thought . . ."

I walked away before she could finish and left her standing there confused and embarrassed. But it was a hollow triumph, and short-lived. For when I returned to my quarters the levee gave way, and the hot tears poured out of me as I sat on the edge of the bed, cursing myself for my stupidity and impatience, cursing Gladys for her cruelty, Stowell for his meddling, even my beloved Gaya for forsaking me when I'd spent the better part of six lives looking for her.

Further Indignities

My trepidation upon leaving the familiarity of Desert Greens was nothing compared to the indignity of my actual departure, a spectacle that escaped nobody's notice. Not forty feet from my quarters, Irma McCleary appeared in her doorway, looking on gravely as two EMTs trundled me down the corridor on a gurney. Edith Messinger, resident big-mouth, watched with keen interest as the EMTs wheeled me past the cafeteria in the middle of the breakfast rush, grist for the rumor mill. Old humpbacked Herman Billet, Danish crumbs ringing his ravaged lips, looked up from his plate of runny eggs long enough to gaze pityingly upon me as the attendants ushered me past. If there was a silver lining to this ordeal it was that Angel was not there to witness my humiliation.

As they wheeled me halfway across the parking lot to the awaiting aid car, a half dozen other morbidly curious octogenarians pressed their wrinkled visages to the cafeteria windows. Secured in the rear of the vehicle, I was subsequently transported to Loma Linda University Medical Center in San Bernardino, where I was delivered with little more ceremony than a pallet of surgical gloves.

Upon admittance, I was subjected to another round of blood

draws at the hands of a nurse, who proceeded to wheel me upstairs to Hematology. There I was left for thirty-five minutes in the purgatory of an exam room with nothing to occupy myself but thoughts of my own mortality, an eventuality that seemed legitimately within reach for the first time since the rise of the Holy Roman Empire.

At last, I might escape the hamster wheel of transmigration and proceed to where the cold, dark rivers flowed, untethered from the ceaseless degradation of the temporal, unstuck from the amorphous sludge of awareness, finally, mercifully emancipated from the relentless trappings of memory. Four months prior, this would have been cause for celebration. But now, even as I was resigning myself to the possibility, I found I was ambiguous about such a future, or lack thereof. What if death wasn't all it was cracked up to be? What if it didn't even exist in the way I'd conceived of it? What if the alternative was hell? God knows, I was no innocent.

The arrival of my physician was a welcome development.

"Hello, Eugene. I'm Dr. Wexler," he said, leafing through his charts. "Sorry about the wait."

Unlike Dr. Talbot, whose good looks and robust manner might have served him well as a movie star or a professional ballplayer, Wexler, with his chalky pallor and baggy eyes, had the look of a man who ought to consult a physician himself.

"Says here you're ninety-two years young. Not bad. How do you feel?"

"Fine," I said.

"No dizziness, no weakness?"

"No," I said.

"How's your appetite?"

"Normal."

"That's good," said Wexler. "Very encouraging."

The man was obviously working up to the bad news, so I spared him the awkward dance.

"Just give it to me straight, Doc."

Wexler set his clipboard aside and lowered himself onto the stool in front of me.

"Well, you're very anemic, Eugene," he said. "Dangerously so. The numbers are concerning. Your hemoglobin is eleven."

"And?"

"It needs to be in the neighborhood of fifteen. At the very least."

"Or what?"

"Or you're looking at acute renal failure, potentially. You're going to need blood, a lot of it, and as soon as possible," he said. "That means sending you back downstairs for a transfusion."

"So, how long will I be here?"

"I'm going to want to monitor you," said Wexler. "A day, maybe two."

"And after that?" I said.

"We'll see where we're at and talk about options."

With that, I was dispatched downstairs once more and consigned to a dreary room in the rear of the facility. The lab tech was only slightly more garrulous than a lamppost.

"My son is AB positive," she observed as she prepped me.

That was amongst her few offerings during the three and a half hours I spent with her, though she monitored me frequently throughout the procedure.

Given the knowledge that I was literally being pumped full of blood much heartier and better fortified than my own, I'd hoped to experience some palpable evidence of such, a quickening of the heart, a certain vigor or alertness. I'd half expected to feel like a new man by the end of it. But that was not the case. The procedure left me weak, feverish, and compelled to urinate. When I relieved myself into the bedpan, the result was a brackish liquid closer to brown than yellow that emitted an unpleasant odor not unlike used motor oil. It seemed that not only did the transfusion fail to reinvigorate my life force or strengthen my will, but it had also left me wasted and somewhat apathetic.

Transferred to a hospital bed, I was assigned to rest in a room split in two by a white curtain, on the other side of which resided an individual who from all indications was insensate and possibly comatose, whose immediate survival seemed dependent upon one or more apparatuses that alternately beeped, hummed, and occasionally (without discernible pattern) gasped suddenly as though expressing a long-held breath. Though they were disconcerting at the outset, I grew accustomed to these proceedings, and after an hour or two my eyelids grew heavy.

I regained consciousness hunched in a dark, cramped space, which I first mistook for my old prison cell in Seville but soon recognized as somewhere else entirely. My heart was beating at a gallop. I was just a boy, tears not yet dry upon my dirty face, alone down there in that dreadful place, and not for the first time, either. My throat was parched, my ragged breaths hoarse from pleading. Fists clenched, stomach cramping, pants still warm from a fresh soiling, there was only my whimpering to mark the terrible silence until I heard footsteps directly above me moving across the wooden floor toward the back door. When they halted their progress abruptly with a decisive creak upon the unstable floorboards at the top of the stairs, I quit breathing and closed my eyes, and willed myself to disappear for the thousandth time.

I awoke with a start in yet another dark space. I sat upright in bed, relieved to find myself back in the hospital room. Never have I been so grateful to hear a sound as I was to hear that incessant beep, and hum, and intermittent gasp of my companion's life-sustaining apparatus in the darkness. Shaken, I lay awake for hours, clinging to those sounds as if my own life depended on them.

When morning sunlight finally penetrated the blinds, I was glad to see a new day. But it wasn't long before Wexler came around to ruin it.

"Eugene, how goes it today?" he said upon entrance, looking like he'd slept fifteen minutes the previous night.

"Can I have my old blood back?" I said. "I'm not sure this is an improvement."

"Trust me, it is," said Wexler. "But only a temporary one."

"Oh?"

"Eugene," he said, "there's no easy way to put this. You're suffering from chronic leukemia."

What followed was a ringing silence so complete that it negated the humming and beeping until the sudden gasp penetrated the silence like an exclamation. I could see there was no use in panicking.

"So, what are my options here?" I said.

"Well, the aggressive option is chemo," said Wexler.

"You mean, shave my head and blast me with radiation? I won't do it," I said.

"In your case," said Wexler, "we're dealing with a blood disorder, so chemo looks different. The affected area is not centralized, so we can't target it in the traditional manner. For you, chemotherapy would be a pill."

"Okay," I said.

"But I have to tell you, Eugene. It's hardly more pleasant than what you describe."

"How unpleasant?" I said.

Wexler clearly did not relish the question.

"Frequent nausea," he said. "Vomiting, fatigue, lack of appetite, constipation, bleeding, bruising—the list is long, Eugene. And whether we shave it or not, you'll probably lose your hair anyway.

And there's the additional risk that it will further damage your kidneys. I'm not gonna lie to you."

"I appreciate that," I said, as badly as I didn't want to hear it. "And the other options are . . . ?"

"We let it run its course and try to make you as comfortable as possible in the interim."

"Until it kills me."

"Yes."

"And how long might that take?" I said.

"Could be two weeks, could be two months, could be a year. There's really no telling."

"But I'm on thin ice."

"With or without chemo, yes," he said.

I took a deep breath and paid it out as a sigh.

"Okay, then," I said.

"You don't have to make the decision right away, Eugene. You can give it a day or two."

"Okay, Doc. I'll mull it over," I said. "When can I go home?"

"Soon."

"How soon?"

"Maybe this afternoon."

Sure enough, I was discharged late that afternoon, having already decided my course of action.

Though consigned to a wheelchair upon Wexler's insistence, I was spared the further indignity of the aid car upon my return to Desert Greens, where I was delivered instead by the DG shuttle shortly after five P.M.

Oh, but those blighted palms never looked so inviting! The perfectly bland architectural concession that comprised the Desert Greens facility never looked so enticing, nor so welcoming. Even the sight of Wayne climbing into his Lexus, oblivious to my arrival, brought a smile to my face. I couldn't stand the guy, but if nothing else, the two of us were connected by association, bound by experience, in addition to proximity. We both loved his grandmother. We both knew I was dying.

Nothing heartened me more upon my return to the Greens than an appearance by Angel shortly after I'd situated myself in my quarters, cozy in my tattered terry cloth bathrobe.

"He's back!" said Angel. "What up, man? I hear they sent you to the hospital. You okay, or what?"

"They just wanted to run a few tests," I assured him.

"And?"

"Turns out I'm old."

"No shit, homie. But you're good, right?"

"They told me to watch my diet," I said.

"So, like, no more croissan'wiches?"

"Exactly."

"Sorry, bro. But check it out: Elana is like one of these vegans now that she's pregnant. I'll get some ideas from her. You'd be surprised, man, it's not so bad. Healthy and shit. Oh, and FYI, we set a date for sure. August twentieth, it's a Saturday. You got Saturdays off, right? Anyway, you better have that Saturday off, because I'm giving you plenty of warning. I need you in my wedding party, Geno. My brother Reuben has got best man covered, but I got you as one of my groomsmen. Gotta get you fitted for a tux and all that. Who knows, Reuben might even make you go to a titty bar, so we gotta get that diet of yours sorted out, homie. I don't need you dropping dead on me at the bachelor party."

I smiled, and even the act of smiling left me weak, as though I only had so many left.

Childhood Redux

So long as I am amending my story, I suppose the time has come to share something of my "real" childhood, for once again I have not been entirely honest in my recounting. My memories of childhood are spotty at times, an irony that is not lost on me, a man who can remember tenth-century Hispania with remarkable fidelity. But trauma tells its own story, something I learned from Dr. Stowell. And that story is often full of omissions.

In fact, I was born and raised in Victorville, just as I have led you to believe. My parents did own the Gas and Go on Route 66, with its mercantile and five-stool lunch counter. So, you see, it wasn't all a lie. While I have characterized my father as an impatient and unsentimental man, ashamed of my awkwardness and other-life propensities (which he viewed as attempts to win attention), that alone does not begin to tell the story of the man.

Roger Miles was a taciturn, moody, and unpredictable presence, around whom I learned to move furtively as a child. A tightly wound individual, my father was brusque in his verbal communication. He was not a drinker, though he was a habitual and aggressive sucker of butterscotch hard candies, which he worked around in his mouth as though he were punishing them. In fact, one could almost gauge the man's temperament by the nature of his sucking. When the candy began to clack against the back of his teeth, he was running out of patience. The faster he worked the confections around in his mouth, the closer danger seemed to lurk. When he bit down and crunched them, compacting them between his molars, that meant trouble, and my mother and I saw the brunt of it. Though my mother did next to nothing to protect me from my father, who beat me on innumerable occasions and shamed me more often still, I don't entirely begrudge her this fact. She was a timid soul to begin with and likely could not see beyond the glare of her own victimhood.

I was an achingly lonely child who longed for connection and could not find it, though it wasn't for lack of trying. In the absence of anyone my own age or even close, I would often besiege customers at the counter, at the pumps, in the yard, in front of the outhouse, soliciting conversation. Often, far too often for my father's liking, I would regale these passers-through with tales of my former lives in Chelsea and Spain and Polynesia. It seemed to me that the customers were generally amused and entertained by my reports, sometimes tipping me nickels and dimes and even fifty-cent pieces as though I were a busker. My father seized possession of every penny of it, frisking me and emptying my pockets at the end of each day. I believe this pocket change was the only reason he abided my behavior for as long as he did.

One morning, a man pulled into the Gas and Go in a beat-up Ford Standard. It was July, and I distinctly remember the fellow was dressed unseasonably in a beige overcoat. No wonder he was irritable; it was 105 degrees. Whoever he was, whatever he was doing in an overcoat, he didn't seem to want much to do with me when I accosted him in the yard, where he smoked a cigarette while my father fueled up the old Ford. He had a crooked nose and a long scar below his ear and looked to me as though he hadn't slept in days.

"Hey, mister, aren't you hot in that coat?" I said.

He measured me up for about three seconds before he made up his mind about me.

"Get lost, kid."

Lonely as I was, and hardly socialized, I was never easily dissuaded as a child.

"At least it's dry heat," I said. "Not like the South Pacific this time of year."

"Whatever you say, kid."

"I crossed it with my father a long time ago."

"That right? Congratulations," he said. "Ain't you got somewhere to be? The schoolhouse or something?"

Again, the hint was lost on me. If anything, I felt that I was making progress with the stranger.

"I lived in Spain, too," I observed. "Over a thousand years ago."

"Thousand years, huh?" said the man in the overcoat, unimpressed.

"You ever hear of the Reconquista?" I said.

"That a restaurant?"

"It was a war. Well, a bunch of wars, really," I explained. "It lasted almost eight hundred years."

He surveyed me again doubtfully through squinted eyes, a plume of blue smoke curling up and over his shoulder.

"Look, kid, I'm trying to think here," he said.

"About what?" I said.

He puffed on his cigarette, squinched his eyes up, and exhaled smoke through a sneer.

"What'd I tell you, kid? Beat it."

He tossed his cigarette on the ground and didn't bother stomping it out. Clueless, but determined to engage him, I followed on his coattails as he strode across the lot and through the front door to the counter, where my father met him to square the bill.

"That'll be a dollar ninety," said my father.

The man fished his billfold out of his overcoat and peeled off two one-dollar bills.

"Keep it," he said. "And get that kid's head checked while you're at it."

My father was no doubt mortified by the suggestion; I saw the storm gathering in his eyes as the man walked out. The instant he sputtered out of the lot in his old Ford, my father began to berate me, nearly choking on his butterscotch candy as he beat me about the head with a knotted rag.

"What the hell is wrong with you, you freak?" he shouted.

It wasn't enough to scold me and send me to my room for the evening, or to simply forbid me from interacting with customers, as a reasonable father might have. No, my father despised me. He resented my very existence, all the shame I brought upon him with my behavior and my "tall tales." Clearly, he yearned to be rid of me, my hunger and neediness and childish curiosity. What was a pocketful of silver coins next to the stigma I represented to my father? The answer is nothing.

For the remainder of the summer, I spent six days a week sequestered in the cellar, away from the public eye and ear. There I remained captive from directly after breakfast until dinner, left to watch the shadows recede through the small rectangular opening at ground level that served as the only ventilation, afraid to make a sound for fear of the consequences. My only companion besides the spiders was the spherical rock I'd found two weeks earlier out back of the Gas and Go, which I'd been carrying around in my pocket ever since. Though it was mostly smooth to begin with, I rubbed that rock almost to a polish, working it in my hands for days on end in the darkness.

On Sundays, I was permitted aboveground but instructed in no uncertain terms not to speak to my father or engage him in any way. I was to remain invisible, lest I suffer a beating—or worse, be committed at once back to the cellar.

Thankfully, I was not unprepared for my captivity. Centuries ago, Assad's dungeon had served to initiate me into the practice and endurance of deprivation. I had only to think of Gaya to give me strength as I whiled away the hours, stomach protesting, rubbing my round rock as though the act might save me. This campaign of isolation briefly ended the afternoon that Mr. Nagy, the man from Gulf Oil, came to pay us a visit.

Mr. Nagy was an important man who had something to offer my father, the details of which I was not given to understand at the time. Only in retrospect would I learn that what Mr. Nagy was offering my father was a buyout, and a very lucrative one, a transaction that would eventually come to fruition despite what transpired that evening, making my father a wealthy man. As such, Mr. Nagy's visit was a matter treated with great import in our household. Such was the evening's significance that even my mother's fine china from Idaho was employed for the sake of appearances. The kitchen table was clothed in white. My mother prepared a pot roast and vegetables. Both gin and wine were on hand for the occasion, though my parents did not partake.

For my part, I was instructed to keep my interactions brief and polite, and not to solicit conversation, nor to speak at all unless called upon. I was to sit upright, mind my manners, and under no circumstances make any mention of my former lives.

"Don't louse this up for me, you little imbecile," my father said, gripping me firmly by the collar.

"Yessir, nossir," I said.

"If you do, you'll wish you'd never been born."

And I stuck to the game plan throughout dinner, as Mr. Nagy

spoke at length about the golden opportunity he was prepared to deliver to my father. Not once was I called upon to speak. It wasn't until after dinner, when Mr. Nagy and I remained at the table alone as my mother tended to the dinner plates and my father retired to the nearby radio to tune in the station in San Bernardino, that I was forced to engage Mr. Nagy.

I remember wanting so badly to impress the man, certain that in doing so I could redeem myself in the eyes of my father, whom, somehow, someway, I still could not hate, or even blame for his senseless cruelty; whose approval I still yearned for desperately, as if I really were the problem all along. Understand: After months sequestered in a cellar in complete isolation, I still wanted to show my father that I was a good boy, to show him I was worthy of his loyalty and affection, and security. In my attempts to charm Mr. Nagy, I wanted my father to see that I was not an embarrassment, nor a burden, but an ally, an ambassador for his cause.

"So, young man, tell me a little bit about yourself," said Mr. Nagy.

What was I supposed to tell the man, that I spent my days clutching a rock and counting spiders in a cellar? That I hadn't a friend in the world? That my parents cursed the day I was born? What could young Eugene Miles possibly impart to this influential man that might impress him?

Before I could stop myself, my mouth was off and running as I began to delight Mr. Nagy (or so I believed) with past-life adventures: firsthand accounts of the South Pacific and the Oregon Trail, of the sights and sounds of ancient Seville, and my luxurious and carefree life as the feline companion of a legendary Victorian poet. My father stood helplessly nearby, pulverizing his butterscotch candy between clenched molars. While I could feel Mr. Nagy looking upon me kindly as I shared my outlandish exploits, it wasn't until

I'd concluded my breathless presentation that I saw the pity written plainly on his face.

My father dismissed me with a subtle but dark-eyed threat, and I retreated to my bedroom, where I could hear my father struggling to account for my behavior.

Upon Mr. Nagy's departure, my father found me cowering behind the bed and proceeded to beat me into a state of unconsciousness, after which I awoke in the all-too-familiar confines of the cellar. Little did I know that I was to be confined there for the better part of five weeks, with only my little round rock for comfort.

I was afforded only the barest of sustenance by my mother, who every other day left a small plate of table scraps and a tin of lukewarm water at the top of the stairs, never speaking a word to me, presumably under orders from my father, who I truly believe wished for me to perish down there. By the third week, I was starving, half the day racked with shivering despite the heat, my thoughts a fog of incoherence. The one notion I could count on with any clarity, the single conception I clung to like a lifeline, was the thought of Gaya and the possibility that someday I would meet her again. Other than that, I was left with only the occasional drone of my father's ball games on the radio through the floorboards, loud enough to recognize it for what it was, but too distant to discern the action.

For days on end, I cried myself into a state of apathy, then cried some more, my appetite fluctuating between ravenous hunger and total inappetence. Finally, I gave up all hope and curled into a fetal position, bathed in the paltry light of the vent, unable to stifle the groans that rose from the very depths of me as though they had a will of their own.

Then one morning a shadow darkened my puddle of light, and I heard a child's voice beckoning.

"Hey, somebody down there?"

Rising deliberately to my feet, I retched from the ensuing dizziness. Fighting off the glare, I perceived a set of legs belonging to the voice.

"Hello?" I said, not recognizing my own voice.

When the boy bent down and peered through the wire mesh, I could see he was wearing a St. Louis Cardinals cap.

"Why are you down there?" he said. "Are you stuck?"

"No."

I didn't dare tell him the truth. How could I explain?

"I'm gonna tell my dad you're down here," the boy said. "He can get you out."

"No, please," I beseeched him. "Don't do that. Just bring me something to eat, anything."

"But don't you want—?"

"Really," I said. "Just something to eat. Anything."

God bless that boy, for, not five minutes later, he returned with three Clark Bars, which he managed to squeeze one at a time through a thin breach where screen met concrete.

I began furiously unwrapping and inhaling the bars as the boy peered through the vent, the brim of his Cardinals cap pressed to the wire.

"You want me to steal some more?" he said. "I think I cleaned them outta Clark Bars, but they've still got Snickers."

"No," I said. "Don't risk it."

"If you say so," he said.

Never in my twelve years had I known such gratitude. I felt the boy's inquisitive, pitying eyes upon me as I licked the foil wrappers clean.

"What's your name, anyway?" he said.

"It doesn't matter," I said. "What's yours?"

"Johnny," he said. "Johnny Brooks."

He reached into his pocket and fished something out and forced it through the narrow opening.

"Here, take this," he said. "In case you need it."

It was, of course, a bone-handled jackknife.

Johnny Brooks was the last human being besides my mother whom I laid eyes on until five days later, when the state authorities, tipped anonymously, no doubt by Johnny Brooks and his father, arrived to emancipate me.

New Life

Despite Dr. Stowell's efforts at Metropolitan to affirm my credibility, Gladys must have seen in my persona not her beloved Euric, but a crazy person in a white robe. Her inability to recognize our history might have driven me insane had life with Oscar not taught me to relish whatever connection I could get. I was determined to make things right with Gladys after my boundary-crossing gaffe.

"You were right," I said to her in the cafeteria. "I stormed off because I was embarrassed. Dr. Stowell says I send mixed signals sometimes because I process my—"

Before I could finish, she cut me off gently and set a hand lightly upon my shoulder.

"Don't apologize, Eugene. I was being presumptuous. I just thought that you were . . ."

"You can rest easy," I said. "I only want to be your friend. That is, I'd like to be friendly. Not overly friendly or anything, just . . . familiar . . . ?"

Gladys extended a hand, an olive branch I accepted greedily. "Deal," she said.

In the coming weeks, I assisted Gladys in her cafeteria duties. We exchanged news of the outside world, both trivial and consequential; talked about movies, books, and virtually any thing else that arose naturally during our conversations. I conspicuously avoided the subject of my past lives, but eventually Gladys began to broach the subject herself, albeit skeptically.

"How can Dr. Stowell be so certain you're telling the truth about these different lives?" she said.

"Ask him yourself," I said.

"I want to hear it from you."

"He's interviewed me at great length," I explained. "He's done tests."

"What kind of tests?"

"Memory tests. Things I could only know if I was really there," I explained.

Gladys turned her attention back to the silverware she was sorting, placing the spoons and the forks in their corresponding chrome receptacles. I can't say she looked at all convinced, but she was at least willing to play along.

"So, what have all these lives taught you?" she said.

"Very little, I'm afraid."

"That surprises me," she said. "One would think with all that experience, a person would learn a few lessons."

"Mostly just the same lessons over and over," I said.

On occasion, Gladys began to offer me small glimpses into her life beyond the walls of Metropolitan. She was quite close to her mother, with whom she often attended the pictures on weekends. I learned, too, that Gladys took night classes at Los Angeles City College in history and psychology.

"I'm fascinated by both," she said. "Right now, I'm leaning toward a psychology major, which is the reason I took this job."

"Well, here I am," I said. "Your first case study. Analyze me all you want; I'm used to it. I'm all yours, Dr. Van Buren."

Gladys looked at me curiously.

"How do you know my last name?" she said.

"You told me," I lied. The truth is, I'd asked another orderly.

"Mm," she said.

Here, Gladys evaded my eyes, turning her attention to the tabletop she was presently wiping down.

Though Stowell of late had ceased inserting himself into our conversations, it still seemed that he was nearby at almost every juncture. I was no longer sure whether to view Stowell as a rival or a benefactor. On one hand, he'd made a habit of upstaging me and subtly exercising his dominion over me as my physician, a reminder to Gladys that I was psychologically less than reliable, and yet, he was also permitting me to extend my rapport with Gladys well beyond professional standards, an allowance that could've potentially compromised his own position. Frankly, I believed Gladys was beginning to trust me more than Stowell did. But still, I sensed I couldn't push her, couldn't rush that intimacy I thirsted for.

"Seen any good pictures lately?" I said, by way of diversion.

Indeed, Gladys welcomed the change of subject.

"As a matter of fact, I just saw *Dark Passage* this weekend," she said.

"And?"

"It made me sad," she said. "That poor man, wrongfully convicted. Then having to change his whole identity. At least Irene was there to save him."

"So, a happy ending?"

"Even that was a little sad," she said. "But Lauren Bacall was wonderful."

"What about Bogart?"

"The usual," she said. "An emotional brick wall. And frankly, I think he looked better with his face wrapped up."

"I thought everyone liked Bogey," I said.

"Oh, he's fine," she said. "But he's always the tough guy. I like a little vulnerability in a man."

The more Gladys and I talked about pictures, it seemed, the firmer the ground I stood on, and the more comfortable she seemed to be with me. We talked incessantly about Robert Mitchum and Kirk Douglas and Betty Grable and Alan Ladd, and meanwhile her confidence continued to bleed into the stuff of real life. She began to tell me about her complicated relationship with her mother, the way the woman didn't quite approve of Gladys's career aspirations, and how it seemed to Gladys that her mother would just as soon see Gladys abandon her studies and settle down and have children with a dentist or an accountant or a banker. Only after she had opened up to me in this manner for a few weeks did I dare solicit intimacy or press her on matters of the heart.

"Have you ever been in love?" I said one day, following her around the cafeteria as was my custom.

It was a lame question, of course, as the answer was as plain as the wedding band she wore on her finger.

"I have," she said, adding a dirty tray to her stack.

"Have you ever lost someone dear to you?"

"Yes," she said.

"Who?"

"My husband, Richard," she said.

I'm not proud of my elation at hearing this news, but it could not have been more welcome, if only to know that there existed a vacancy in Gladys's heart.

"How did you lose him?" I asked.

"He was killed in the war."

"I'm sorry," I said.

But that didn't seem like nearly enough. This intimacy seemed to demand something more. Or perhaps I was just a shameless opportunist.

"Maybe you'll find Richard again in another life," I said. "I found you, didn't I? Just like you promised me I would. It took me a thousand years, but here we are."

Gladys shook her head, as if to scold me.

"No, Eugene. I'm not going to play that game with you," she said. "I made no such promise, and you know it."

Technically, she was right; Gaya had never promised me anything, only suggested the possibility that we might meet again.

"You remember, somewhere in you," I said. "I know you do."

"There's nothing to remember," she said. "I was never there, Eugene."

"But you were, just as sure as I was."

Gladys looked at me sadly, which came as a relief, considering I was pushing the envelope.

"I'm sorry, Eugene. But I don't think you were there, either," she said.

"I most certainly was," I said. "Ask Dr. Stowell."

She set her own stack of green trays atop mine and looked me kindly in the face.

"Was Dr. Stowell there with you?" she said.

"No, of course not," I said. "But he'll vouch for me. He'll tell you that I'm not crazy."

"Of course he will," she said, patting me on the wrist. "I don't think you're crazy, Eugene. I just think you have a vivid imagination."

She was essentially calling me a liar, but in an affectionate way that quickened my heartbeat and gave me hope. I found myself falling for Gladys on her own terms, with or without Gaya. And Gladys, for her part, became daily less resistant to my intimate forays, and gradually more tolerant of my persistent assertations, no matter how thoroughly she disbelieved them.

"Eugene, we've been over this," she said. "You can say it all you want, but that doesn't make it true. Neither of us ever lived in Spain. We met right here at Metropolitan. Isn't it enough that we're friends now?"

She was right, of course. It should have been enough, more than enough. But as much as I was falling for Gladys on the strength of her own virtues, I could not give up so long as I knew Gaya was in there somewhere. And despite Gladys's denials, I felt I was getting closer, that she was getting closer, that eventually we might bridge the thousand-year gap.

Stowell, himself a third party to our burgeoning intimacy, grew progressively more willing to entertain the possibility that Gladys embodied a lost fragment of my distant past, and that maybe, just maybe, despite a complete lack of demonstrable evidence, my recognition was not mere wish fulfillment. Perhaps Stowell's willingness to take this leap was his own wish fulfillment. If Gaya were ever to corroborate my claims, Stowell would have the most sensational case of the century on his hands. If he could demonstrate in two separate subjects an a priori knowledge of shared past events, he would redraw the perimeters of human psychology. In permitting me to continue my intimate course with Gladys, his ambitions were clearly crossing some ethical lines, but Stowell saw this potential symbiosis between me and Gladys as an opportunity. Probably his ambition was getting the best of him, but I was grateful nonetheless for the encouragement.

"It's time to push her a little," he urged.

"But what about boundaries? You're the one who said—"

"You must get closer," he insisted. "You might be the only key to unlocking her memories. Sooner or later, you're bound to trigger something."

Stowell wanted it to be true almost as much as I did. Like me, he wanted to distinguish himself. And so, with his blessing, I resumed my campaign to reach Gladys, convinced that the more I familiarized her with the story of Euric and Gaya, the more likely it would come back to inhabit her as it did me. It's true, these methods were highly suggestive, if not coercive, but what did my heart care about scientific methodology? While Gladys proved increasingly willing to indulge me, she still could not see the truth.

"I can't remember what didn't happen to me, Eugene. It's a great story, though. I could see Hedy Lamarr as Gaya. Or maybe a blonde, like Veronica Lake."

"What about for Euric?" I said, accepting the detour.

"Maybe Ray Milland?"

Forgive me if I was a little insulted. But Ray Milland looked like somebody's dad. I saw myself, at least from the remove of ten centuries, as someone a little more rugged and handsome.

"I was thinking more along the lines of Mitchum."

"He's kinda creepy, though. And not vulnerable enough."

There was that word again, *vulnerable*. Perhaps Gaya's age-old trauma was the trigger to firing Gladys's memory? I'd told her the love story with no success; maybe the unpleasant parts of our story were what she needed to hear.

"You may not remember it," I said, "but we killed Assad's minion in the cellar when he came for us."

"You keep saying *we*," she said. "I did nothing of the sort."

"We stove his head in with a hatchet. Surely you remember that?"

"That's awful," said Gladys.

"And you're right," I said. "You didn't kill anyone. It was me. But

I was protecting you, just as you'd protected me, hiding me away in that cellar. Had the man discovered me in your cellar and lived to tell Assad of it, you stood to be punished as harshly as I."

"Then what happened?" she said, willing to indulge me.

"In the middle of the night, we hauled his body in your barrow, just as you had transported me halfway across Seville. And when we reached the edge of the city, we dumped him in the river. We stood on the bank and watched the current take him away. Now do you remember?"

"No," she said. "It sounds like something from Murder Incorporated."

"We were only doing what you had to do for the cause."

"Quit saying *we*. I would never do such a thing," she said.

"And just how can you be so sure of that, Gladys Van Buren, when all you've seen are the tangerine groves of Inglewood and the First Presbyterian Church? You may not remember it, but you were as tough as they came, sister. More Barbara Stanwyck or Ida Lupino than Donna Reed."

"Is that so?" she said, her interest rekindled.

"You weren't afraid of anybody," I said. "You wouldn't back down in the face of any obstacle. You were the most confident, committed, self-possessed person I'd ever met. More than anyone I'd even dared to imagine."

Gladys was blushing now.

"And courageous," I said. "And tough as nails. Don't forget how Assad's men beat you, how Assad himself split your lip. How they broke your nose and blackened your eyes, and still you wouldn't talk."

"That's terrible," said Gladys.

"They killed your father," I said.

"My father?" she said.

"Yes. And don't forget how they locked you away for weeks on end to wallow in your own filth. How he starved you until—"

"Stop!" she said. "Eugene, this is an awful story."

"But it's not. It's heroic, it's—"

"No," she said. "I don't like it, Eugene. I don't want to hear any more."

No Longer a Liability

Whatever else I could say about Assad, he was a man of his word. He made good on his end of our arrangement, immediately dispatching food and water to Gaya. But again she would not take it, nor, predictably, would she volunteer any information regarding the resistance.

"I'd rather die," she said.

"Don't say that," I beseeched her from my cell. "You must eat. What good are you to the cause if you are dead?"

"Dead, I am no longer a liability," she said.

When the guard came the third day, Gaya again refused to touch her food.

"Why must you be so stubborn?" I said. "Eat!"

"And be beholden to them?" she said. "Never."

"Starvation is not the answer."

"It appears to be the only answer," she said.

Hours later, I was summoned to Assad's chamber, where he was eating his supper, a far cry from the gruel I'd been living on below. My mouth watered at the sight of fresh meat.

"It seems I was shortsighted," Assad said, clutching a leg of lamb. "I'm told she won't eat."

"I'm working on that," I said.

"Have you managed to gather any information?"

"She won't talk."

Assad set his leg of lamb aside and wiped his mouth with a cloth napkin.

"Perhaps the guards could persuade her?" he said.

"No," I insisted. "I will persuade her. Give me time."

"You'd better hurry," he said. "I'm told she's fading fast. Where the body goes, the mind follows. And once her mind goes, she's useless to me."

But Gaya remained steadfast in her refusal to eat. Again, the following day I beseeched her for hours to reconsider, knowing that if she did not take nourishment soon, things would surely come to a head with Assad, who was not nearly so patient as Gaya gave him credit for.

"They'll torture you if you don't eat."

"Let them try," she said. "They will get nothing from me."

"They will make you suffer."

"So be it," she said. "I do not take it personally. Our side would do the same. These are the rules of war."

"Why are you doing this to me?" I said.

"This has nothing to do with you."

"But it does, Gaya. Don't you see, I—"

"Don't say it," she said.

Finally, I was forced to accept that this woman who had shown me the only kindness and confidence I'd ever known, this woman who had more resolve and courage in her little toe than I had gathered in a lifetime, was stubborn beyond any measure, and that she would never give up her ground, no matter how horrific the consequences, and she was running out of time. Thus, I took it upon myself to protect her, for something had to be done.

When next I was summoned to Assad's chamber, it was clear that he was discouraged with the lack of progress.

"I'm told she still hasn't eaten. I'm afraid it may be time to try a different approach," he said.

With my back to the wall, I attempted a bold new tack.

"She may not eat," I said. "But she's begun to confide in me."

"Oh?"

"From what I understand, the resistance is gathering in the east," I said.

"The east?" Assad said, somewhat dubiously.

"A small faction near the coast," I said. "In the hills west of Águilas."

Águilas, a place about which I knew next to nothing, was the furthest I could think to lead Assad astray without pointing him north and risking exposing the real resistance. Moreover, I knew that Águilas would force them to travel through the mountains, a journey that might take weeks, valuable time for any hope of keeping Gaya alive.

"Nonsense," said Assad. "I've heard no rumblings from Águilas. Your lover must think me a fool to believe such a thing, when every intelligence tells me the threat resides in the north."

"That's what they want you to think," I said.

Assad entertained this notion momentarily. It was impossible to tell whether he was leaning one way or the other, but I couldn't take the chance.

"They're not stupid," I said. "Does it not stand to reason that the resistance would hope to deceive you and your superiors? They cannot match al-Andalus in might; thus they must rely on their guile."

This suggestion seemed to persuade Assad somewhat.

"How many men?" he said.

"That I don't know yet."

"Find out."

While I had succeeded temporarily in circumventing Gaya's torture or execution, I had failed to resolve the predicament of her starvation. My only recourse was to inform her of the plot that I had already set in motion, to convince her that in diverting the Berbers' attention to the east, I was operating in the best interest of the cause. That there was still hope for her, for us. And given the time, we might find another way out of this place besides death.

"Don't you see?" I said in the darkness. "We're more valuable to the cause alive than dead. Even from right here in our cells we can serve the resistance by way of diversion."

I hardly expected that this idea would persuade her, but I had to attempt something before Assad was moved to force the issue.

"And when they discover we're lying?" she said.

We! She said *we!* There was hope, after all!

"That could take months," I said.

"But when they do?"

"We can get out of here somehow."

"How?" she said.

"That remains to be seen," I said. "But with enough time we can figure a way, I know we can."

"And if we can't?"

"In that case, we will only be facing the same dilemma we face now," I said. "But don't you see? We will have helped the cause."

In the next cell, she stirred for the first time in days, and I nearly swooned from relief. My idea had captivated her. I heard her climb to her feet and begin to pace slowly about her cell. When she spoke again, she lowered her voice to a conspiratorial hush.

"You have done well," she said, her voice but a whisper. "Sending them to Águilas was brilliant. In doing so, you've proven what I suspected all along: that you are more than worthy, and that you could help the cause, just as I told my aunt. But Assad must not suspect this subterfuge. It must look as though I am telling you these things in confidence. And we must continue to misinform him."

"Of course," I said.

"Next time, you will tell them that we are a disorganized bunch, that there is much infighting amongst the fledgling resistance."

"Understood," I said.

"Tell Assad our people are half starving and that they are ill equipped for battle. But don't oversell the idea," she said. "Tell him they are righteous in their indignation and highly motivated. This will sound like the truth. You must prepare him to fail in his pursuit. You will warn him that they are likely to be elusive, that they migrate in small bands from Águilas to the south, sometimes as far as Almería, and inland as far as Baza. This will buy us even more time."

I knew that when Gaya said *us*, she referred to the resistance, but I could not help but think of *us* as her and me. Oh, how that notion brightened the darkness. Moments later, Gaya began to partake greedily of the cold slop left in her cell, and my heart thrilled.

"Euric," she said, her plate of slop presumably clean.

"What is it?" I said.

"You once asked me why I would help you, why I would shelter you from Assad and his men, and I could not say, not at first. Call it a hunch. But now I see you clearly. I see what you've done for the cause, and I see that it has nothing to do with the cause. Everything you've done, you've done for me."

"It is true," I said.

"And you've asked nothing in return."

"But I have," I said.

"Only that I help myself," said Gaya.

"That is enough," I said.

"It's not," she said, then retreated briefly into a thoughtful silence.

When she resumed speaking, her voice was clearer and stronger.

"I have become a hard woman," she said. "Bit by bit, I've allowed it to happen—by balking at kindness, by rebuking love, by stifling my own yearnings. I've told myself every step of the way that these were necessary sacrifices, that my focus must remain singular, that I am nothing more than an instrument of the resistance."

"But you are not a hard woman," I pleaded. "Far from it. You're generous and faithful and—"

"Stop," she said. "It's my turn to bestow praise. It is you, Euric, you who are generous and faithful, you who have protected me, have all but submitted your life to save mine, a sacrifice of which I am unworthy."

"But it's not true, you—"

"Shush," she said. "And being true to the nature I have chosen, I've shut you out, accepted your loyalty while offering you nothing in return. And yet, you've remained steadfast in the face of my every discouragement. Your commitment is admirable."

And there it was, the acknowledgment, or near-acknowledgment, I'd always yearned for. Never mind that it arrived in a stinking cell below the ground from which there was probably no escape. Eleven centuries later, those days in captivity, down in the dank confines of a Moorish dungeon, deprived of light, and dining on inedible gruel, were amongst the brightest days of all my lives. If not for the two feet of wall separating us, I might have held Gaya in my arms. I might have died there happily. Every moment of every day I relished the possibility that someday I would.

Gaya grew stronger and more talkative with the passing days. From her cell, she fed me misinformation loud enough that the guard might hear it were he of a mind to listen and thus corroborate my report. Every few days I convened with Assad in his chamber, where I relayed Gaya's intelligence. While he was hungry for these bits of information, they did not always agree with him.

"A ragged bunch, are they?" he said dismissively. "By your own logic, they'd like me to think so, wouldn't they? Don't think I can't see a trap from three hundred miles away."

"How could they possibly know you were coming?" I said. "We could no more get word to them than the two of us could lay siege to the city from the confines of our cells."

Assad considered me, a knifelike glint of suspicion in his eye.

"Unless," he said, "it was your plan to be imprisoned all along. How do I know you are not messengers sent to guide al-Andalus into the jaws of the resistance?"

"I should think we might have guided you there sooner, before you started starving us to death."

"Ah, but then, what could be a more convincing subterfuge than that?" said Assad.

"You are overcomplicating things in your mind," I said. "You asked me for information in return for food. If I am to feed you misinformation, what is to stop you from serving me tainted food?"

Assad considered me closely again.

"I have at turns overestimated you and underestimated you. Now I see definitively that you are much cleverer than I ever suspected," said Assad. "Let's hope that your cleverness does not betray you. I have already sent a party east to Águilas, and another south to Almería. They will both proceed to Baza from there. We shall know within a matter of weeks if you are lying to me or if this is a trap. And if either proves to be the case, it will be the end of you."

As doomed as this ploy seemed to be, it was a risk I had to take, and one destined to cost me dearly.

To Forgive Life

"Death must be so beautiful. To lie in the soft brown earth, with the grasses waving above one's head, and listen to silence. To have no yesterday, and no tomorrow. To forget time, to forgive life, to be at peace."

Oscar's words, not mine, and despite my vast experience, I cannot attest to the accuracy of his assumptions. I only know that I clung to them like never before in the days after I made my decision to end my life naturally.

Whispers began circulating around the Greens minutes after the hospice team arrived for my orientation. Soon, inquisitive denizens began idling about in the hallway outside my room, a few bold ones rubbernecking for a glimpse of the proceedings through my open door. Amongst those foraging the halls for crumbs of intelligence was big-mouth Edith Messinger, who would no doubt have a field day with my impending demise. Edith would be the first one to start digging up the soft brown earth and tossing shovelfuls carelessly over her shoulder. Her inaugural disclosure would be the flammable stuff of pure speculation, disbursed less than surreptitiously in the commons or the cafeteria, perhaps to Herman Billet, who didn't hear so well, or maybe Bud Brewster, not exactly the most discerning individual, or Iris Pearlman, who loved to talk. Bud, or Herman, or Iris, would then put the flame to those waving grasses until soon the news of my nearing expiration would spread like wildfire, straying further from the truth with every new gust of innuendo.

I heard it's some kind of cancer.

Rectal cancer.

I heard it's blood cancer.

Apparently, he's bleeding from the rectum.

The doctors give him six months to live.

He's got six weeks to live.

They say he'll be dead within the week.

The story of my death, like the story of my life, would be a study in disinformation.

It wasn't long before Angel caught wind of the news. Around four thirty, he arrived with his cart to tend to my quarters.

"You lied to me again, bro."

"I'm sorry," I said. "I guess I just didn't know how to tell you."

"How bad is it, homie?"

"Bad," I said.

Angel slumped perceptibly, God love him.

"So, like, you're just giving up? No chemo or anything?"

"It's gonna get me one way or another," I said. "I don't want to spend my last days fighting an uphill battle. The doc says the treatment can be worse than the disease."

"Rectal cancer, I heard. Damn, ese. Does it hurt?"

"It's leukemia," I said.

"Aw, man. That's even worse."

A brief silence settled in as Angel processed the news.

"So, like, how much time until . . . ?"

"Nobody can say," I said.

Angel shook his head dispiritedly. "That sucks."

"Ah, well, I've had a long run," I said.

"You gotta make the wedding, though, right?" said Angel.

"I cleared my calendar, didn't I?"

"You scared, dog?"

"Heck no. As long as your wedding's not at one of those little Vegas chapels."

"Seriously, man."

"Nah," I said.

"Geno, you're a lot braver than me."

"I'm lying," I said. "I'm plenty scared."

"Maybe you won't come back at all this time," said Angel. "That's what you want, right?"

"I'm not holding my breath," I said.

"You never know," said Angel. "You gotta keep the faith."

Faith. Maybe that was the problem. It had always seemed a fool's proposition to me, even as a cat. History tells us that Oscar sipped champagne on his deathbed, which is more than I can say for poor Whiskers, who was put out to the curb with no more ceremony than a sack of potato skins after Oscar was jailed for indecency. Life after Oscar was not kind to me. Within two days, I lost an eye in a street fight over the meager pickings of a cast-off chicken leg. Ravaged by bloodsucking fleas, riddled with worms, eye socket oozing a foul-smelling goo, I stalked the streets of Chelsea listlessly, unloved and all but unnoticed. My once-lavish pride abandoned me. I stopped grooming myself. I starved until there was nothing left of me but blighted skin and wasted bones. I grew weaker and weaker until I lost all interest in eating or drinking.

Finally, heartsick and utterly defeated, I lay down to die in an alley, yearning for that soft brown earth, those waving grasses, that silence and peace. History doesn't tell us whether my carcass wound up on a rubbish heap, half consumed by vermin, or my good eye shucked clean from its socket by a magpie. I was not set free. On the contrary, I endured that living hell only to come back in my present form, a lovelorn soul destined to be alone. So you'll forgive me if I find the notion of faith an elusive one.

"I've got a favor to ask," I said.

"Anything, homie."

"As you know, I have no family, not so much as a distant cousin that I know of. No long-standing friendships. My executor is an attorney named Sherrard in San Bernardino, whom I've only met once," I said.

"What do you need, Geno?"

"The hospice people, they've asked me to pick a personal advocate."

"Of course. I got you, dog. What do I do?"

"I don't really know the extent of it. Mostly just be there for me throughout the evening when things get worse. Make sure I'm comfortable."

"I can do that."

"You'll be compensated, of course," I said.

"Nah," said Angel. "I couldn't take your money, man."

"I insist," I said. "It's in the budget. Somebody's gonna get paid."

"But like, how does that work, if I'm already getting paid by this place?" said Angel.

"The hospice folks said they can clear it with Wayne. I'm sure he'll go for it. You won't be the only one assigned to me, there's a whole team of people. It really shouldn't interfere with your job much," I said. "You'll just swing by and check on me once in a while, make sure I've got my pain meds, make sure I'm comfortable, empty my commode, if it ever comes to that."

"So, let me get this straight," he said. "I'd be getting paid twice?"

"Yeah."

"If you say so," said Angel. "I guess I could use the extra cash with the baby and all."

"I'll try to linger as long as possible, so you can leverage the situation," I said with a wink and a nudge. "Who knows, maybe I can hold out a year."

But Angel wasn't in a joking mood. "C'mon, dog," he said. "Who's to say you can't beat this thing?"

"Perhaps," I said.

"But let's not talk about it like that, bro," he said. "You're gonna beat this thing."

"Maybe. But I don't want to stick around too long," I said. "I may as well move along to the next chapter. Who knows, maybe I'll be a concert pianist, or a professional ballplayer. Maybe I'll cure cancer."

"Maybe you'll find Gaya again," said Angel.

As much as I appreciated the sentiment, I was no longer clinging to any such hope. My only hope now was that my death would finally offer me the closure I so yearned for.

The Determination

"First of all," said Dr. Spencer, "I'd like to wish you a happy eighteenth birthday, Eugene."

"Yes," Dr. Maxwell chimed in. "Happy birthday, Eugene."

I sat across from both men at a folding table in an unfurnished office in the rear of the facility, facing the lone window, the glass of water directly in front of me already beginning to sweat. Frog-eyed Dr. Spencer, squat and stocky, and silver-haired Dr. Maxwell, lean and statuesque, were both bespectacled, and both holding clipboards and clutching pens.

"As you know, Eugene," said Dr. Spencer, "we're here to review your discharge status now that you're no longer officially a minor and therefore a ward of the state. Do you understand the purpose of this interview?"

"Yes," I said.

"You're aware that the purpose of this interview is to determine whether you're mentally competent for release?" said Dr. Maxwell.

"Yes," I said.

"And what is your personal opinion on the matter?" said Dr. Spencer.

"By all means, I'm ready," I said.

Dr. Maxwell scratched out a note on his clipboard.

"Tell us about Dr. Stowell," he said without looking up.

"What about him?"

"Where is he presently?" said Dr. Spencer.

"Gone," I said.

"Gone?"

"Yes."

"How can you be sure?"

"Well, he's not here, is he?"

"You tell me," said Dr. Spencer.

"If he was here, he'd be talking. Trust me."

"When is the last time you saw Dr. Stowell?" said Dr. Maxwell.

"Two and a half months ago," I said.

"Explain your relationship with Dr. Stowell, if you would."

My eyes sought refuge in the square of blue sky out the window as a wisp of cumulus cloud drifted past.

"Our relationship was mutually beneficial. He believed me," I said. "And I needed to be believed at the time."

"Believed you about what?"

"About having lived before," I said.

"Why do you think he believed you?" said Dr. Spencer.

"Because he wanted to, I suppose."

"What was the benefit for Dr. Stowell? Why do you suppose he would want to believe you?"

"Ambition," I said.

"Ambition to . . . ?"

"To distinguish himself," I said.

"Distinguish himself as . . . ?"

"A pioneer in the field," I said. "I was the case study of the century. I was going to make him famous."

"Were you sorry to see Dr. Stowell . . . go?" said Dr. Maxwell.

"No."

"Do you know where he went?" said Dr. Spencer.

"Presumably, back where he came from."

"And where is that?" said Dr. Maxwell.

"Impossible to say."

"Do you think Dr. Stowell will be back at any point in the future?" said Dr. Spencer.

"No," I said.

Spencer made a quick notation on his clipboard.

"Tell us about your relationship with Gladys Van Buren," said Dr. Maxwell.

"She was my friend."

"Was this friendship reciprocal?" said Dr. Spencer.

"Yes."

"How can you be sure?"

"Because she told me," I said.

"Mm," said Dr. Spencer.

"Why did she stop working here?" said Dr. Maxwell.

"You'd have to ask her supervisor," I said.

Maxwell jotted down a note.

"Did you ever suggest to Miss Van Buren that you'd known her in a past life?"

"Yes."

"Do you still believe that you knew Miss Van Buren in a past life?"

"No," I lied.

"Do you believe that you've lived past lives, Eugene?" said Dr. Maxwell.

"Not anymore," I said.

"Why not?"

Here, I stared out the window once more at a cloud shaped like a seahorse.

"Because believing as much has not served me well," I said.

"How so?" said Dr. Spencer.

"Isn't that obvious?" I said.

"Why do you think you were placed here, Eugene?" said Dr. Maxwell.

"Because I was sick in the head."

"Was?"

"Yes," I said. "Was."

"And you feel that is no longer the case?"

"That is correct," I said.

"Why is that?" said Dr. Maxwell.

"I feel different."

"How so?"

"I feel . . . not sick," I said. "Normal."

"And what does that feel like?"

"Like I got a good night's sleep."

"You said you stopped believing in your past lives because they did not serve you well," said Dr. Spencer.

"Actually, I said that the belief did not serve me well."

"What is the difference?" said Dr. Spencer.

"Very little, I suppose. The lives themselves never served me well, either," I said.

"So, you *do* believe you've lived before?" said Maxwell.

"I used to believe," I said. "I choose to no longer believe as much."

"You choose?" said Dr. Maxwell.

"Yes."

"So, then, you are acknowledging that these past lives exist?" said Dr. Spencer. "You just choose to ignore them."

Once again, my eyes sought the square of sky out the window.

"Yes? No?" said Dr. Spencer.

"Yes," I said.

Dr. Spencer's pursed lips hinted at a frown as he and Maxwell simultaneously scribbled notes.

"But that doesn't mean I expect anyone else to believe they exist. There's a difference," I said.

"Mm," said Dr. Spencer.

"They're not delusions," I said. "They're my lives, nobody else's."

Maxwell and Spencer exchanged a knowing glance, then both looked at me pityingly from across the table.

"What?" I said.

Dr. Spencer was now officially frowning.

"They're not hurting anyone," I said.

"I want to thank you for answering our questions today, Eugene," he said.

"Yes, thank you," said Dr. Spencer. "And happy birthday."

Maxwell looked a little rueful as he scratched out a final note on his clipboard.

Wellness Check

It's not like I needed a doctor to tell me that my life was winding toward its end. The world's interest in prolonging my captivity seemed to wane with each passing day. Daily, the tether slackened. For six days, I existed in a medicated fog. My thoughts ran thick as molasses. So dull were my senses, so unconditional was my apathy, that I might have left my body and never known it. Every four hours, Angel rolled me over like a sack of oats so I wouldn't develop bedsores.

On the seventh day, I quit the drugs completely, and while the discomfort returned immediately and with a vengeance, so, too, did my appetite and mental acuity. Sometimes suffering is the better option. In the afternoon, Wayne dropped by for a wellness check. Rather than linger in the doorway as usual, he rolled my office chair to my bedside, where he straddled it like a horseman. No sooner was he settled than he produced a roll of Life Savers from the pocket of his khakis.

"Life Saver?" he said.

"You're too late," I said.

"Ha. You sure?" said Wayne. "Butter-rum. You know, like but-terscotch."

"I'll pass," I said, my eye twitching.

Mercifully, Wayne replaced the unopened roll in his pants pocket, sparing me the discomfort of his incessant clickety-clacking.

"So, how are you feeling?"

"Not great," I said.

"Would you rather I leave?"

Normally, I would've welcomed the opportunity to be rid of Wayne, but in recent days my opinion of virtually everything had softened, and that included Wayne.

"Eugene, I owe you an apology," he said.

"Oh?"

"I guess I sort of ambushed you with the stuff about my grandma. That was bad form on my part. Very unprofessional."

"Don't you think, Wayne, that taking this job in the first place was sort of unprofessional, I mean, given the circumstances?"

"You got me there," said Wayne. "But there was more to it than that. The truth is, I wanted out of LA anyway. My job at the hospital was a rat race, my ex-wife was engaged to one of my colleagues. And I figured out here I might do some good, you know? It seemed like the right decision at the time. I love the desert."

"And how has that worked out?" I said.

"Meh," he said. "I miss the sushi."

Wayne stood up and moved across the room, where he plucked the picture of Gladys and me at King George's off the dresser. Resuming his seat at my bedside, he gazed at the photograph.

"So, you ready to talk about it?" he said.

"It may not be the story you're expecting," I said.

"I want to hear it."

"Bring me a glass of water," I said.

....

A few months before my eighteenth birthday, things began to change for me at Metropolitan. The more familiarity I fostered with Gladys, the further I managed to engender intimacy, the less Dr. Stowell seemed to be hovering around. And without the mediating influence of Stowell, I believe Gladys viewed me less as a patient and more as a person, a confidant, a friend.

"It's been almost five years since Richard was killed, and there are still days I can hardly get out of bed," she said.

"I know the feeling," I said.

"Mother says I need to move on. She insists I need to meet some-one new," she said. "Oh, she's so pushy. Always after me to abandon my studies and settle down with a banker. She says college is no place for a woman. You'd think we were living in the Dark Ages. Why are you smiling?" she said.

"Am I?"

"You most certainly are. You have a big stupid grin on your face. Is there something you find funny about all of this?"

"I just can't see you with a banker," I said.

"Neither can I," she said. "Oh, Eugene, the worst part of it all is that I'm beginning to think Mother is right. I'm practically failing my psychology class."

"What about history?"

"Better," she said. "But between this job and my studies and the fact that I don't want to get out of bed most days, it just feels like too much."

I reached out my hand to her, and to my delight, she accepted it.

"Eugene," she said. "If it's not too personal, may I ask how you came to be here—at Metropolitan, I mean?"

"It's a long story."

"But I like your stories," she said.

"You probably wouldn't like this one."

"I understand," she said. "Forgive me for prying."

"I was a ward of the state," I said. "They put me here when they decided . . . well, I'm not sure exactly what they decided. That I was crazy, I suppose."

"Why did they decide that?" she said.

"Because I didn't stick anywhere, I guess. They put me in all kinds of foster care, but it always went south, every time. Everywhere I went, something bad happened. Never mind that the bad thing happened to me; that didn't seem to matter. They just figured I was unable to assimilate in normal society, so they put me here."

"What kind of bad things?" she said.

"I'd really rather not talk about it."

I'm ashamed that I wasn't stronger in that moment, that I couldn't put a brave face on my suffering in the presence of Gladys. But merely broaching the subject of my youth laid waste to my carefully constructed defenses. At the very thought of what I'd endured in that cellar, all the rest of it, a lifetime of anguish and affliction flooded in, and I was powerless to stop the tears.

Shaken by this display, Gladys squeezed my hand harder and allowed me to rest my head upon her shoulder.

"Oh, Eugene, you poor thing," she said.

Perhaps Dr. Stowell, having witnessed this scene from a distance, perceived that I no longer needed his help to qualify me or earn Gladys's confidence. Maybe that explained his absenteeism in the coming weeks. Or maybe he'd attached himself to a more sensational subject than Eugene Miles, the thousand-year-old man; some other troubled soul to distinguish his work. Whatever the case, his absence was soon conspicuous.

"Where's Dr. Stowell?" Gladys asked one afternoon in the cafeteria. "I haven't heard from him in weeks."

"I think he's gone," I said.

"Really?"

"It looks that way."

"Good riddance," she said.

I watched a smile take shape on her face as she bent to retrieve a lunch tray.

"You think it's a good thing?" I said.

"Of course it's a good thing," she said. "It's great. It means you're getting better. What do you need him for? He was so overbearing, so full of himself. I like you much better."

"Me?"

"Yes, you," she said.

"But why?"

"Because you're sincere," she said. "And you're funny."

"Me, funny?"

"And you're vulnerable," she said. "I find that a rare quality in a man."

Suddenly my ears were burning. Had she really called me a man? Had she really chosen me over Stowell? How had we arrived here so quickly? I really wasn't that funny. It had to be the vulnerability.

"But if you knew Stowell was a delusion, why did you indulge me? You even spoke to him as if he was there."

"Because I figured you needed him."

The next day, Gladys didn't show up for work. Assuming she had a dental appointment, or a cold, or some family obligation to attend to, I survived the morning. But such was my active imagination that by afternoon I was fretting over some terrible demise; perhaps she was killed in a house fire, or struck by a streetcar like Consuela's husband.

When Gladys failed to appear the following day, I began making inquiries amongst the doctors, the receptionists, the orderlies, and anyone else I could collar who might offer me some insight. At every attempt I met with a brick wall.

It was a custodian named Osgood, a man half a foot taller than me, pushing a mop, who finally offered me clarity on the matter.

"Young lady?" he said. "Nice figure, pretty brown eyes, little mole under the nose?"

"That's her," I said.

"Quit, pretty sure," he said.

"Why?"

"Hell, I'm about one paycheck from quittin', myself," he said.

"Why?"

Osgood pursed his lips and shook his head. "Place like this ain't for me," he said. "Place like this starts workin' on your head, if you know what I mean."

"Boy, do I know what you mean," I said.

I was crushed at this news, of course. It seemed that all my living had been in vain. Osgood, seeing that I'd taken her absence hard, tried to cheer me up the second week.

"You got bigger problems, my man," he said. "You gotta find your way out of this place yourself. I'll tell you what, it won't be long for me."

"Yes, but you've got a choice," I said.

"Not a good one," he said. "But I see your point. I hope you get out of this place. I ain't been here for but two months, and I know what they say about you living them other lives, and I'm not entirely sure what to make of that, but far as I can see, you ain't no crazier than Dr. Maxwell himself."

Two days later, Osgood didn't show up to work, and it was then I accepted for the thousandth time that I was officially cursed, for I had lost any hope of a sympathetic audience. I retreated once more to my quarters, back to my bedsprings and my paint drips, where I scarcely saw the light of day for weeks to come. The orderlies persuaded me to eat, to shower and shave twice a week, but to do little else. I might have welcomed the counsel of Dr. Stowell through that dark interval, but he, too, had abandoned me.

I languished for what must have been a month and a half in Gladys's absence, each day indistinguishable from the next. I was back where I'd started at Metropolitan. It seemed that all was lost.

Then, late one morning as the sunshine was angling through my window to no avail, a new orderly shook me in my bed and told me I had a visitor. Of course, I had no earthly idea who it could be. Wozniak or Doris come to check on me? Consuela? None of them seemed likely. Despite the possibilities, I was scarcely compelled beyond a vague curiosity as I padded down the hallway in my stockinged feet. Until I reached the commons.

There, seated in the lounge, a splash of radiance in a gray world, garbed in an orange and yellow sundress, her cream-colored clutch set before her on the tabletop, was Gladys. Just the sight of her awakened my every flagging sense in the beat of a heart. And it wasn't enough just to look upon her as I approached oh-so-casually, an effort that took every ounce of restraint I could muster. Closing my eyes, I could smell her before I even took a seat across from her: roses and gardenias, and the slight chalky scent of powder.

"Hey, I passed my psychology exam," she said.

"That makes one of us," I said.

Smiling sadly, she patted me on the hand, and for the first time in weeks I didn't tense at the touch of another.

"It won't be long, Eugene," she said.

"Hard words to swallow for a thousand-year-old man," I said. "Came to see your crazy friend, huh?"

She withdrew her hand and busied it shifting her purse on the table to no purpose.

"You're not crazy, Eugene," she said. "But you are my friend."

"Then you believe me?" I said. "About Spain, about Oscar, about—"

"Not exactly," she said. "But I do miss your company."

How could that be? What compelling reason had this young woman to fraternize with the likes of me? So far as I knew, beyond the grief of losing her husband she was not damaged in any way. She was bright, lovely, four years my elder; surely the larger world had something more promising to offer her than eighteen-year-old Eugene Miles?

"Of all people, why would you miss me?" I said. "Surely you could do better for company?"

"Eugene," she said, "you're the most interesting person I know."

"Interesting like a case study, you mean? Am I extra credit?"

"No," she said. "Interesting like a person."

"Why did you quit your job, then?" I said. "Just like that, without even telling me?"

"Because I was afraid."

"Of me?"

"Of a lot of things," she said. "But yes, you were one of them."

"I would never hurt you," I said.

"I know you wouldn't," she said. "That's not it. It doesn't matter, does it? I'm here. Isn't that what matters?"

"Yes," I said.

How did it all work in this life? What were the guiding principles of the indefatigable phenomenon of existence? After all my lifetimes, I still wasn't any closer to answering these questions. For all the bad fortune I'd endured, for all the terrible hands I'd been forced to play in all my lives, there were miracles like Gladys, like Gaya, a light shining out of the abyss.

Gladys continued to visit me every Saturday in the lounge. She reenacted the matinees she'd seen with her mother: *Nightmare Alley*,

Possessed, A Double Life. She told me about her new ancient history class and how it energized her.

"I mean, for all our so-called advancements, have we really come that far from the Romans or the Greeks or the Egyptians?" she said.

"The bathrooms are nicer," I observed. "And we have electric razors now. And glow-in-the-dark stuff."

"Oh, you're so funny, Eugene. How do you think of these things?" she said.

I lived for my Saturday visits with Gladys. I began preparing for them, combing my hair and wearing shoes. I even took to donning a button-down dress shirt for the occasion, ill fitting though it was, having formerly belonged to Osgood, who had gifted it to me on the eve of his final day.

Gladys was always in a dress, usually something bright, her hair arranged any number of ways, pulled back, or in a bun, or hanging loose and natural. Invariably, her scent was a revelation, a tropical paradise for olfactory receptors accustomed to the thick but indefinite scent of cafeteria food with undertones of bleach. But more than anything sensual, more even than the warmth and ease of Gladys's manner, it was her capability and confidence that hypnotized me, as with Gaya before her. She was an island of calm in rough waters. Unlike Eugene Miles, forever set upon and tossed around by outside forces.

"I've filed a formal appeal to the hospital that Dr. Maxwell and Dr. Spencer reevaluate your status within ninety days," she said. "In the meantime, I've managed to secure you supervised outings on Sundays."

"Outings?" I said. "To where?"

"Anywhere you want," she said. "Within reason."

"Supervised by whom?"

"By me," she said.

"But . . . how did . . . who . . . ?"

"Isn't it wonderful?" she said.

It was beyond wonderful, it was miraculous, and so unexpected that it rendered me speechless.

"I was thinking we could take in a picture," she said. "*California* is playing at the Hitching Post next Sunday. We could go to lunch first."

Next Sunday? Hollywood? It was all too much to believe.

"This isn't a gag, is it?" I said.

"Of course not," said Gladys.

"But I don't have any . . . I don't know how I could pay for . . . There's a trust from the settlement, but I don't know if . . ."

Gladys smiled and patted my hand once more.

"It'll be my treat," she said.

When we parted, I floated across the lounge and down the corridor, half convinced I'd dreamed my good fortune. Never in my eighteen years had I had anything to anticipate, let alone something so deeply yearned for. My destiny was bound to thwart it, somehow, someway; a policy oversight, a question of liability or legality, or maybe just Gladys's cold feet. Whatever it was, it would prevent her from following through. Eugene Miles never got what he wanted.

But this time I was not stymied by fate. The following Sunday, Gladys came for me as promised and checked me out with no more ceremony than would be required to check out a library book. We took a Red Car to Hollywood, where we ate scalloped chicken à la king and drank RC Colas at the Brown Derby and talked about Vivien Leigh and Veronica Lake and Claude Rains and Basil Rathbone, about ancient scripts and the Khufu ship, Cretan bowls and papyrus scrolls, the heliacal rising of Sirius and the flooding of the Nile.

After lunch, we attended a matinee of *California* at the Hitching Post on Hollywood Boulevard. The picture delivered, mostly. When Trumbo promises Lily he'll return to the army to atone for his desertion, Gladys took my hand in hers and gripped it firmly in the darkened theater.

After the picture, we spilled out onto the sidewalk and immediately began to chatter.

"So, what'd you think?" she said.

"Never trust a man named Coffin," I said.

"I don't like it when they go crazy," she said. "Even the bad guys."

"Oh, Gladys," I said. "Why do you always take the pictures so personally?"

We strolled around for several hours, peering in windows and soaking up the pageantry of Hollywood. But as evening approached, and it was time for me to return to the Metropolitan, my spirits began to flag, for my situation seemed hopeless. As we stood at the Highland stop, holding hands, I wanted nothing more than to never go back, yet I hadn't the courage to do anything but. Where would I go and what would I do? Eugene Miles had never cared for himself.

"I've got to get you out of there," she said.

"How?"

"I'll keep appealing," she said. "I'll pester them until they can't stand it anymore. They'll have to let you go just to get rid of me."

I believed her, I had to, or I'd have gone crazy. Suddenly, at least for the moment, the possibility seemed real.

I ceased my storytelling momentarily and looked across at Wayne straddling the office chair.

"So, what happened?" he said.

"She tried," I said. "She wrote letters to the health board, to her state representative; she even appealed to the hospital administrators in person. But the reality was that with no immediate family to harbor me and no safety net to catch me, my fate was consigned to the doctors."

It seemed I'd never get a fair shake in this world, no matter how many lives I led. A young man of burgeoning appetites, a young man daring to yearn for something beyond safety and security for the first time in his life, a young man hopelessly enamored with this woman, and there I was, stuck in a hospital with little hope of release.

Unfinished

There were minutes, even hours, when my old vitality returned, but on balance, I seemed to grow weaker by the day. Gone were my lunches with Angel out on the green, let alone the possibility of an outing to Los Angeles, or even Victorville. Most days I didn't get out of bed for more than an hour or two, usually to puzzle at my desk. But the act of puzzling itself no longer served its purpose, to while away the hours, which now slipped away of their own accord. My recently undertaken thousand-piece Seville sidewalk scene seemed destined to remain unfinished. It now seemed incumbent upon me to instead fit all the pieces of my own life together into something resembling completion, to achieve some kind of closure hitherto unknown in any of my previous incarnations in order that I might, just might, leave this world behind once and for all. It was worth a shot.

Despite my diminished capacities, I found myself quite occupied throughout my waning days. Between the respite team, Wayne's increasingly frequent wellness checks, and the steady presence of Angel, my social calendar was busier than ever before. For eight years, not a solitary visitor, and now my dance card was full. These frequent visitors were not unwelcome; quite the contrary. None were

more welcome than Angel, upon whom I became increasingly dependent not just for company but for toileting, and even dressing on
those days when I could still muster the ambition to do so. Angel
seemed to take naturally to caregiving. He had a gentle touch. None
of the more personal tasks seemed to faze him in the least, whether
it was emptying my bedpan or dressing and undressing me.

One afternoon when he was helping me out of my thin cotton
gown, he saw for the first time my scars, four raised lines running
more or less perpendicular at a slant from just above my waist to just
below my shoulder, each about an inch wide and about eight inches
long, still pink and shiny after eight and a half decades.

"Whoa, man, what happened here?" he said.

Without thinking, I said, "Got tangled up with the business end
of a harvester when I was just a boy. Not that there was anything
worth harvesting out here in the damn desert, but my father was
stubborn that way. Hard to believe the marks are still visible."

"Dang, dog," said Angel.

"It just looks bad," I said. "Truth is, I hardly even remember it."

It seemed I was growing softer and more forgiving of the world
by the day. I had even learned to enjoy Wayne's company, so long
as he wasn't molesting a Life Saver. Our next visit wasn't even in
Wayne's usual wellness capacity; I simply called him into my room
through the open door as he was passing by in the corridor.

"Eugene," he said. "How goes it?"

"How about you?" I said.

"Not too shabby. Shot an eighty-two at Spring Valley Lake yesterday."

"Is that good?"

"For the likes of me it is."

"Well done," I said.

With no more encouragement than that, Wayne swung the office chair around and straddled it at my bedside.

"So, are you ready to tell me what happened after you didn't pass your second review?"

"Yes," I said. "But you might wanna get comfortable. This could take a while."

All I had to look forward to at Metropolitan was my Sundays with Gladys, who inexplicably chose to love me, even though her mother wholly disapproved of the relationship. Or maybe because of it. With our visits limited to Sundays, the other six days of the week were a delirium of anticipation. The quotidian drudgery of Metropolitan, 144 hours of institutional monotony, isolation, and terrible food, was endurable so long as I had my Sunday afternoons with Gladys. *Welcome Stranger* at Grauman's, *Code of the Saddle* at the Hitching Post, *Heartaches* at the Hawaii on Hollywood Boulevard. We lunched at Chasen's, the Derby, the Pig 'n Whistle, Gladys footing every penny of it.

"I have a trust," I assured her at every restaurant and box office.

"Don't be silly," she said each time. "You'll get even with me eventually."

Indeed, I had every intention of doing so. Eugene Miles was no pauper. While on the surface he may not have seemed a young man of great prospects, on paper he was not without means. The only problem was that the not inconsiderable settlement awarded to me by the state of California from the seizure of my parents' assets was placed in a trust that would remain beyond my grasp until my twenty-fifth birthday.

"Don't worry about money," she said. "You're too young to worry about such things."

Something dismissive about the way she said it made me bristle with insecurity.

"Too young for you?" I said, my ears burning at the urgency of the question.

"Relax," she said. "Grow into yourself, Eugene."

Though I resented what I perceived to be the patronizing overtones of the statement, Gladys's prescribed course of action was nothing if not apt, and the fact that she had any stake in the game at all was a small miracle, so I let it pass without rebuttal. But I'd been right to worry. I was losing her. My novelty was wearing off. My youth was starting to show to this twenty-three-year-old widow who had already been to college and worked at a mental institution, who dreamed of being a history professor and yet could not escape the influence of her mother.

Each Sunday, Gladys seemed to be preparing me for the ultimate disappointment. The touch of her hand seemed somehow less engaged and more businesslike as we strolled the sidewalks of Hollywood. Rarely did we speak of the future. And yet, more than ever, she seemed to depend upon me as a confidant.

"Mother is relentless," she said. "She won't stop pushing Vernon Niemeyer on me."

"Who's Vernon Niemeyer?" I said.

"An optometrist."

An optometrist! How could a mental patient possibly compete with an optometrist when he couldn't even see his own future? I was doomed.

"But I thought she wanted you to marry a banker," I said.

Not that I could compete with a banker.

"Does this Niemeyer have . . . intentions?" I said.

Gladys paid out a sigh, already weary of the subject.

"If he does, he's too awkward or too aloof to let them be known," said Gladys.

"Maybe he's just shy."

"Maybe," she said.

I was dying inside. Imagine having to entertain a conversation about Gladys's future that didn't include me. But what choice did I have? So central had Gladys become to my very existence that I was committed to being whatever she needed me to be, so long as I was indispensable. And the approach seemed to be working, for Gladys clutched my hand a little bit tighter as we waited for the Red Car, and when we parted that evening, the grip of her hand was more impassioned than ever before.

But the following Sunday, as we were dining on tuna melts at Barney's, the matter of Vernon and her mother reared its head once more.

"Oh, he's fine, I suppose," Gladys said. "You were right. He's just shy."

"Mm," I said.

"He's actually quite handsome in the right light."

How could she torture me so? How could she be so kind as to accept me without judgment, to adopt me as her pet, and yet be so cruel as to subject me to the possibility of this other man?

Gladys squared the bill, and when we left Barney's, the unwelcome subject of Vernon followed us out onto the sidewalk.

"Oh, I could get used to him, I suppose, but I could never love him," she said. "Not the way I loved Richard."

Deceased or not, the mention of Richard was another sucker punch to the solar plexus. Was she testing me or merely tormenting me?

"Talking to Richard was like talking to you," she said. "I could say anything without fear of judgment. I just can't imagine saying the things I say to you to Vernon. He's so . . . safe."

It seemed a reckless mood took hold of Gladys with this revelation. In retrospect, it had probably taken hold of her the moment I'd become anything more to her than a mental patient.

"You know what?" she said. "I'm tired of convention. I'm tired of doing what the rest of the world sees as my duty! What did Richard's duty ever get him but an early grave?"

"At least he died a hero," I observed.

"And that's supposed to console me?" she said. "Have you any idea of the loneliness I've endured?"

"I think I have an idea," I said.

"And who have you lost?"

I might have backpedaled there, but I was emboldened by the very candor that Gladys had broached herself.

"Who have I kept?" I said. "What do I have left? Do you suppose you're the only person who has lost what is most dear to them?"

"I'm sorry, Eugene," she said. "Of course you've known loss. How could I even say such a thing? You're right, I'm being selfish. I'm a terrible person."

"You're not," I said. "I didn't say that."

"But I am," she said.

"Gladys, you're the best person I've ever met," I said.

That's when it all came unwound. That's when any semblance of good judgment took leave of Gladys.

"Let's catch the car downtown," she said.

"But it's after four o'clock," I said. "Shouldn't we start—"

"C'mon," she said.

Grabbing hold of my hand, she began running down Santa Monica Boulevard, and I had no recourse but to follow. On the car ride downtown, Gladys seemed to be intoxicated by her own heedlessness.

"Who cares what my mother or anyone else thinks?" she said. "You only get one time around."

"Well, if you're lucky you only get one," I said.

That's when Gladys did the unthinkable: She turned to me and kissed me right there on the streetcar, the longest, most fervent smacker these lips have ever known. I was breathless by the time I extricated myself from her advance.

"You're one of a kind, Eugene. You know that? C'mon, let's get off here," she said.

Gladys hopped off at Union Terminal and dragged me along with her. She began leading me briskly toward the heart of downtown with no discernible plan. I was both exhilarated and anxious at this unscheduled development. Soon we arrived in the Flower District, an explosion of color like I'd never before seen, red and orange and purple and yellow. Booth after booth, block after block, of cut flowers of every conceivable variety. The smell of them hung in the air like some paradisical vapor, overpowering the miasma of grit and smog and exhaust that permeated the rest of the great teeming city.

"Buy me some flowers, Eugene," she said.

Before I could tender my feeble reply, Gladys was already fishing around in her purse for the money.

"You pick them," she said. "I'll wait right here. Make it a surprise."

As Gladys sat on the curb, as radiant as any bouquet herself, I proceeded up and down the block collecting an arrangement worthy of my affection. The result was a mélange of red and white roses and purple orchids and yellow snapdragons with one gigantic white hydrangea. Maybe flower arrangement wasn't my specialty, but Gladys must have appreciated my effort at least.

"Eugene, it's . . . stupendous," she said when I presented her with the bouquet.

She clutched the arrangement prominently at her side as we strode arm in arm, south down Spring Street, then aimlessly about town on side streets, block after block, until we ended up once more in the heart of town. I could have walked arm in arm like that forever. Never in all my life had I glowed so! For once, I was the hero of my own story! With Gladys on my arm, I was a giant amongst men at five foot seven and a half. And I could only guess that Gladys was feeling the same. For why else would she stop suddenly in the middle of the sidewalk in front of a dumpy hotel in Skid Row and suggest the unthinkable?

"Let's get a room," she said.

I blushed to the roots of my hair at the suggestion.

"Here?" I said.

"Yes."

"This is no place for someone like you," I said.

"Eugene, I'm not even sure who I am anymore," she said. "It's liable to be very affordable, don't you think?"

"But I'm due back at the hos—"

"Sshh," she said, redoubling her grip on my hand, pulling me through the front door to the lobby, where she approached the desk with no hesitation at all and booked a room, paying in advance at the behest of the clerk.

The Oviatt was everything the Flower District was not: drab and dingy, and smelling of not bougainvillea and tulips but stale cigarettes and mop water. The red-carpeted stairs seemed to sag beneath our every step as we ascended to the third floor, thumpity-thump, and down the hallway to 312.

I shall not elucidate the act itself, but to say it was executed enthusiastically and, it seemed to me, anyway, reciprocally for the duration of perhaps forty minutes. No reservations were heeded, no precautions taken. We were as candid in our lovemaking as in our conversation. Afterward, to my embarrassment, I cried softly for reasons I could not quite comprehend. Gratitude was amongst the emotions inciting my riot of sensations as I listened to the rise and fall of our breathing, staring up at the water-damaged ceiling. Despite our squalid environs, anything seemed possible in those hushed moments.

Until Gladys broke the silence.

"Maybe this was a mistake," she said.

"I warned you this wasn't a place for somebody like you," I said.

Indeed, a cursory inventory of the peeling wallpaper and shoddily painted molding, the window sealed closed by countless careless coats of paint, the bedsheets smelling of starch, was all the confirmation one would ever need to support such an argument.

"We should have gone to the Biltmore," I said.

"No," she said. "I mean, all of it. You, me, that this even happened. What was I thinking?"

Instantly besieged by confusion, I launched myself into a panic state. I had no clue what to make of Gladys's quick turnabout or how to respond to it, let alone remedy the situation. What had I done? Was I a terrible lover? Or had she finally glimpsed in the dreary light of the Oviatt Hotel that I was unworthy of her affections? My mind was spinning cartwheels. What more could I do to persuade this woman that I was the right choice, that despite my miserable prospects, my questionable stability, and my status as a ward of Metropolitan, I was worthy?

"Maybe you're right," she said, much to my relief. "Maybe it's just this place. Let's get out of here."

Without further ceremony she climbed out of bed, dressing hastily as I followed her cue. On our way out the door, Gladys stopped, returned to the nightstand, opened the drawer, and filched the Gideons Bible.

"What the heck?" she said, still reckless in spite of her misgivings. "Something to remember the place by."

By the time we descended the groaning stairwell to the lobby, Gladys was almost back to her old self, but I was still off-kilter from her conflicting messages, still raw and a bit jittery from the shock of it all. Something had gone wrong upstairs and I still didn't know what, but I knew in my gut that it was more likely attributable to me than the lousy room.

At the foot of the stairs, Gladys crossed the lobby purposefully, with me right in her shadow as she pushed through the front door and paused immediately in the middle of the sidewalk to draw a breath of fresh air. There was a drunk holding up a lamppost out front, and I caught him ogling Gladys shamelessly.

"C'mon," I said, taking Gladys by the elbow.

"Hey, toots," said the drunk. "Nice set of gams you got there."

Presumably accustomed to such harassment, Gladys merely blushed. But when the louse reached out and grabbed a handful of Gladys's rump as we passed by, something inside me snapped. It wasn't just my most recent failure upstairs but a lifetime of anxiety, my guilt, my shame, my powerlessness, the overriding sense that I was nothing, nobody, no more worthy of Gladys's heart than that lousy stewbum; all of it came to a head in that instant, and before I knew it, I was on top of the man, battering his face with both fists long after I'd made my point, until the clerk rushed out of the lobby and pulled me off him. Already there was a crowd of people gathering around.

Nose bloodied, the drunk managed to regain his feet with the help of the clerk and staunched the bleeding with his filthy shirtsleeve.

"What the hell's wrong with you, Mac?" he said. "I didn't mean anything by it."

Before Gladys and I could effect our retreat, there was a beat cop on the scene, and shortly after that the LAPD came for me in a squad car and hauled me off to the station.

That was the end of my Sundays with Gladys.

Wayne sat in the swivel chair, agog, as though some great mystery had been revealed to him.

"So that's when it happened," he said. "Grandpa Vern never even knew."

"About us?"

"About my mom," he said. "You'd have to be pretty good at math, I suppose."

"What are you talking about? What's there to know about Nancy?"

Wayne looked at me searchingly until it was clear my ignorance was not feigned.

"Wait," he said. "You really don't know? She never told—? Of course, why would she if . . . ? And if you never saw her again . . . ?"

"Told me what?" I said.

"And all this time I just thought you were an asshole. You never even suspected . . . ?"

"Suspected what?"

Wayne gave me one last concerted look.

"That my grandmother was pregnant. That Nancy was your daughter," he said.

Had I not been flat on my back already, surely the shock of this revelation would have put me there.

"But . . . how can you be sure she was mine, if . . . ?"

"She knew," said Wayne. "A woman knows. It's in the journals. And besides, Nancy looked just like you, right?"

"Looked?" I said.

"She passed away two years ago," said Wayne.

"But . . . how did . . . ?"

"Stomach cancer," he said.

"But if . . . why didn't Gladys tell me if . . . ? If she was my . . . ? Why did she . . . ?"

But the answers could not have been more obvious. On every count the answer was me; if it wasn't my lack of prospects, it was my immaturity, or my mental instability, or my being a thousand years old. Of course no woman in her right mind would start a family with me, even if it was my child. Of course she'd find a better option if one was within her reach. Who could blame her? My failures were even greater than I'd ever imagined.

There in my bed, I was suddenly beset by the crushing weight of shame, by the sheer extent of my ineffectualness. I'd had seven lifetimes to mold myself into someone worthwhile, and I was still an abject failure, still unlovable, still unclaimed, still unconnected to the larger world by any meaningful measure because nobody, not one person, had ever claimed me without relinquishing me soon after. I was forever an orphan.

Then it dawned on me.

"Well, wait a minute," I said, looking at Wayne as though for the first time. "Then, that means you're . . ."

"Yes," said Wayne. "I'm your biological grandson."

Sound and Fury

My mood continued to grow increasingly wistful as the inevitable approached. How much loneliness and isolation had I endured to reach this juncture? How many connections had I missed, how many opportunities had eluded me, how many relationships had I failed to forge?

I could forgive the world almost anything much more easily now, its cruelty and its senseless design, knowing that I would soon leave it behind, if only temporarily. Suddenly, I was a bereaved father, and a grandfather. As far as I could tell, Wayne no longer begrudged me. I suppose my side of the story had won him over, and he could see his grandmother's part in all of it. Not only did my life suddenly have biological implications, I had found in Angel a true friend. Why should I want to leave the world now that I was telling my stories at last, that I finally had a sympathetic audience, a stage upon which to strut and fret my hour?

"What was she like as a mother, Nancy?" I asked Wayne, back the next day, again straddling the office chair.

"She was the best," he said.

"Were you her only child?"

"I had a younger sister, Leigh Anne," he said. "Gone, too, I'm afraid. Complications from COVID last May."

My heart plummeted.

Wayne set a hand on my shoulder. "You would have liked her," he said. "She was quite a bit like Grandma Glad."

"How so?" I said.

"Adventurous. Kind. Supersmart. She looked like Grandma Glad, too, same dark brown eyes, but not quite as tall. She even had a little mole under her nose."

After all my histories, recent and ancient, real and fabricated, here I was learning about an entire legacy I never knew I had.

"Do you have a picture?" I said.

"I can bring one," he said.

"I'd like that."

"Can I get you anything?" said Wayne.

"Nah, I'm fine."

"How's the pain?"

"Not too bad," I said.

The truth was that pain and discomfort were my constant companions. Not only did my every joint ache, so, too, did my every gland, and despite my meager appetite, my swollen belly felt overfull at all times.

"Life Saver?"

"Okay," I said. "Why not?"

Wayne produced an open roll from his pants pocket, the silver lining scrunched and tattered at the open end.

"I think yellow is pineapple, how about it?"

"Sure."

"Mmm, I've got watermelon," he said.

Even though the damn thing was clacking against the back of his teeth, somehow, for the first time, it didn't set me on edge.

....

As my passing drew nearer, I found my focus easily diffused, my attention easily distracted. My mind was wont to wander, my thoughts more fluid than concrete. Because of this lapse, I could only read for twenty minutes at a time before my concentration failed me or my mind grew weary. In an unsolicited gesture, Angel began reading aloud to me at daily intervals, even staying after his shift sometimes to finish a chapter of O'Callaghan's wonderful—if occasionally misinformed—*A History of Medieval Spain*, liberally peppered with Angel's responses to the subject matter.

"I dunno, Geno," he said upon reading about the expulsions that followed the Reconquista. "Seems to me like the Christians were less tolerant than the Muslims."

"You're not wrong," I said. "And we haven't even gotten to the Inquisition yet. But if we were intolerant it was because the Moors had set upon us against our wills. They were not our guests, not our gracious hosts; they were our conquerors. But of course, for me, it was much more personal than that."

Even at a glance it was clear that Assad was irritable, brow furrowed, no hint of that game smile upon his face. Nor did he greet us on this occasion with his customary pretense of nonchalance. No, Assad was all business as we kneeled before him in the candlelit chamber.

"As you might have guessed, my men have arrived back from the coast," he said. "And what do you presume they discovered there?"

"Forgive me," I said to Gaya urgently. "I've betrayed the resistance. I was only trying to ensure that—"

"Stop!" yelled Assad. "You will insult me no further with this mockery. Do you really think I'm that clueless?"

Even as I cast my eyes down, I could feel Gaya leering back at Assad defiantly.

"I have called you because you've broken the terms of our pact," he said. "I kept you around in good faith in exchange for credible information. You not only failed to deliver, but you also willfully engaged in subterfuge. For this, there will be dire consequences. While you may consider them to be cruel, these are the rules of engagement."

"Kill us," said Gaya. "Go ahead."

"That is exactly what my superiors would have me do. But I now see that in doing so, I'd be letting you off easy," said Assad. "For all the trouble you've put me through, it is incumbent upon me as a protector of al-Andalus to make this more difficult for you."

"Torture us, then," she said. "If you wish to sate your appetite for cruelty."

"You misunderstand me. It is not an appetite for cruelty that I serve," he said. "It is my duty to al-Andalus, no more and no less. No doubt, your people would do the same. You have willfully defied our governance, you have subverted valuable resources, you have lied, stolen, and killed for your 'cause,' which, as far as I can see, is only yourselves. But I shall not kill both of you. No, I shall kill but one of you. And you, thief, I shall force you to choose."

My blood froze in my veins.

"So," said Assad. "Whose life will it be, your lover's or your own?"

"Mine," I said without hesitation.

Assad looked at me meaningfully.

"I suspected as much," he said. "In somebody else it might be a noble gesture. In you, it's just predictable. Guard," he called.

Angel leaned in breathlessly from his place on the office chair.

"No way," he said. "So, this is it, homie? This is where you die?"

"No," I said. "On this occasion, Assad did not honor his terms."

"You mean . . . ?"

"In choosing myself, I had chosen Gaya, because Assad knew her life was of more value to me than my own. Don't you see? I should have said Gaya. I had no interest in living in a world without Gaya anyway."

"So he . . . ?"

"Proceed," Assad ordered the guard.

"No!" I yelled. "Gaya!"

Straining against my bonds, I jumped to my feet and tried to dissuade the guard, but he kicked me to the floor, where I landed with a stupefying impact. Before I could protest further, Assad himself placed his foot on my neck to restrain me.

Desperately, I watched the scene play out, my cheek ground into the grit of the floor.

Gaya did not budge, nor utter a word, but despite her façade of defiance, she was shaking visibly as the guard positioned himself behind her and unsheathed his sword.

"The sonofa— He did it right there in front of you?" said Angel.

"No," I said.

"Then, what?" said Angel.

"He ordered the guard to stop at the last instant."

"And what happened?"

"He let her go," I said.

"But . . . why?"

"To punish me," I said.

"But if he saved her, then . . ."

"He took her from me just as sure as if she'd died. For he knew I would never see her again."

"So, then he did kill you after all?"

"No," I said. "He locked me back up."

"For how long?"

"I can't say."

"Did you ever get out?" said Angel.

"Yes," I said. "Eventually."

"But you never found her?"

"No."

"So, what happened after that?"

"I lived," I said, fighting back a grief so old it defined me. "And lived and lived."

"What about Gaya?"

"I never saw her again."

An Uneventful Life

My arrest outside the Oviatt spelled the end of me and Gladys. Not only was it our last supervised outing, it was also our last visit. I did not receive so much as a letter from Gladys for the remainder of my stay at Metropolitan. As they say in the modern parlance, I was ghosted. And who could blame Gladys?

Despite my devastation, I did not allow myself to wallow as I had the first time I'd lost Gladys. Instead, I compartmentalized my anguish and surrendered to the tedium of institutional life as though Gladys had never existed, resigned to the possibility that one day they'd have to set me free. And when that day came, I would start a life without her.

It took six years to persuade hospital administrators that I was competent for release upon my twenty-fifth birthday, by which time Drs. Maxwell and Spencer had both retired. I left Metropolitan with a single change of clothing and forty pounds of books. The benefactor of a sizable, though not extravagant, trust, I was able to rent a "furnished" apartment off Normandie on West Maplewood. The flat was a small, shabby affair, consisting of a single room with a kitchenette and a tiny bathroom splashed with pink paint and black tile. As for the furnishings, there was a single bed, a desk, and a chair that toggled between the desk and a small dining table suitable for two. It wasn't much, but it was sunny, and centrally located, and mine alone.

Within a month, I secured employment at the Union 76 filling station on Wilshire, pumping gas, and cleaning windshields, and filling tires. I wore a uniform consisting of gray coveralls, which I laundered on Sundays, and a white cap emblazoned with the Union 76 logo. Most of the service boys, Chet, and Phil, and Henry, and Pete, were in their late teens, while the manager, Don, a thick-waisted prematurely balding fellow, was somewhere in the neighborhood of his late thirties. Without meaning to, I was following in my father's footsteps, grease beneath my fingernails and a persistent whiff of petrol following me everywhere I went.

Thus, I began leading a normal life for the first time. I worked every minute of my eight hours with a fastidiousness that did not escape Don's notice. The truth is, I enjoyed the work of greeting the people, small-talking with them if they were so inclined. I even grew to like the smell of gasoline. After work, on the way back to my flat, I walked to the grocery, where I almost always exchanged pleasantries with the checker on duty. I usually ate with the radio on for company, KFWB or KHJ or KNX, then read my history books until I turned in for the night.

Weekends, I went to the pictures or caught the Blue Bus to Santa Monica, where I'd gaze at the ocean or sit beneath the pier with my eyes closed, listening to the distant pounding of the breakers and the hiss of the frothy swash, and let my past lives wash over me, ebbing and flowing with the surf. I never spoke of these lives to anybody and had no intention of ever doing so again. Had I entertained any urge to talk about them, I would have had a difficult time finding an audience anyway, for I had no friends to speak of, only my work associates, whose concerns were mostly of an adolescent variety: girls, and parties, and the popular music of the day. I was lonely but not completely unhappy. Free at last from institutional life, I was content to exist as a face in the crowd. Though it might seem an uneventful life, it was a consistent one, and I needed that, for my life up to that point had been nothing if not inconsistent. Not since my days with Oscar had I known such pleasant predictability and routine.

One day I was pumping gas at the Union when a powder-blue Chevy Bel Air pulled up at the opposite pump. As soon as Henry started filling her up, the driver, a tall, lean fellow in a baggy gray suit, climbed out and stretched briefly before proceeding inside to Don at the front desk. That's when I noticed the kids in the backseat and the woman in the passenger seat, applying mascara in the rear-view mirror. I immediately recognized her.

"Gladys!" I shouted, waving my hand.

When she did not respond, I stopped pumping and left my station, all but running to the passenger door of the Chevy, where I rapped on the window, spooking Gladys, who dropped her mascara wand with a start, then bent down to retrieve it before rolling down her window.

"Yes?" she said. "Can I help you?"

"Gladys, it's me!" I said.

She looked at me unsurely but seemed to register nothing familiar.

"Eugene Miles," I said.

All the color left her face at once, and her eyes darted instinctively to the two girls in the backseat before returning promptly to me, agitated.

"Eugene," she said. "I . . . it's so good to see you!"

Though she sounded somewhat less than thrilled, it might have just been the shock of seeing me again so unexpectedly.

"What are you doing here?" she said.

"I figured the uniform would be a dead giveaway."

"Right. Of course," she said. "So you . . . ?"

"Yeah, they finally let me out. Maxwell and Spencer both re-tired, and the new regime saw me for what I was, a pussycat."

"That's wonderful," she said, but she still sounded a little pan-icky.

"Looks like you've been busy," I said, indicating the girls in the backseat with a nod.

"Yes, I certainly have," she said, her eyes seeking out her hus-band, who was still at the front register, conversing with Don.

"Have they got names?" I said.

"Oh, yeah, right, this is Donna, and this is Nancy."

"Pleased to meet you," I said.

But the girls just sat there silently. Was it me? Did I frighten people somehow?

Gladys began to fuss with her purse, replacing her mascara and generally digging around as though looking for something else.

"I wondered what happened to you," I said. "You just . . . disap-peared."

Gladys was clearly mortified by now, and I suppose I couldn't blame her, confronted out of the blue by a former mental patient who believed himself to be a thousand years old, a man whom she'd slept with, whom she'd watched beat a hobo half-senseless, and—I now know—with whom she had conceived a daughter.

"I owe you an apology for never coming back, Eugene. My life was very . . . complicated at the time," she said.

I had so many questions, so much pent-up confusion and sadness and anger, but I knew for once in my life that the past was really the past, and that dredging it up would benefit no one.

"Nah," I said, waving it off. "You had bigger things waiting for you. I understand. Besides, I sort of lost it in front of the Oviatt."

This acknowledgment seemed to disarm her somewhat.

"We did have some good times, though, didn't we?" she said.

Only the best of my life, but I didn't dare say as much under the circumstances. Before I could conjure an alternate reply, her husband took his place in the driver's seat.

"Vernon, this is Eugene, an old friend from college," said Gladys.

"Pleased to meet you, Eugene."

"Likewise," I said without extending a hand through the window.

"Well," said Gladys. "It was good to see you, Eugene, really. I'm glad to know you're doing well."

"You too," I said. "You have a beautiful family."

And that was that. Gladys walked out of my life yet again.

The remainder of that day, I was distracted as I replayed the encounter with Gladys in my head again and again, looking for some shred of deeper meaning, some secret message Gladys might have imparted that only I could understand. My preoccupation didn't go unnoticed by Don.

"Miles, what is it with you today?" he said. "Get your head out of the clouds. You've got someone on pump six."

Indeed, my head was somewhere in the ether. For days, I waited hopefully for Gladys's return, alone or with family, any opportunity to be in her presence. Days turned into weeks, and I reasoned that I had probably scared Gladys off with my familiarity, or she would have returned by then, or left some sign or hint of her whereabouts. Or maybe it wasn't that easy for her, maybe she lived clear across the basin in East Los Angeles, or in Orange County. I rationalized beyond all reasonable measure, until finally my hopes began to wane as weeks turned to months, months to years, and years to decades.

The next time I saw Gladys was on the TV, twenty-one years later. I was still living in the same apartment off Normandie.

By then, I was working as a stenographer downtown, but I never saw any reason to leave the old flat, which suited my simple needs. One evening, while I was eating a frozen turkey dinner and watching my twelve-inch black and white Toshiba, the KNXT news ran a human-interest story about a history teacher at Rubidoux High School in Riverside who had won eleven thousand dollars on a TV game show. They cut to the teacher with the reporter, and again I recognized Gladys immediately. Her hair had gone mostly gray, but she still had the same high cheekbones, the same intelligent dark eyes and full lips, and yes, the little mole beneath her nostril.

It turned out that the trivia question that had ended her fortuitous run on the quiz show was about the Macedonian dynasty, specifically Constantine VII. Upon learning this I was outraged at the difficulty of the question. I'd actually lived during a portion of Constantine VII's reign, and I couldn't have answered that question with a gun to my head, so how was a high school teacher from Riverside supposed to answer it? But Gladys was so gracious in her brief interview. I guess eleven thousand dollars was quite a bit of money back then, but Constantine VII was still not a fair subject in my estimation.

God, how I missed Gladys, even if she wasn't Gaya as I'd once so fiercely believed. How I yearned for those long-ago conversations, those meandering walks through old Los Angeles, that intimacy, that candor, shoulder to shoulder through those classics of the cinema, marking our Sundays with the great stars of the day, Claude Rains and Henry Fonda and Gene Tierney, those meals at Barney's and the Derby and Chasen's, patty melts and Swiss steak, that electric conversation and the easy silence.

"What do you plan to do with your winnings?" the interviewer asked Gladys.

"Well, first, I think I'll go to Spain," she said.

The interviewer passed it back to the anchor, who wrapped up with some smarmy commentary, which I scarcely heard because my mind was already in Riverside.

I had to see Gladys; it was imperative. I couldn't stand not seeing her again; I'd go crazy.

"Wait, but how did you find her?" said Wayne from his place at my bedside.

"The phone book, dummy. I knew her name, I knew she was in Riverside; it didn't take Sam Spade to figure that one out," I said.

"And so you just called her out of the blue after all those years? And what, Grandpa Vern answered?"

"No, your grandmother," I said.

"And what did you say when she answered?"

"Gladys, it's me. Eugene!"

"Eugene?"

A brief silence set in, and I knew I'd better start talking fast.

"I just wanted to congratulate you on the game show!" I said. "I just saw the story on KNXT. What a kick!"

"Oh," she said. "Well, um, thank you, Eugene."

"That Constantine VII question was an outright travesty! Obviously, they just got tired of you taking their money."

She let out a nervous half laugh. "Eugene, how did you find me?" she said.

"The phone book, dummy."

Again, the line went silent, and I knew I couldn't afford to let the silence last.

"Hey, I owe you a dinner," I said. "A lot of dinners, actually. A lot of movies, too, for that matter."

"Eugene, I . . . I've been married to Vernon for nearly thirty years. I'm not in the habit of—"

"I don't mean a date, Gladys. Just old friends catching up. Hey, we can talk about history, and movies, and—"

"Eugene, I'm really not sure that's such a good idea. . . ."

"I'm lonely," I said, and it was the truest thing I've ever said. "I just want to talk, you know, like old times. Please."

Persuading her in such a manner, by bluntly soliciting her sympathy, was not my proudest moment. But I'd always been honest with Gladys, so why stop now?

We met the following Saturday in West Covina, at King George's Smorgasbord, a venue I picked for its relative proximity to Gladys, so as to make things as easy as possible for her. The place was a dump, but the Derby or Barney's or any of our old haunts were too far from Riverside, and too symbolic to boot. I needed this to go smoothly.

"So, it *was* a date?" said Wayne from the swivel chair.

"No," I said.

"Coffee is a catch-up," Wayne said. "Dinner is a date."

"It was 1977, Wayne. Nobody went out to coffee. Besides," I said, "I half expected Vernon to show up with her. Or the girls."

I was careful not to dress up for the occasion, and I certainly didn't bring flowers. I had next to no experience with these occasions. Friendly, but not too familiar, I told myself. Don't bring up Metropolitan or the Oviatt, stick to those Sunday outings, those great pictures, and those glorious evening walks. Ask her about her job. Talk about history.

I arrived ten minutes before Gladys and chose what I reasoned to be the least private table in the middle of the dining room, not fifteen feet from the buffet. I ordered two glasses of wine and immediately regretted it as being too presumptuous, and almost called the order back. But before I could, Gladys walked through the door in the modest attire of jeans and a high-necked blouse.

"Gladys!" I said, standing to greet her with a handshake. "So good to see you."

"And you," she said.

"So, what's it like to be rich and famous?"

"Ha!" she said. "I wouldn't go that far. But a few people have recognized me from the show."

Though she demurred, I could see that I'd flattered her.

"Shall we?" I said.

We grabbed our empty plates and silverware, still hot from the dishwasher, at the head of the buffet and began working our way through the line. Gladys went straight for the Brussels sprouts, I for the green bean casserole. We both scrupulously avoided the meatballs.

"And how are your daughters?" I said, slopping some mashed potatoes on my platter. "They must be all grown up now."

"Donna just graduated from Pepperdine with a degree in fine arts. And Nancy is a social worker," she said.

"Any grandchildren?"

Gladys seemed to hesitate at the question.

"A grandson, yes. And what about you?" she said, changing the subject. "Did you ever marry?"

"No," I said.

"Any hopefuls?"

"Not even close," I said. "I've been meaning to get a cat for twenty years. If anybody can relate to cats, it's me. I mean, I used to be one, right?"

Gladys looked a little uneasy with the reference. It was my turn to change the subject.

"So, you chose history over psychology?" I said.

"Actually, it chose me," she said. "I find it so fascinating."

Our glasses of wine were waiting for us when we returned to the table. Gladys didn't seem to mind, as she soon took a healthy sip from her goblet.

"So, what eras do you teach?" I said.

"Ancient, medieval, and twentieth century," said Gladys.

"Medieval, eh?"

"The kids love it," she said. "Especially the boys."

"Tell me," I said, unable to resist the temptation. "What are your thoughts on the Moors conquering Spain?"

"At least they brought culture," she said.

"They ruined the Visigoths."

"They elevated the Visigoths!"

"Oh? And how is that?"

"By educating them. By freeing them from feudalism," said Gladys.

"No, no, no," I insisted, an edge of annoyance creeping into my voice. "That's not how it was at all. The Moors didn't cross the Strait of Gibraltar to save the Visigoths! The Christians, the Jews, nobody asked the Moors to come grace them with their culture."

"But that's just it," said Gladys. "There was no culture before the Moors!"

"Oh, ho, ho," I said. "Is that a fact? No culture? Gothic culture was not culture? Visigothic law was not law? What about all the basilican architecture that survives to this day?"

"The Moors brought science, they brought art. They encouraged diversity."

"Ha! They tolerated diversity, there's a difference."

"No, they encouraged it," she said. "The Moors enlightened Spain. The Moors didn't erase anyone, they didn't shove their culture down anyone's throat."

"But they did in an everyday sense. They made you feel like less. Trust me, I was there."

With that, Gladys stiffened slightly, looking ill at ease.

"I thought you were beyond all of that," she said, her eyes gravitating toward the nearest exit.

"All of what?" I said.

"Past lives," said Gladys.

"And why should I be beyond them?" I said. "They are part of who I am."

"Eugene, they're delusions," she said.

"If I could be over them I would, believe me," I said. "But they're not delusions."

"What about Dr. Stowell?" she said. "Do you still believe in him?"

"Of course not," I said. "He was a delusion."

I really didn't like where this conversation was headed, either, so I switched gears abruptly once more.

"Hey, did you see *High Anxiety*?" I said.

"Yeah."

"What did you think?"

"It made me uncomfortable. Particularly the setting. You didn't find it unsettling?"

"It was a comedy."

"I guess I don't think mental illness is funny," she said.

Clearly, Gladys and I had grown apart. Ten minutes, and already I was running out of subject changes. Family was a brick wall. History was a bust. And movies were trending in the wrong direction.

"The pictures were better back in the golden era," I said. "Don't you think?"

"Absolutely," she said.

"Remember *Dark Passage*?"

"That was a good one," she said.

"What about *California?*"

"I remember seeing it with you at the Hitching Post. We ate at the Barney's afterward."

"The Derby, actually, beforehand. What a great afternoon that was," I said.

That's all I wanted, some acknowledgment that I ever meant something to somebody, some proof of my existence. And once again, Gladys had granted me as much.

"Hey, I brought my Instamatic," I said. "What say we get a picture?"

Before Gladys could answer, I flagged down a busboy and fished the camera out of my coat pocket.

"So, this is the picture?" interjected Wayne from the swivel chair, clutching the very picture in question.

"Yep," I said.

"How about that?" said Wayne. "You've got a hell of a memory, Eugene."

Impossible

My condition grew precipitously worse in the days after I let Wayne take the picture with him. I seemed to be getting weaker by the hour, and my appetite was almost nonexistent. It's not that I didn't want to eat; my body just wouldn't accept nourishment. Everything tasted like burnt copper on my tongue or smelled like a teakettle left on the burner overnight. The discomfort in my joints was almost impossible to endure without drugs, and most days I didn't even get out of bed to use the bathroom, but submitted to the ignominy of the bedpan, which Angel, or one of the other orderlies, emptied. And yet, I was in a good place mentally. I was enjoying the company. It seemed that between Angel and Wayne, I always had a friend at my bedside.

"So, after the buffet, that was it?" said Wayne, customarily straddling the swivel chair. "She ghosted you again?"

"I honestly don't think she meant to," I said. "Her life was already so full, I think her good intentions simply failed her. I called two or three times over the next year and even left a message once, but I never heard back. Then, eight years ago, thirty-seven years after our last visit, Gladys appeared again out of the blue."

I had been at Desert Greens for nearly four years and in that time had not had a single visitor, thus I was incredulous when a liaison from the front desk, a young woman named Frieda, came to my quarters to inform me that I had a visitor.

"Impossible," I said.

"I'm quite sure," said Frieda. "Come see for yourself."

Who could it possibly be? I wondered. Sad as it sounds, I could not think of a solitary person on earth who would come to visit me, unless it was a lawyer, or a banker come to tell me that my trust had all dried up.

Imagine my shock and delight when I saw it was none other than Gladys awaiting me in the commons, now a woman of some eighty-nine years of age. Never mind her diminished stature and slightly humped back, nor her wispy white hair thinning in patches. A lifetime of wrinkles and skin tags could not disguise her beauty: the perceptive brown eyes, the haughty cheekbones, the native intelligence and confidence that shone all around her like an aura— Gladys, my true, my one and only, friend! The mere sight of her was like a shot of adrenaline. Not five minutes prior, I had been bereft of will, totally indifferent to the world outside the prison of myself, and suddenly I was gregarious, self-assured, imbued with the sort of charm I'd always wished I'd possessed.

"So, there you are, I've been waiting for you," I said. "I thought you'd never show up. Boy, that must have been some traffic jam."

She laughed as though in spite of herself.

I reached my hand out to her, and like a small miracle she took it. Oh, how good that felt, to cradle her hand in mine for the first time in half a lifetime.

"Well, come on, let me show you the greens," I said.

Back then, the greens were actually green, the palms were young and supple and meticulously manicured, a far cry from the shaggy, blighted specimens they would become. The picnic tables were brand-new back then, smooth with shellac and sturdy. And the Ord Mountains were still the Ords, craggy gray-brown and timeless on the horizon.

"It's nice here," she said. "Nancy and Donna have been trying to get me into one of these places since Vernon passed."

"I'm sorry to hear it," I said.

I wasn't lying with my condolence, but at the same time my heart was beating triplets at the possibility of Gladys's joining me at Desert Greens. Wasn't that what she was hinting at?

"How recently did he pass?" I said.

"Six years," she said. "Six years that feel like thirty."

"Maybe the girls are right," I said. "Maybe a change of scenery would be good. I really can't say enough about this place. The facilities, the resources, the amenities, the staff."

"I could never leave my house, not willingly, not after all I've been through with it: the girls, Vernon, all my years at Rubidoux. No, I'm staying put for as long as I can hold out."

"I'm telling you, the food is pretty good here," I said.

"You've always made me smile, Eugene."

"I only wish you would've given me more chances," I said.

"Me too," she said. "I brought you a little keepsake." She produced a book from her cumbersome purse. "Do you remember?"

She handed me the old Bible, and I felt my face color, for I recognized it immediately as the Gideons Bible she'd filched from the Oviatt Hotel in what felt like another life, and everything came rushing back, all the shame and embarrassment and confusion of my undoing. The years had scarcely dulled any of it.

"I had never been with anyone except Richard," she said.

"And you chose me," I said.

"I did," she said. "And I have no regrets."

I had so many questions for Gladys that I didn't know where to begin, so many old emotions I'd been carrying around, all of them suddenly as raw as if Gladys had broken my heart yesterday.

"I don't understand," I said.

"I was young," she said. "And I was scared, and I wanted somebody to save me, even though that ran contrary to who I was."

"And I wasn't going to save you?" I said.

"No," she said. "It didn't seem so."

Of course, she was right. I couldn't save her if I couldn't save myself. She'd given me every opportunity to prove myself and I had failed. To make her explain her decision all these decades later seemed unfair.

"Gladys," I said, "it's a reasonable explanation, it really is. But you don't owe me one."

"I do," she said.

"No," I said softly, and I held my finger to her lip. "You're here now. And that means the world to me."

Gladys set her hand atop mine and smiled. How was this happening? And why? After all this time, why did she find her way back to me? More than I needed to know why she'd abandoned me, I had to know why she'd found me again.

"Why did you come?" I said. "After all these years?"

"I've been thinking about you," she said.

My heart thrilled to hear her say such a thing. I was eighty-five years old, but I may as well have been eighteen all over again.

"How did you find me?"

"The phone book, dummy."

"And why were you thinking of me?" I said. "Was it my dashing good looks? My magnetic personality?"

"Well," she said, "about a year and a half ago, after my hip surgery, I had a, well . . . I don't quite know what to call it. Not a dream, not a memory, but a sort of vision."

It was happening. It was finally happening. I knew it in every fiber of my being. She'd finally found her way back to Gaya.

"What was the vision?"

"It was a man with his face pressed to the floor. A large man in a robe was standing on his neck. The man on the floor was desperate, there were tears running out his eyes and puddling on the floor. It was like he was pleading directly to me. He kept calling out a name."

"Gaya," I said.

"Yes," said Gladys.

There it was at last.

"So, you believe me?" I said. "You finally believe me!"

"No," she said. "Not exactly."

"But . . . how could you know? How could you see me if . . . ?"

"I don't know," she said. "Suggestion, maybe. Coincidence. Maybe it was the painkillers."

"No, Gladys, it wasn't," I said. "It was destiny, just like I told you the first time I met you."

"I don't think so," she said. "But whatever it was, I took it as a sign. I knew I had to see you. To say goodbye."

"Goodbye? You just got here," I said.

She smiled sadly, like she'd smiled at me a lifetime ago when I'd first professed my affection for her.

"I'm dying," she said.

"Dying? Dying of what?"

"Who knows?" she said. "I just know it's coming."

"After all these years, you drove out here from Riverside to tell me that? Did a doctor tell you you were dying?"

"I don't need a doctor to tell me," she said.

"Gladys, what's wrong? Why are you saying this? Do you want to die, is that what you're saying?"

"That's not it," she said. "But I suppose I do, now that you mention it."

"What's so bad about your life that you want to die?"

"Nothing," she said. "It's just time. Oh, but let's not be gloomy. What about you, what's going on in your life?"

"Most mornings I don't want to get out of bed, and I haven't had a visitor since I moved in here. What else do you need to know?"

"I'm sorry, Eugene," she said.

"Oh, it's not that bad," I said. "I do puzzles, I read books."

"No," she said. "I'm sorry for the pain I caused you so long ago."

She was causing me pain right then, though she didn't know how much. Finally, she was back in my life for all of twenty minutes, and already she was threatening to leave again.

"Come live here," I said.

"You're not listening," she said.

"They do bingo on Wednesday nights. You can play up to four cards."

"Eugene."

"They've got yoga classes," I said.

"Eugene."

"Please," I said. "You can't leave me again. This has been going on for eleven centuries."

"Stop that," she said.

I reached across the picnic table and took both her hands in mine and squeezed them a little harder than I intended to.

"Why?" I said. "Why do you always have to go?"

Gladys extricated her hands, then picked up her bag and got to her feet.

"Where are you going?" I said. "They've got a great chicken salad in the commissary. Here, sit back down. We haven't even talked about movies yet!"

"It was good to see you again, Eugene."

"Gladys, you can't go."

But she strode slowly on her artificial hip across the green, looking back just once to smile that sad smile of hers. Then she turned around again and walked out of my life. Eight days later she walked out of her own life. This life, anyway. I got the call from her daughter Nancy two days after the fact. I thought that was a nice gesture.

When I opened my eyes, I saw Wayne was crying in the swivel chair, and my own eyes began to burn.

"She's in a better place," I said.

It took all the strength I could muster, but I swung my legs around and sat up in bed and got to my feet, and leaning down, a little nauseous from all the movement, I put an arm around Wayne's shoulder and hugged him as best I could manage.

Recognition

Spanish history was officially a wrap, and Angel, God bless him, was reading me Oscar now, *The Picture of Dorian Gray*. I was clearly about to become history again myself, so I figured why not read something with a beating heart, something concerned with the living? I should have learned my lesson way back in Chelsea and governed my life like Oscar governed his, with no other responsibility than to enjoy excess and create beauty. Instead, I'd essentially let my life live me, accepted my circumstances too readily, while taking the bruises and heartbreak and isolation all too personally, unlike Oscar, to whom the whole endeavor was a celebration. But then again, Oscar died at forty-six.

"I dunno, ese," said Angel, setting the book aside. "This is kinda creepy. Who wants to live forever and not get older? That's some billionaire shit, right?"

"It was a different time," I said. "You have to understand that Oscar, his stories, his plays, his essays, they flew in the face of Victorian convention. They were about excess; they were about expression in an era of repression."

"Okay, whatever you say, homie, you were his cat, I guess I'll take your word for it. Probably just over my head. I still like the history better," said Angel.

My God, I'd become selfish in my old age. Poor Angel had listened and listened and listened to me, served me and served me and served me, read to me and read to me and read to me, and what did he get in return, save for an old man concerned exclusively with his own needs and interests? Though my days were numbered, I still had time to be a better friend to Angel.

"How's Elana?" I said.

"She's good," he said. "She's big in the stomach, really showing now. Don't tell her I said that, though, she'll kill me. I like it. I think it's hot. But don't tell her that, either."

"When are you gonna bring her by?" I said. "How am I supposed to tell her anything if I never even meet her?"

"I was gonna bring her last Saturday," he said. "But she was in full-on wedding mode."

"You nervous?" I said.

"Hell no, not about the wedding," he said. "I'm relieved. I thought for sure she was gonna dump my ass, bro."

"She'd be crazy to leave you," I said. "What more could anyone want from a companion? You're kind, loyal, adventurous. . . ."

"Nah," he said, waving it off. "I ain't all that, dog. All I know is, I can't wait to be a pops, you know? I wanna do all the stuff my old man never did with me. Play catch, go fishing, coach her softball team, all of it."

"'Her'?"

"Just a hunch, homie. Whatever it is, I just wanna be there for my kid, really be there—not partway there, all the way there. I know I was scared at first, but now that I know the baby is coming, it's like she can't come soon enough. I can't wait to hold her, you know, this little bitty life made from Elana and me. Who cares if we don't have a lot of money? Not like I ever had any in the first place, right? What matters is just loving her. Man, I can't wait."

Without warning, my eyes brimmed with tears at the simple purity and rightness of Angel's enthusiasm, a development that did not escape his notice.

"Yo, what's wrong, ese?"

"Nothing is wrong," I said. "It's what's right. I'm just so . . . happy for you, for your child."

Angel rested a hand on my shoulder.

"Aw, hell, dog, you don't gotta cry about it," said Angel.

"I just can't imagine it," I said. "Being loved the way you and Elana love your child, who isn't even born yet, who doesn't even have a name."

Angel gave my shoulder a consoling squeeze as I tried to contain the rush of emotion, an effort that only liberated a second wave of tears. I could see that this response had aroused his confusion somewhat, and that this confusion was edging toward concern.

"I'm sorry," I said.

"You don't need to apologize, bro," he said, gently massaging my bony neck.

With this encouragement, I was able to staunch the tears, but not the welling of emotion.

"You know those scars?" I said. "The ones on my back?"

"Yeah, dog, those were intense."

"Well, they weren't from a harvester," I said. "They were from my father. He whipped me so bad once with a belt that all these years later you can still see the marks."

Angel looked stricken by this news, as the color drained from his face.

"Aw, man, Geno, I . . . I never knew it was that bad for you."

Then Angel did something wholly unexpected, but so welcome

that the tears recommenced. He set *Dorian Gray* aside on the night-stand and he leaned down and worked his arms around my slumped shoulders and wrapped my wasted torso in an embrace and pulled me close. He didn't let go, didn't say a word, for a good ten or fifteen seconds. When he finally relinquished his grip and stood upright once more, he wiped the tears from his own eyes, then immediately chased off the melancholy.

"Hey, look, I gotta cut out," he said. "Tomorrow is the ultrasound. Elana's mom is coming over in the morning, and I gotta stop at the store for a bunch of stuff."

"Are you gonna find out the sex?"

"Yeah, Elana, she don't like surprises much," he said. "She wants to do the whole nesting thing. Me, I just wanna know blue or pink, so I can start knocking out the nursery."

"I think it's a boy," I said.

"Nah, it's a girl," he said. "So long as it has ten fingers and ten toes, I'm happy either way."

"Good luck tomorrow," I said.

"Thanks, Geno."

That night, I dreamed for the first time in weeks, dreamed of the high desert, of snake holes and creosote bushes, long horizons shim-mering in the heat. In my dream I was a boy, but not myself, a dif-ferent boy, with a mother and a father who cherished me. I stood between them, high upon a mesa, gazing over a split-rail fence, splintered and bleached by the sun, at the plateau spread out be-low us, at once thrilled and terrified by its immensity. My father squeezed my hand as though to reassure me.

"Does it go on forever?" I said.

"No," he said. "It just seems that way."

Then, still clutching my hand, he reached up with his other hand and mussed my hair.

"Kiddo?" he said.

"Yeah, Dad?"

"Everything's gonna be okay."

You'd think that after such an encouraging dream I might awaken refreshed. But I awoke the next morning parched and listless, as though I'd trudged clear across the very desert I'd dreamed of. I had no appetite, nor any intention of leaving the bed that day. I closed my eyes throughout most of the morning and tried to resume my slumber, but sleep would not have me.

When I finally lifted my head from the pillow with considerable effort, I discovered a green-speckled lab notebook sitting atop my bedside table, its white label marked "VI." It required all my strength to reach out and take hold of the little book. When I had it in my clutches, I jockeyed my bed into an upright position and opened the notebook. I was astonished to find that it was one of Gladys's journals, now seventy-five years removed. I could only assume that Wayne had left it, perhaps as a token of our new bond.

Settling back against my pillow, I donned my reading glasses and, with trembling hands, began to read Gladys's tight-looping cursive with equal parts rapture and trepidation. I need not have been apprehensive, for Gladys's words came, as always, from a place of kindness. To hear her voice, so far removed and yet so familiar, was a revelation. Tears of gratitude soon blurred my vision, for I was holding Gladys right there in my hands.

The final fifteen pages of the journal comprised Gladys's recounting of the end of our love affair, and I shall not tell it here, for it is not my story to tell. Everyone must tell their own story. Suffice it to say that what I did not find in Gladys's telling was an explicit declaration of her unconditional love for me, nor a satisfactory resolution regarding its sudden conclusion, besides the baby, which she knew was mine and not Vernon's. What I did find, after I put the journal down, was inside me: the comfort of knowing that Gladys, kind and conflicted, curious and impulsive, was someone who still lived in my heart and my mind, and that she had never left me after all, and nothing, not life or death, could ever take her away from me. She would always live inside of me so long as I remembered.

No Easy Task

Angel returned on his day off, and as promised, he brought Elana with him. They found me weaker than ever before, but, heartened by their appearance, I rallied all the vitality I could, which was enough, just barely, to sit upright in my bed.

"You're not supposed to be here today," I said.

"This is a social visit, ese."

I noticed immediately that his nose ring was back in place.

"It's back," I observed, flaring my nostrils.

"Yeah, she thinks it's sexy, bro, what can I say?" said Angel, nudging Elana. "She made me put it back in."

Elana smiled shyly. I liked her immediately: her kind, lively eyes, that shy smile that belied what I knew to be her willfulness, the way she touched my wrist gently when I was too weak to reach up and shake her hand.

"I've heard so much about you," she said.

"You're even more beautiful than Angel described," I said.

"He warned me you were a charmer," she said, blushing nonetheless.

"I'm gonna grab something from my locker," Angel said, ducking out into the hallway. "You two get acquainted."

Elana smiled down at me in my bed.

"So, we finally meet," she said.

"I'm sorry you have to meet me like this," I said. "So weak and useless."

"Don't you dare," she said. "It's an honor to meet you. I know how much you've helped Angel."

"Me, help Angel?" I said. "I think you've got that backward."

"I know about your pep talks," she said. "He says you helped him *man up*—that's how he put it. He also said that buying all that baby stuff was your idea."

It might have been my turn to blush if only my blood could've moved fast enough. As it was, I was barely able to manage the weakest of grins, but don't think Elana's words didn't mean the world to me. That I had been anything to Angel beyond some peculiar old geezer in his line of work was a victory. That I'd helped guide him in any way felt like a small miracle. How long since I had been of any real consequence to anybody? Fifty years, eleven hundred? When had anyone ever benefited from my guidance? The answer until now had been never, as far as I knew. And maybe Angel and Elana were just being kind in giving an old man credit; I wouldn't put it past them.

"He's even gonna tell his dad about the baby," she said.

I wasn't sure what the implications of that were. God, what a heel I'd been. Only now did it occur to me that Angel had never so much as mentioned his father or mother, or any family beyond his brother Reuben, and his aunt Olivia who made the tamales, and his cousin in Downey, whose name I didn't even know. Hardly once had I solicited any information about his immediate family.

"Angel hasn't spoken to his dad in four years," Elana explained.

"That's wonderful," I said. "I mean, not that he hasn't talked to him, but that he's gonna tell him."

"I'm proud of him," said Elana. "He's really owning his past. His dad disowned him when he was running around with . . . well, let's just say the wrong crowd. It's why he moved out here."

"And his mother?"

"She died when Angel was eleven," said Elana.

For months I had burdened Angel exhaustively with my own past, a past that stretched far beyond any reasonable scope, and yet, what did I know of his? Next to nothing. I had so many questions, so much I wanted to know about Angel, yet it was clear I was running out of time.

"He doesn't talk about his past much," said Elana, as though my thoughts were visible to her.

"Not like some people," I said.

"So, did you really live in Spain?" she said.

"Yes," I said.

"And you were a cat?"

"Not in Spain, but yes."

Elana smiled politely. She didn't look very convinced, but who could blame her? That she was willing to indulge me at all, to grace me with those kind eyes and that smile, was more than I could ask for under the circumstances.

"Sometimes I feel like I've lived before," she said. "Nothing like you. Just flashes, you know, little moments of . . ."

"Recognition?" I said.

"Yeah, like déjà vu."

Just then Angel returned from his locker with a crumpled sweatshirt in his fist.

"Did you tell him?" he said.

"I left that for you," said Elana.

"Tell me what?" I said.

"You were right, it's a boy, Geno!" said Angel.

"How about that?" I said.

Angel donned a huge, stupid grin.

"It was pretty obvious from the picture, if you know what I mean, dog. You should have seen the size of his—"

"Oh, stop it," said Elana.

"Congratulations," I said.

"Actually, he wanted a girl," said Elana.

"That's not true!" said Angel. "I just said I *thought* it was a girl."

Clearly, it didn't matter either way; they were both thrilled. How I envied the child who would soon be delivered to their care. To be born in love, to be wanted, to be anxiously and lovingly expected.

"I'm gonna call my aunt Inez and tell her the news," said Elana. "I'll let you two visit. Baby, remember, we have to be at my brother's apartment by five."

With that, Elana fished her phone out of her purse and stepped out into the corridor.

"So, what are you gonna call him?" I asked.

"Haven't decided yet," said Angel. "I threw Eugene out there, homie. But Elana wasn't having it. She says it sounds like an old man. Sorry, bro."

"She's not wrong," I said.

"I shortened it to Geno, but she said that sounded like a mob boss."

"You'll think of something," I said.

"Yeah, we got time. But the wedding is right around the corner. So, like, we gotta hurry up and get you fitted for a tux, Geno. How about next Saturday? I could pick you up, and we could hit the mall. I talked to Wayne and he said you could leave if you're up to it."

How could I tell him? Especially on a day like today, when I was too weak to lift my head? But I had to let him know early in the game; I owed him that. And I wanted to give him and Elana their gift now, while I was still here, so I'd know that they got it.

"Angel, I've been meaning to talk to you about the wedding," I said.

"I told you, bro, don't worry, we've got your transportation covered. Elana's brother, Emilio, is gonna pick you up. His van's got a
lift, straps, all that, you can be in a wheelchair the whole time."

"It's not that," I said.

"I could probably just have a tailor come here and get your mea-
surements and all that, no biggie. It ain't rocket science, right?"

"No need," I said.

With all the strength I could muster, I lifted my arm and reached
out to take hold of his wrist.

"Listen to me, Angel," I rasped. "There is nowhere in the world
I'd rather be than up there with you and Elana when you make your
vows. Nowhere at all, do you understand?"

"Of course," he said. "That's the point."

I squeezed his wrist weakly. God, but I hated to disappoint him.

"But I don't think I'm gonna make it, my friend."

"Aw, c'mon, Geno," he said. "I know you think you're checking out tomorrow, but we're talking three weeks here. You got
this, dog."

I can only imagine how pathetic I must have looked to Angel:
rheumy eyed and wasted; pale, knobby, and wrinkled; skin hanging
off my ancient bones like melted wax.

"I'm not gonna make it," I said. "Really. I am so sorry."

I watched the knowledge settle in, and Angel looked stoic, but I
swear to you his chin began to quiver ever so slightly and his eyes
moistened, and in that moment, how could I do anything but fall in
love with him all over again? He truly was an angel. My angel.

"I understand, Geno, I do," he said. "No pressure, bro. But you
never know, right?"

"Do me a favor," I said.

"Anything, ese."

"On the dresser there's an envelope," I said. "I apologize in advance for the handwriting."

Angel walked to the dresser, picked up the envelope without reading the front, and presented it to me.

"No, it's for you and Elana," I said. "It's my gift."

He inspected the envelope: "For Angel and Elana," it said in the uneven scrawl of a second grader.

"So, like, am I supposed to open this now?" he said.

"Save it for the wedding," I said. "Just don't lose it."

"Of course not," he said.

"No, really," I said. "Don't lose it."

Inside the envelope was a card, something I'd had Wayne pick up, nothing fancy, just "Congratulations!" embossed in sparkly silver upon the front of a cream-colored card. Inside the card was a note: "For Elana and Eugene on their wedding day: Congratulations, and may your love endure for many lifetimes."

Along with the note was a personal check for $17,500, which amounted to all that was left of my savings, minus the $23,364.54 reserved for clearing my ledger and putting me in a casket. So, you see, even if I'd wanted to stay, I wouldn't have had the money to pay my rent on this earth much longer. But that's beside the point.

Elana reappeared in the doorway, smiling, the bulge of her belly noticeable but not conspicuous.

"Aunt Inez wants us to name him Pablo," she said.

"Pablo?" said Angel. "Pablo is fine for a baby, but he's not gonna be little all his life!"

"It was my great-grandfather's name," said Elana.

"It sounds like a circus act," said Angel. "What do you think, Geno?"

I may have been a slow learner, but eleven hundred years had granted me enough sense to stay away from this one.

"That's for you two to decide," I said.

"What about Berto, or Felix, or Oscar?"

"I don't like any of those," said Elana.

"Well, I'm not naming him Pablo," said Angel. "He'll have a complex."

"You don't have to name him right now," I observed into the brief silence.

"He's right," said Angel.

My heart was full, but my battery was empty. Never in my life had I been so tired. I was still holding Angel's wrist, afraid to let go because I knew it was the last time I'd ever touch him. But he didn't need to know that. So I reached down deep and mustered a smile.

"You kids run along," I said. "I'll see you on Monday."

"You'll still be here, right? Promise me," he said.

"I promise."

"It was great to finally meet you," said Elana. "I'm sure I'll see you before the wedding."

With all I had left, I reached out for her hand and set my ravaged lips to it and planted a dry kiss.

"The pleasure was all mine," I said.

Angel rested a palm atop my head and mussed the wispy remnants of my hair.

"Love ya, bro," he said.

Then Angel turned and took Elana's hand as though it was the most natural thing in the world, and they walked out of my gloomy quarters, out of my life and into their future. My eyes burned watching them go, and I thought: May nothing ever separate them, nor come between them, nor strike their love down.

If I've learned anything in eleven hundred years, I've learned this: It's no easy task finding love, and more difficult still holding on to it, so hold on tight, as if your life depends upon it, because it does. And get ready to hurt, my friend. Because this life will break your heart again and again.

If you do dare to open your heart, you will come to understand, as I have, finally, that love is not a force of nature but a capacity, a willingness.

And you may learn, as I have, that it might not be necessary to wander the earth ceaselessly in search of your Gaya, or your Oscar, or your Gladys. Your Angel. If you're willing to open your heart, it's possible you will find that love is right in front of you.

Acknowledgments

Heartfelt thanks to my wife, Lauren, and my kids for inspiring me, and for enduring me when my head is in the work. Big gratitude to my early readers: Josh Fernandez, Thomas Kohnstamm, Craig Lancaster, Zachary Cole, and Tim Teehan. Huge thanks to McKaila Allcorn for her medical expertise. Big ups to my wonderful team at Dutton, in particular Emily Canders, Lisset Lanza, Tiffani Ren, Cassidy Sachs, Stephanie Cooper, Aja Pollock, and my editor and champion, John Parsley. And of course, a huge thank-you to my long-suffering agent and advocate, Mollie Glick.

About the Author

Jonathan Evison is the author of the novels *Small World; All About Lulu; West of Here; The Revised Fundamentals of Caregiving; This Is Your Life, Harriet Chance!; Lawn Boy;* and *Legends of the North Cascades.* He lives with his wife and family in Washington State.